ACCIDENTALLY MARRIED

JEAN ORAM

Accidentally Married © 2018 by Jean Oram

This is a work of fiction and all characters, organizations, places, events, and incidents appearing in this novel are products of the author's active imagination or are used in a fictitious manner. Any resemblance to actual people, alive or dead, as well as any resemblance to events or locales is coincidental and, truly, a little bit cool.

All rights reserved, including the right to reproduce this book or portions thereof in any form whatsoever, unless written permission has been granted by the author, with the exception of brief quotations for use in a review of this work. For more information contact Jean Oram at JeanOramBooks@gmail.com.
www.JeanOram.com

Printed in the United States of America unless otherwise stated on the last page of this book. Published by Oram Productions Alberta, Canada.

LIBRARY OF CONGRESS CATALOGING-IN-PUBLICATION DATA

Oram, Jean.

Accidentally Married / Jean Oram.—1st. ed.

p. cm.

ISBN 978-1-928198-44-4 (paperback)

Ebook ISBN (primary) 978-1-928198-36-9

1. Romance fiction. 2. Romance fiction—Small towns. 3. Small towns—Fiction. 4. Blueberry Springs (Imaginary place)—Fiction. 5. Interpersonal relations—Fiction. 6. Veils and Vows—Series. 7. FICTION / weddings. 8. FICTION / marriage. 9. Romance fiction, American. 10. Man-woman relationships—Fiction. 11. Romances. 12. FICTION / Romance / Contemporary. I. Title.

First Oram Productions Edition: March 2018

Cover design by Jean Oram

ACKNOWLEDGMENTS

Thank you to everyone who helped with this book from my wonderful and generous Beta Sisters (Donna Wolz, Margaret Cambridge, Sharon Sanders, Sarah Albertson, and Jude C.) to my editors (Tessa Shapcott and Margaret Carney) and proofreaders (Erin and Emily). You're all amazing—thank you for taking the time to help me make Jill and Burke's story become even better.

A NOTE FROM THE AUTHOR

While I was dreaming up this series the idea of someone getting married accidentally and not recalling it captured my imagination (and made me laugh). And, for me, the idea of finding love in an unexpected place is equally appealing as I believe that's the beauty of love—you never know where and when it will happen, and with whom.

I had a lot of fun writing Burke and Jill's unexpected love story and I hope you enjoy it as well.

Happy reading,
Jean Oram
Alberta, Canada 2018

Accidentally Married

Thank you for letting us "authors" crash your back scene!

xo Jean Oram
2019

CHAPTER 1

Jill Armstrong swiped a damp hand down her skirt and took a deep breath. She pulled on the glass door to the building's workout room. Locked.

Another roadblock in her plan. She should just go home. Pretend she'd never found out about the document in her hand. Pretend she'd never come here to try and tell Burke Carver.

A skinny security guard approached Jill from the other side of the locked door and frowned at her attire—heels and a skirt. No visitor badge.

Burke, who she could see on a treadmill about thirty feet beyond the door, would surely notice if the security guard tossed her out.

Stick to the plan and there would be no disasters. That's the way life worked. She'd fallen to the siren call of spontaneity last April and now look. Disaster.

Jill made an unlocking motion with her hand, and the security guard raised his pale eyebrows. He made a sweeping motion, indicating that if she wanted in, she needed an access card. She repeated her motion. The man's shoulders moved as though he was heaving a tremendous sigh over her stubbornness.

She rattled the door. "Let me in."

The security guard cracked it a few inches. "You need an access card to enter."

"I'm here to see Burke Carver." Jill pressed a hand against the door's cool glass, stepping forward.

A few weeks ago she had been delighted when the bank finally approved her latest application for a business loan—until she realized why. It had had everything to do with Burke Carver, the man who'd refused to consider a partnership with her small company a mere ten months ago.

Jill held the large manila envelope against her chest and surreptitiously wiped a palm against her skirt once again. She had a pretty good feeling Burke would remember her, but she wasn't as certain he'd recall the way their few drinks in the conference hotel bar had culminated in the disaster currently tucked inside her envelope. Although it was possible he recalled more than she did. But if he had, they surely would have had this upcoming talk almost a year ago.

She was confident he was going to believe she'd been playing him. And even worse, she'd gained weight in the past few months and no longer had the slim build he tended to gravitate toward and he... No, it didn't matter what he thought. She just needed him to do his part to make their little problem go away. Quickly.

"No access card, no admittance," the guard said nervously.

"Trust me," she replied, tone firm. "He'll want to see me, and he will have your head if he learns I came all this way only to be sent home." It was only two hours from her hometown of Blueberry Springs to the city of Dakota, but it wasn't that often that she made the trek.

The man slowly stepped away from the door and Jill smiled curtly while pushing past. The workout room smelled of disinfectant, warm bodies and machines, reminding her of the hours she'd spent in the basement workout area with her father as a teen. Her twin sister, meanwhile, had spent her time upstairs with their mother learning how to curl hair and apply makeup.

Across the workout area, Burke was still on the treadmill, his body moving in a fluid, captivating way. His calf muscles rippled as they propelled him forward on the machine, his hair flopping as he landed before pushing off again, moving at a pace that would surely leave most people winded.

Jill strode over, trying to ignore how her reflection was following her across the room in the long panel of mirrors to her right.

Burke was laughing with a woman on the neighboring elliptical machine. She barely had an ounce of body fat, her hair was in a perfect, smooth ponytail, her makeup not at all impacted by her workout...because she wasn't even sweating.

How was that possible? Then again, Jill had once looked like that—and her twin sister still did, as she hadn't gained the same ten pounds Jill had over the past few months. Okay, fifteen after an ice cream binge.

"Burke?" His name came out sharply, and he turned, eyes narrowed. His even, powerful stride faltered. He quickly regained his rhythm, legs pumping.

"We need to talk," Jill said.

His open expression had changed, shadowing his face. This was where he said no. "Make an appointment."

Frustration and anger pounded inside Jill and she reached over to slap the treadmill's emergency stop. The machine came to a quick halt.

"I *said* we need to *talk*."

His gaze traveled to her gut and she instinctively sucked in. Less than a year ago they'd shared a million laughs, dinner, drinks, his room. And more, according to the document she was holding. But she was *not* a new mom looking for her partner to pay up.

Burke's gaze had flicked to the security guard, who was

standing behind Jill. She shot the nervous man a dirty look and he backed up a step, his Adam's apple bobbing.

"You'll want to see this," Jill said, as Burke restarted the machine.

"I'm not taking proposals right now." He was just about up to his previous pace again. "Excuse me, I'm working out."

"Fine." Jill moved to the vacant treadmill on the far side of Burke and used it for support as she shucked off her heels. She stepped onto the machine, placing her envelope in the magazine holder.

"What are you doing?" Burke asked.

"Joining you."

He stared at her while she started the machine.

This was such a horrible idea. Absolutely horrible. She'd been too busy to work out much over the past year and she was going to be sweaty and panting within thirty seconds. Not to mention what she was about to do to her sister's borrowed pantyhose.

"Here," Burke stated. "Wearing that? Just so you can speak to me?" There was a twinkle of something in his eyes. Reluctant respect for her moxie, perhaps? He had reacted to that in the past —and she'd found that powerfully heady.

"Yes," she said primly. The machine was going too fast and she had to jog to get her feet back under her as she worked to control the speed. "If your secretary was a bit more helpful…" She paused to suck in a breath. "I could have made an appointment—" she exhaled "—where we could discuss this in an office like civilized adults."

Oh, man. She was already panting.

"So your stalkerish harassment isn't a coincidence?" he said, his tone dry.

"There's no such thing as coincidence." Coincidences were like a Trojan horse. They looked like a gift to get you to let your guard down, then they led to nothing but disasters. Plans were the only things you should trust.

Burke stopped his machine and flicked a white towel over his shoulder. He was watching her again, his gaze back on her belly. "Let's talk somewhere more private." He gave the woman he'd been chatting with earlier a nod, then without a word began walking away. Jill scrambled to follow, hustling to reclaim her abandoned heels.

Burke was moving swiftly through the maze of clanking weight machines and she caught up just as he opened a stairwell door.

As the door closed behind her, he turned, arms crossed. The concrete landing suddenly felt too small, too closed in.

"Hi," she said breathlessly. His gaze was traveling over her slowly, noting changes, perhaps. "I didn't have a baby, if that's what you're thinking."

He shot her a sharp look. He turned, walking up the flight of stairs, his hands clenched around each end of his towel. "Tell your friend Emma Carrington I said hello. You can also tell her my decision hasn't changed since last year, despite her recommendation."

Emma had set up the meeting between them at the conference, her name opening the door for Jill, who ran a small botanical business. She'd been hoping to partner with Burke's large online store that specialized in eco-friendly clothing. Jill had hoped he'd agree to feature her products as add-on items.

She had been small potatoes, according to him. She got that, she did. But he hadn't even looked at her growth plan.

She lowered her voice. "I'm here about something else. Something more...personal."

Burke turned to face her and she swallowed, feeling suddenly as though the enclosed stairwell was way too warm. His look had intensified, bringing out his handsomeness. The sharp lines of his jaw strengthened; his dark brown eyes turned practically black. Without a word he began taking the stairs upward, two at a time. She took her time following him, trying to prevent her heart from blasting out of her chest. She'd needed a week to summon the courage to come here, and she'd only done so because she knew it would be worse in the long run if she didn't.

One floor up, Burke held open the massive door to his company offices, letting her pass. Then he led her through a large open area dotted with thriving potted plants and streaming with natural light that filtered through the large offices that were glassed in along the outer walls. No flickering fluorescent lights, just sunshine and the odd soft LED floor lamp to brighten a sitting area or work area. Desks speckled the edges of the space, Jill noted, with several offices off to the left and right, and one large one straight ahead. Just about everyone looked up with a smile, ready to wave, until they caught their boss's expression.

Wordlessly, Burke strode into the large office, saying over his shoulder, "Close the door."

He sat in a bamboo executive chair with worn cushions and faced her, fingers pressed in a steeple like he was about to give thanks, his eyes boring through her with that familiar intensity.

Jill took the chair across from him and nervously handed him the envelope. Nothing but the whir of his computer fan filled the silence as he looked at the vital records document.

As he skimmed it, she braced herself for what would surely be an explosion.

MARRIED.

He was married? To Jill Armstrong.

No, he would most certainly remember that.

"Is this your idea of a joke?" Burke rose from his desk, his mind running through the possible implications of the marriage certificate being valid. None of them were good. He was betting that if this was real there wasn't a prenuptial agreement.

He'd fought for this company through one divorce and won. He wasn't going to lose it now.

He placed his hands on his desk and leaned forward, snapping, "Is it?"

Across the desk, Jill's eyes were wide, her head mutely shaking back and forth.

He tried to rein in his rage, but found control was out of reach. He swept a hand down his face, collecting sweat from his workout. He had a meeting with a potential, much-needed financial backer in fifteen minutes. He'd planned to finish his run, shower, and arrive fresh with a clear mind.

Not…this.

He had trusted Jill. She was smart, strong, and he'd been certain she understood what he was willing and able to offer, and that she was not in need of anything more. He'd always been careful, choosing women who were happy to stand on their own two feet and didn't want or need a relationship or text the next day. Women who only wanted him to help burn off their stress.

No strings. No commitments.

And no flipping marriage. Didn't she know the rules?

No, she was playing an entirely different game. He hadn't partnered his business with hers last April, so she'd gotten him drunk and married him. Now she was here to claim her marital assets.

Man, he was a fool. He'd admired the way she hadn't taken the rejection of her business proposal personally, and he'd even considered looking her up since then. The night after her pitch they'd accidentally ended up sharing a few shots of tequila in the conference hotel bar, in the middle of a wedding party that was taking place around them, luring them to join in with the celebrations.

He'd woken up the next morning with a massive headache, his memory full of blanks, and an empty bed. After a few months of silence, he'd assumed everything was cool.

Obviously, it wasn't.

Something huge had gone down during that blank spot in his memory. Something bigger than waking up to find a puzzling, one-inch-long comma tattooed to the inside of his right wrist.

But now he wasn't so sure she *hadn't* taken things personally that night. She'd found a way to partner with him, after all. Why, though, had she waited this long to tell him? What trap had she laid in order to take advantage of him?

And *married*? How on earth had she convinced him to say those two little words of marital agreement that he never planned on uttering again for as long as he lived? He'd proved he wasn't capable of marriage and all that went with it, and he wasn't the kind of man who needed to learn his lessons more than once.

"I've already looked into an annulment," she said quietly, ignoring his outburst.

His mind stopped.

Annulment? She wanted to pretend this had never happened?

"Good," he said, easing back in his chair. "You know, I remember every night of my life except that one." He cleared his throat and sat forward again. "But what matters is how we fix this—quickly and quietly. How do we get this marriage considered invalid?"

A married man, one who was the founder and owner of an ethical, green company, did not take the governor's daughter to a ball, as he had a few weeks ago.

It didn't matter that it had been a business move—he'd been seeking corporate tax breaks and Governor Martinez had suggested they talk at the event. Burke had agreed. Then there had been the issue of a ticket. But it turned out his daughter, who was in need of a date, had an extra.

The press had acted like there was something between the two of them, despite Burke telling Autumn he wasn't interested in a relationship. But the media attention had made her eyes dance. He hadn't been able to shake her ever since.

Reporters would go nuts if they found out that he, a man who never committed, had been married the whole time. Especially to a woman whose curves could rival that of a racetrack. Dangerous. He didn't recall her being so curvy the last time he'd seen her, and his eyes kept being drawn to the dip in her waist before the flare of her hips. Her shapely legs.

"There is a slight hitch," Jill said, drawing his attention back to their conversation.

Burke froze, then wiped a hand across his mouth, but the feeling that he'd lost control of something very important didn't go away.

"What do you mean?" he croaked.

"As you know, I'm looking to expand my business." Jill was avoiding his gaze and his right leg began jiggling with pent-up energy.

"So am I." He'd put nearly every asset the company owned—as well as his own—behind their latest push for growth.

"I applied for a loan."

He nodded. So had he. And yesterday it had been denied—a move that puzzled the company's accountant. The team at Sustain This, Honey, had taken a calculated risk by financially extending themselves, knowing that with the right moves they'd make that money back in a conservative six months, if not sooner.

They counted on him to personally create a financial bridge that he'd unexpectedly been unable to raise. That meant he needed to go into his next meeting fresh, calm and on top of his game, so the potential investor felt confident in stepping up. And Jill and her marriage problem wasn't helping him stay calm and collected.

She studiously kept her eyes trained on the edge of Burke's

desk, then the wall to his right, which was coated with whiteboard paint where he'd written out their growth plan's timeline.

Jill spoke, her tone even. "They approved the loan based on my husband's credit rating."

Burke's mind stopped working as he processed the statement.

Husband's credit rating.

Husband.

That was him.

His credit.

His recently denied loan application was because of her?

No. That—*this*—had to be a nightmare.

"Burke?" Jill asked gently. Her tentative, but curious tone brought him back to the conference hotel bar where they'd spent hours chatting. He'd been sitting alone in the boisterous pub, thinking over the day, and had turned to see who was speaking to him. The lights had been behind her, giving her dark hair depth. Someone had popped a confetti bomb to celebrate the partying bride and groom, and Jill had jumped forward, landing in the V between his legs, her palms, hot and sure, pressing against his thighs as she'd steadied herself. She'd laughed it off, embarrassed by her overreaction to the loud crack, but the contact had sent a shiver down his spine. A shiver of longing.

As she repeated his name now, in his office, that same anticipatory shiver ran through him again like a conditioned response.

Longing. Longing for his wife.

Married.

No, not him. No way.

Not trapped.

Not again.

A funnel of rage whipped through him.

"Get out." He came around his desk. He didn't want to even think about the level of deceit she'd gone to in order to get that loan. "And pay back the loan immediately."

He reached for the door, stopping when she stuttered, "I —I can't."

"You took it, you pay it. You did *not* have my authority, and I will sue you into the ground for this, you hear me?"

He was losing control.

Of his emotions, of his company.

If she defaulted, everything would be lost. People depended upon him. He had a staff of twenty-five just outside that office door, people who trusted him not to mess up, not to let his grip slip. And somehow he had. The personal loan he'd counted on to help the company was now out of reach.

Tears streaked down Jill's cheeks as she snatched the document from his desk.

"What are you doing?" he demanded.

"I paid for this copy. It's mine." She swiped at her wet cheeks, her spine straight. Her chin was jutting out and she looked fierce even with the tears.

But the tears. He didn't expect someone like her to be reduced by his sharp tone.

She'd used him, hadn't she? Used him to get the loan, so she could expand when he hadn't allowed her to partner with Sustain This, Honey. And now she was using tears to try and soften him.

Jill was babbling at high speed. "I swear I didn't know, Burke. I wouldn't have transferred it to my vendors. It wasn't until Wini —the loan manager—was teasing me weeks later about keeping a secret husband that..." She paused to gulp, steadying herself. "I'm so sorry, Burke. I really am. It was so embarrassing and confusing. I'll fix this. I promise."

He studied her, feeling uncertain by the depth of her emotion. But he couldn't trust her, could he? The tears could be fake. This could have all been orchestrated.

"Just tell me where to show up for this annulment."

CHAPTER 2

Jill let herself into the judge's chambers. One annulment coming up. One loan to be paid back as outlined in the plan she'd emailed Burke a few days ago.

Plan set. Life soon to be back on track.

Burke was already sitting across from the judge's desk, his jaw hard, muscles twitching with pent-up emotion. He was handsome. And very, very angry.

Angry enough to actually sue her? He wouldn't sue his accidental wife, would he?

Jill pulled the second visitor's chair a few feet beyond his reach and sat down.

He was intimidating in his dark power suit, and she was glad she'd taken the time to put on a wool skirt and silk blouse, even if they were a tad too tight.

"Jill Armstrong?" the judge asked as she entered the room, her robe flowing behind her. She was tall, her expression severe. She exuded a no-nonsense attitude. In other words, she was perfect.

Jill stood. "Present."

The judge's mouth twitched in amusement. "And you are Burke Carver, correct?" she asked him.

"Yes," he replied.

"We're here to annul your marriage?"

Burke spoke for them. "I don't recall marrying Jill. She drugged me. The marriage and all goings-on, as well as marital entitlements, are therefore null."

The judge raised her eyebrows as she seated herself.

"I did *not* drug you!" Jill said with a gasp. And they'd already settled things in regards to neither of them requesting any 'marital entitlements' from the union.

"You may be seated," the judge told Jill. "Burke, you were under the influence when you took your vows?"

"Yes. My consent should be considered—"

"Jill? Were you under the influence?"

She nodded. "I assume so. I don't recall the ceremony."

"That makes things easy," the judge said, closing the file folder that had been open on her desk.

"She's meddling with my business," Burke said, "and I would like to reserve the right to sue her."

Jill gasped again, and added hotly, "I am *not* meddling and there is no reason to sue me."

Without facing her, he said, "Explain the loan you haven't paid back. The one you obtained through deception. The one where you borrowed against my credit, and without my signature."

Jill shrank in her chair. "That was a mistake, and I emailed you a schedule for paying it back."

"How did she borrow money without your knowledge?" the judge asked, leaning forward, pen poised.

Burke fumed. "I don't know."

"Did you forge his signature, Jill?" the judge prompted. "Was he a cosigner?"

"No. It was an honest mistake made by my bank when they

checked my credit rating and found I was married," Jill squeaked.

"Please, can we just annul our marriage?"

"Now that you have my money, sure, why not?" Burke grumbled, arms stiffly crossed.

"It's not like that," Jill said tightly. "And it's not like one little loan against your credit rating is going to break you until I get it paid off."

"I have mouths to feed."

"You have children?" she asked, sitting back in surprise.

"You withheld this knowledge from Ms. Armstrong?"

"Employees," Burke said sharply. "They have children. Families. Medical needs. Mortgages. Tuition payments."

"Are you cohabiting?" the judge asked.

"No. Never," Jill said, fingers interlaced in her lap.

"Did you consummate your marriage?" the judge asked.

"I don't know," Jill said, feeling flustered by the personal question and Burke's attitude. Was he really thinking of suing her? "And I didn't borrow *that* much money."

"You don't recall the consummation?" The judge seemed amused. "Have you ever woken up together?"

Jill nodded. "Yes, once. And I gave him a schedule for paying back the loan."

"The next morning she just left," Burke said. "Didn't even tell me we were married."

"Was I supposed to stick around for breakfast? And for the record, I don't recall our marriage any more than you do."

"So you consummated the marriage?" the judge confirmed.

Jill shifted uncomfortably. "Yes."

She had flashes of memory of her and Burke. Of kisses that seared her soul, so hot she could barely breathe just thinking about them and the way his mouth had trailed over her skin. She was certain that had been after committing themselves to each other, as when she'd awoken in the cocoon of warmth of his arms, the alarm clock said five thirty. She'd quietly collected her things, including her three-page business proposal, which had been resting on top of her dress in its brown envelope. She'd folded it up, stuffing it in the nearest hallway trash can on her way to the elevator, impressed that she'd managed to stay in possession of the papers all night.

She now realized it likely hadn't been her proposal, but instead their marriage certificate, which, according to her research, had been issued from the late night chapel on Shalina Avenue, just a few blocks from the conference. A chapel where, she'd then confirmed, they had indeed been married—at three in the morning.

"Normally being under the influence would be grounds for an annulment, but this is a uniquely messy situation," the judge informed them. "I can't grant your request. You need to apply for a divorce."

"What?" Burke sprang from his chair. "I need her out of my life and out of my business before she takes everything. This marriage is her fault and it's not fair that I should be punished for it."

"I am *not* the only person who said 'I do,'" Jill declared, standing to face him.

"I would never agree to marry you. You had to have drugged me."

"I've had enough." Jill scooped up her purse, afraid she was going to cry. Her first husband had been a piece of work and years ago she'd wasted enough big fat tears over him. She wasn't going to do that over some man who was nothing more than a drunken mistake.

"I don't deserve your attacks," she said, tipping her chin up, "just because you're feeling scared because I made you feel something that night." She jabbed him in the chest. They had laughed all evening. She still remembered that. Their heads tipped together, the look in his eyes... It had been heady, and it had felt right. Enough that they'd let go of their hang-ups and gotten hitched.

That wasn't all her fault. He was just as much to blame.

She thanked the judge and stalked into the hall, slinging her bag's strap over her shoulder.

"You planned this all along, didn't you?" he shouted after her, hurrying to catch up. "Marry me, act like it's all 'oops' and take what you want, then discard me like I never mattered."

Jill whirled, arms flung out to show him he couldn't intimidate her. "You use women. You look down on businesses smaller than yours. *You* used *me*. And *you* messed up *my* life."

"Your life? What about mine?"

"Was there something to mess up?" she asked coolly. "Your socialite of the week is upset to find out she's been kissing a married man?"

"You're—you're..." Burke was shaking his finger, at a loss for words. Some man she'd married. He couldn't even look her in the eye.

"I'm *what*?" she spat.

"Your blouse is unbuttoned."

She looked down and clasped her hands over her exposed bra. The top two buttons across her chest had come undone in her outburst, revealing enough lingerie to be inappropriate in any setting outside a strip club or a photo shoot for undergarments. She furiously tried to fix her shirt, but one of the buttons was missing. Holding a hand over the gaping fabric, she faced Burke with burning cheeks.

"I have flashes of memory..." She tried to put words to the question she needed to ask, despite her deep humiliation. "Do I have to worry about STDs?"

"I use protection. In fact, I *insist* on it. And I don't sleep around nearly as much as you believe."

"Was there a used condom in the room?"

Burke's lips were moving in a silent tirade. Finally he said, "Seriously?"

"I deserve an answer."

"I *always* use protection, Jill."

"Good." She turned and began walking again.

When would she ever learn? Make a plan, stick to the plan. Don't let spontaneity or charming men woo you. That was a recipe for ruined goals. Her ex, Hayes Hayward, had swept into her life like one wonderful coincidence. He was hot. He was smart. And he liked her—not her twin sister, Jodi. Not only that, he knew the restaurant business as well as accounting, and was more than happy to help out while sweeping her off her feet.

Everything had seemed absolutely perfect until a few months after their marriage, when he'd unceremoniously left. Not just with her heart, but with a stockpile of cash that had been supposed to be going toward the bills to keep the doors of The Café in Blueberry Springs open. She'd been embarrassed and horrified at how easily she'd been had. In one fell swoop she'd lost her job, her sister's job, her marriage, her trust, her reputation and so much more.

With the help from local police officer and friend Scott Malone, she'd caught up with Hayes. After a little persuasion from Scott—who'd sworn her to secrecy over what he'd threatened on her behalf—the money was returned. All but thirty thousand, which she'd ended up raising on her own to pay the café owners. They hadn't kept the restaurant open, though, saying it wasn't worth the headache any longer.

It had been years since that mess with Hayes where he'd made her look like a trusting fool. Jill had worked hard to correct her image around Blueberry Springs, and she wasn't going to give Burke the chance to add another blemish to it. She was going to quietly divorce him and move on, not add another juicy tidbit to the gossip mill. Not this time.

"What was I thinking, marrying you and then consummating

it?" she muttered, her own self-loathing creating a wave of nausea.

"I'm good in bed," Burke said defensively, falling into step beside her.

"Not good enough that I can actually remember."

Liar.

She remembered a lot of it. *A lot.* And it had all been good. Really good.

She hid her smile as she saw him fighting with himself, resisting the urge to react to the arrow she'd sent straight at his ego.

Instead, he slipped out of his suit jacket and awkwardly tried to slide it around her shoulders as she walked.

She shrugged it away. "What are you doing?"

He sighed. "Just take it. I'm not the worst person you could have married."

"That has yet to be proven." His comments in the chambers, as well as about possibly suing her, still stung.

She didn't want his jacket, but he was already helping her into it, forcing her to stop moving as he carefully did up the buttons for her. The tender gesture was confusing after his sharp words, and the comforting warmth of his jacket dampened her eyes. She made sure she looked down until she had her emotions back under control.

When she finally glanced up, there was a softness in his gaze that appeared apologetic.

"I'm going to burn this jacket when I get home," she said, lifting her chin. "I hope you know that."

To her surprise, he laughed. "You're an awful wife."

"And you're a worse husband."

"Then there's nowhere for us to go but up."

BURKE FELT like the world's biggest heel. He'd been raised by his aunt to be a better man than one who shouted at women and made them feel horrible. And in public, no less.

If Aunt Maggie heard about how he'd treated Jill back there, she'd have his ear pinched in her grip so fast it hurt just thinking about it.

The stress had to be getting to him. His quest for market expansion being blocked by Jill, and her inability to immediately free up his credit, was making him twitch. His team had invested heavily in creating valuable momentum and now it would all be for nothing. Lost.

He had to find an answer and it was most definitely not marriage. That was *never* the answer. Women left. And when they did, they had a tendency to take down everything around them, like an angry kitten with a vendetta against draperies and glass vases. Absolute and total destruction.

What had he been thinking, uttering "I do"?

"Let's find a divorce lawyer," he said, moving forward to hold the outer courthouse door for Jill, letting the February cold into the building in the process. She strode out on high heels that made her hips sway seductively. At least his suit jacket—the one she was intent on burning—was covering her, so he'd be less likely to become distracted and forget what he was supposed to be doing.

"I forgot my coat." She turned suddenly and he bumped into her, his hands going to her waist as her fingers dug into his shoulders for balance. He had a flash of memory of her bright eyes meeting his in the dim light of his hotel room. It was a good feeling that washed over him, one of contentment.

He clung to the shard of memory, willing his mind to bring forward more. It did.

He was on his back, smooth sheets beneath him. Jill was smiling, her long dark hair brushing his chest, his hands on her warm waist, her cool fingers resting on his shoulders.

It was she who had been haunting his dreams for the past several months, causing him to wake with a muddled mind over what was memory and what was fantasy. Sweet and strong, unpredictable Jill.

Most one-night stands didn't leave him feeling like he had that next morning.

Most one-night stands also didn't leave him married.

He quickly stepped back from her, brushing off the collision with an apology. He caught sight of the judge, already out of her robe, briefcase in hand as she headed home for the night. She gave him a sly smile full of meaning. She thought there was something between him and Jill?

Well, there wasn't.

And he could guarantee there never would be, because she had the power to destroy everything that mattered to him.

They returned to the coat check, hurriedly claiming their belongings. Jill went to unbutton his suit jacket so she could return it to him, shifting away to try and hide her wrecked blouse from a school group that was milling about underfoot as their teacher tried to organize them and the stack of coats retrieved by the attendant.

"Keep it for now," Burke said gruffly. "Let's go."

She pushed her hands into the sleeves of her winter jacket and followed him out.

But once free of the building, at the bottom of the concrete steps, Jill made a sharp right turn, leaving him behind.

"Hey!" He held up his arms as if to say *"What the heck, woman?"*

She turned, her look impatient. "Well? Are we getting a divorce or not?" She pointed to a sign across the street. Big red letters that said Divorce Lawyer were hanging over a glass-fronted business.

"That'll do."

They jaywalked, the late February sun weak, but welcome

after a dark and bitter January. He'd planned on holding the door for Jill, but she beat him to it, holding it for him instead.

"I got it." There was no way he was walking through that door before her.

"Now you're the gentleman again?"

"You're still wearing my jacket, aren't you?"

"Oh, so that makes your earlier unkind words acceptable?"

He cringed. "No. But maybe it helps make up for them."

"It's going to take more than an act of kindness to make up for being a callous you-know-what."

He sighed. "It already feels like we've been married for a million years."

She gave him a dark glare before moving through the door to speak to the receptionist, requesting an immediate appointment.

"Can you come back tomorrow at three?" the woman asked, after checking her appointment book. Her hair was impossibly large, and she had a pencil stuck in its white-blond heights.

Jill turned to Burke in question. "Tomorrow?"

He faced the receptionist. She had withdrawn the pencil and had it poised above her date book, her heavy eyebrows arched in question.

"Do you know anyone in town who can fit us in today?" He smiled charmingly. "Jill's from out of town."

The receptionist checked her delicate gold watch. "Sorry. Most offices have already closed for the night. But if you and your wife want to come back tomorrow I can give you the three o'clock opening." She flipped through a file folder on a desktop rack beside her, then handed them two copies of a list. "Here are the things we recommend you bring to your first meeting."

Burke eyed the items, muttering, "I think it was faster to get married than divorced." He asked the receptionist, "Do we really need all of this? We're ready to sign papers and part ways."

"Bring everything tomorrow at three." The woman tucked the pencil back into her hair. "Don't be late."

Burke stepped away from the receptionist's desk and scanned the list again. "Think we wrote a prenup?"

"I'll check the trash for cocktail napkins." Jill had already tucked her list in her purse and was pushing her way outside.

"I think I had mine tattooed on me."

"Yeah?" She crossed her arms, watching him as he came through the door. She seemed suddenly wary. "Where?"

"Guess."

"I'm guessing it's not above your heart."

He smacked his left butt cheek with a grin and she rolled her eyes.

"You're kind of fun for a stodgy old wife, you know." Even though she was still ticked at him, he could see a spark of humor lighting her blue eyes.

He remembered laughing with her in the hotel bar, blue, red and yellow wedding ribbons clipped to her hair by someone in the wedding party. The colors signifying good luck and good fortune. His gut had been aching from laughing at her hilarious fake commentary for the hockey game playing on a TV screen to their right.

Outside the office the sky was already starting to darken, giving the city of Dakota a drab, empty and lifeless feel despite the rush hour traffic.

"Let's grab supper and strategize for tomorrow," he said, waving the intimidating list of personal assets and other documents the lawyer expected of them. More so for him, since he owned a corporation.

Jill tightened her coat around her torso as a breeze swept down the street, rattling a soda can that had been tossed in the icy gutter. "There's nothing to strategize."

"Come on, I know a great place just a few blocks from here." He began walking, trying to coax her into following. He should really ask for his suit jacket back and go back to his office to catch up on the work he'd been unable to focus on since hearing about their marriage.

But he didn't want to. He told himself he wanted to take Jill out for supper only to ensure he didn't awaken tomorrow to find her wanting blood. His.

"There's no reason to dine together."

"It's only supper. And you live a few hours from here, right?"

She nodded.

"Let me at least feed you before shipping you off home."

"Are you trying to apologize for being mean earlier?"

"Maybe. Yes." He held out his hand. "I promise I won't bite."

"Maybe I like a little bit of playful biting," she retorted, giving him a sassy look as she hesitantly fell into stepped beside him.

"I wish I could remember if that was totally true or not."

They took a few steps in silence.

"This is awkward, isn't it?" she asked.

"A bit." Mostly because he kept having X-rated flashbacks from their night together. And the more time he spent with her, the more he recalled. It was nice filling in the gaps, but it was also disconcerting. All this intimate history between them and yet out of his reach.

They walked quietly, both caught in their own thoughts. About half a block from the cozy Italian place Burke was heading for, he was pulled from his internal musings by someone calling his name. He looked up to find himself outside the restaurant MacKenzie's. Or, as he referred to the place, the deal sealer. Both for business and personal reasons.

There was a crowd of well-dressed people mingling in the dusk, as diners came and went, their breath escaping as clouds in the brisk air, and he recognized Tiffer Garbanzo, the owner of Get There Media, watching him with amusement, hands tucked into his knee-length wool jacket.

"Well, well, well. If it isn't Burke Carver with yet another beautiful woman." Tiffer came forward to shake Burke's hand, his wife, Babette, taking in Jill as she joined them.

"Good to see you." Burke kissed Babette's cool cheek. "As gorgeous as ever."

She blushed with the compliment, pleased.

For over a year Burke had been unsuccessfully trying to get Tiffer to sign a deal with Sustain This, Honey to help his company expand to global markets. But the man, an expert in foreign markets, had always brushed him off with a polite excuse about being overbooked. Burke knew STH wasn't too small and his niche was right up Tiffer's alley. The man could make anything with a hint of environmental sustainability the next It Thing. Burke needed him and Tiffer kept rebuffing him, making Burke assume the rejection was somewhat personal.

And he knew why, too. Tiffer was conservative about marriage and relationships, and every time they met Burke seemed to be with a new woman. Just like tonight.

Tiffer gave Jill a polite, dismissive smile. Jill reached out to introduce herself, but Tiffer turned to his wife, giving her a light kiss.

Jill looked affronted, and Burke said pointedly, "This is Jill Armstrong. She owns a line of medicinal creams and soaps created in the beautiful mountains, from ancient formulas founded by the Ute people. She's looking to expand." He paused thoughtfully, "Although I'm not sure you...hmm. No, never mind."

Tiffer narrowed his eyes, while Jill watched the men curiously.

"All of her products are all-natural, as well as environmentally friendly," he told Tiffer. "Good for people, good for the earth."

"Is she working with you?" Tiffer asked. "Who are you working with?" he demanded, focusing on Jill.

She eyed Burke with a bright gaze, looking for the best way to follow his lead. She looked so pretty with the cold air pinking her cheeks.

"Oh, you probably haven't heard of Tiffer," Burke said apologetically, placing a hand on her lower back. "He expands companies like ours. He specializes in the global market. He turns pennies into dollars." He glanced to Tiffer to add, "She's independent. Good luck convincing her to work with you."

"Independent? Very smart. Keep your cards close to your chest. But you know, sometimes it's good to delegate tasks to companies that are niche experts. Get There Media is well versed with how products like yours fit into the global marketplace. Why don't you join us and we can talk shop," Tiffer offered. He nudged Burke aside, guiding Jill gently between the fake potted trees lining the restaurant's outside entry. She was moving stiffly, obviously not so impressed with Tiffer or his sudden change in interest.

Burke looked up at the black-and-silver sign of the popular restaurant filled with tycoons and wannabe tycoons. This could be so easy. So, so easy.

Once inside, either Jill would make a deal with Tiffer, which would allow her to pay back Burke sooner rather than later—maybe even with interest—or the two would decide not to work together, allowing Burke to woo Tiffer and maybe even drop the fact that, legally, Jill was more than just the flavor of the week. And thus putting him in the man's favor at long last.

Tiffer and his wife moved ahead to change their dinner reservation, and Jill fell back a step, hissing to Burke, "I'm not ready to talk to a global marketer. My company isn't—"

"This is an amazing opportunity, Jill." Burke huffed warm air into his cupped hands, trying to warm them.

"He's condescending."

"Just talk to him. The networking alone—"

"Everything all right?" Tiffer asked. "The maître d' is ready to seat us."

Burke and Jill inhaled as one, placing fake smiles on their faces.

"We *need* this, Jill," Burke whispered under his breath, while nodding at Tiffer. "Please just play along and see where this happy coincidence takes us."

Jill bristled, and for a moment he thought she was going to leave. Instead she muttered, "Fine, shoot yourself in the foot and see." She marched ahead, leaving Burke to wonder what she meant. She'd already fallen into step beside Tiffer's wife and the two women were chatting as if they'd known each other for years.

Once seated, Tiffer ordered himself a scotch and soda, his wife giving a small wave of her hand when asked by the waiter.

Tiffer pointed at Burke. "Drink?"

He shook his head, then turned to Jill.

"I'll have one, please," she said, lifting her wrist to catch the waiter's attention. She'd removed her winter jacket, but was still sporting Burke's coat. The cuffs of her blouse and the suit jacket fell back, revealing a wide leather bracelet on her left wrist. It didn't go with her outfit, piquing Burke's curiosity.

"But make mine a gin," she added.

It wasn't long before it became clear that Jill wasn't ready for Tiffer's services. She couldn't maintain that kind of rapid expansion and still maintain the integrity of her handmade products.

Tiffer was glaring at Burke like he'd set him up.

Which he kind of had.

"You know, STH is still in the market to expand globally," Burke said casually. "We've built valuable momentum in the past six months and are poised to—"

"Sorry, Burke," Babette said, reaching a hand to stop him. "What does STH stand for again?"

"Sustain This. Sustainability is vital to our organization, from product creation to the end of its life."

"What's the H stand for?" Babette asked.

"Honey," Burke said quietly, taking a sip of his ice water.

"That's an amusing name," she said, a hint of laughter dancing in her eyes.

Jill was watching, her head tipped to the side.

"My assistant thought it was funny," Burke said. "Sort of an in-your-face joke that ended up becoming the company name." He focused on Tiffer again. "So as I was saying, we're ready to break into the global market. In particular we feel there is growth potential in the European arena and we—"

"Change your name." Tiffer was looking uninterested, bored even.

"Would that influence your decision in regards to partnering with us?"

"No, that's simply a helpful piece of business advice."

There was a moment of awkward silence.

Burke wasn't fond of the name, but he wasn't changing it.

"It's kind of sassy, isn't it?" Jill said. She was smiling slightly, considering the name. "I think there's some marketing potential there in terms of standing out from the crowd. Catch their attention with your name and then—"

"Shall we order?" Tiffer asked, opening his menu. "Sorry to rush things along, but Babette and I have tickets for the theater."

Jill quickly opened her menu, looking embarrassed, and making Burke dislike Tiffer for being the cause of it. "The chicken is good," he said to her.

She closed her menu, setting it gently on the linen tablecloth. "Sounds perfect."

"I'll ask my marketing team to focus on branding," he said to Jill. "Say, Tiffer…how are your new client openings?"

"It's been a busy quarter," he said, not looking up.

"I'll bet. Is there anything we can do at STH to position ourselves better for a future partnership?"

"Look, Burke," Tiffer said, placing a palm on the table, his expression one of sincerity, "I hate to make it personal, but I find married men tend to act less erratic and take fewer risks."

Burke wanted to feel insulted, but a part of him wondered if it was true.

"They tend to have more stable businesses, make fewer rash decisions," the man added.

"My business is stable."

"How can you build a solid foundation and stay focused when your personal life is in flux, with women coming and going from your world? I know it seems old-fashioned, but it's simply a personal preference I've developed after years as a leader in my field."

"Would this be a good time to tell him we're married?" Jill asked quietly. She was staring at Tiffer. "It seems odd that something like that could influence your potential to create a deal, but I do understand. We all have our own...thing. It's about what we're most comfortable with." She had placed a linen napkin across her lap earlier and now she ran it through her hands, as though debating leaving the table.

"You're married?" Tiffer asked, leaning back in his seat. He was scrutinizing Burke, who barely dared breathe.

Babette looked tickled, and she leaned across the table to ask Jill in a confiding tone, "How did you manage to tie this man down?"

"The bed sheets were too thick," Jill deadpanned. "You know how they are. I had to use rope."

Burke coughed on a sip of water as an image flashed through his mind of what his life could be like under different circumstances. Him with Jill. Partners having each other's backs. Breaking down the doors of business.

Shaking the bed frame every night.

Well, okay. He needed to focus.

This *was* about business. He had nothing to offer in the commitment department.

Even if Jill did catch him off guard in ways that made him want to spend more time with her—the woman he needed to divorce.

Jill needed to shut up.

She wasn't helping anything.

She was just so fed up with men like Tiffer, who treated others as though they were beneath him unless he could gain from them. She'd felt an unwarranted need to step in and help Burke, which showed her just how messed up her head was at the moment.

She didn't want the world to know she'd made yet another marital mistake, and here she was, announcing it. Gossips in her hometown of Blueberry Springs had finally stopped mentioning Hayes a few years ago and how he'd run off on her after blindsiding her with the theft. Then after that, they'd enjoyed discussing how long she'd "pined" for Devon Mattson, her rebound that had lasted almost two years. And then along comes mistake number three: Burke. Just another illustration of how Jill would never find love and was still making rash, desperate decisions.

She needed to stick to allowing the dating service she'd hired, We Win Your Love, to choose—scientifically via a trusted algorithm—her Mr. Right and Forever. Algorithms didn't fall prey to charm, spontaneity and fun, causing them to make poor decisions.

"When was your wedding?" Babette asked. "Was it big?"

Jill opened her mouth to reply, but the words stuck there. She didn't have a "story" ready for public consumption. Especially since Burke had been publicly seeing the governor's daughter, Autumn Martinez, since their marriage. Jill hated to admit it, but she'd been jealous when she'd seen a picture of them in the paper, grinning while cutting the ribbon together at a new city park.

Burke might still be involved with Autumn, who was publicly on the prowl for a husband.

"It was...it was a private affair," Jill said honestly. She glanced at Burke. She felt as though she owed him one. She'd borrowed against his credit, albeit unknowingly, and she could tell that stressed him out. Sure, she had a careful, meticulously outlined five-year plan where she'd steadily expand her business, taking it slow and easy while performing her full-time work at All You, a cosmetics company. She would think and strategize before taking each step so she didn't end up ruining another business by not staying on top of everything.

She could tell he needed Tiffer in the way he put up with the guy being slightly pompous and condescending. Assumptive. Men like Burke walked away from guys like that. And he wasn't walking.

She'd spoken up, thinking it might change things for Burke, but she really shouldn't have.

They were arranging to get a divorce.

Tomorrow.

That would not help Burke look like a stable man in Tiffer's eyes.

Burke slipped a hand along the back of Jill's chair, joining her conversation with Babette. "After we made the decision, we moved quite quickly. Didn't we, Jill?" His thumb ran over her shoulder, and she shivered at the contact.

"We did," she admitted. "Kept it unconventional. No rings. No gown."

"Just a top hat and veil."

Jill glanced at him. Did he recall their wedding? He gave a small nod as though savoring the memory, trying to bring more of it to mind.

"You make it sound as though that was all the two of you were wearing," Babette said with a tinkling laugh.

Burke let out a short chuckle. "Jill wasn't as immune to my charms as she believed, that was for sure."

"I think it was the other way around. You admired a woman who could keep you in line."

Burke chuckled again, warming her.

"I like her," Tiffer said to Burke.

"She doesn't back down," he'd replied, with a smile twisted with wry humor as well as a hint of admiration and attraction which sucker-punched Jill's desire to keep picking at him. It was that same look he'd given her in the conference hotel's bar when she'd said to heck with being proper and had let it all hang out, like she was one of the guys. But like today, she'd been done up as a sexy businesswoman. His type. Not a small-town gal with a hobby business who preferred to wear jeans and eat tasty doughnuts. Or ice cream. Or perhaps a sundae with whipped cream and chocolate syrup. And those crunchy little cookie bit toppings.

That attraction wasn't real. But she found herself wishing it was.

"How did you meet?" Tiffer's wife asked.

"The Metro Conference," Jill said. "I'd been hounding him for a meeting for months."

"Are you going again in April?" Babette asked Burke.

"I'm not sure."

"Oh, you have to! We've booked a suite and Tiffer will be taking proposals all weekend."

"You gotta show off your new wife, Burke." There was an unspoken dare in Tiffer's words, and Burke, who still had his arm along the back of Jill's chair, stiffened.

"Maybe if we're not too busy with world domination by then," he said, smiling at Jill.

"Oh, I'm certain we will be." She returned his smile, feeling like they had each other's backs.

"Tell you what." Tiffer sat back in his chair, and the way he studied Burke made Jill want to jump to her husband's defense no matter what was coming. "Meet my team at the Metro Conference. Make your pitch."

"It would be my pleasure," Burke replied.

"Bring your wife."

"Our businesses are separate."

"Bring her."

Jill resisted the urge to say *"I'm right here, stop talking like I'm not."*

"Would you like to come?" Burke asked Jill, his jaw flexing. It was a little more than two months away from now. Surely they'd be divorced, and strangers again by then.

She teased Burke, "Share a room this year?"

"We did last year, so why not again?" His voice was low, rumbling, and her mind flew to her scattered memories of their wedding night.

Suddenly it was very warm in his sports coat.

"Great. The newlyweds will be there," Tiffer said without amusement, as salads were placed on the table. "If the team likes you and your proposal, we'll sign Sustain This, Honey. You know our old base fee?"

"I do."

"It's increased by 18 percent. Will that be an issue?"

Jill could tell Burke was trying to act cool even though inside he was fist-pumping to his success.

"Not a problem," he said in a controlled voice.

A tension settled over the table as though the two men had challenged each other to a duel and were waiting for the other to break the rules of combat first. Jill placed a hand over Burke's, which was clutching a fork. His gaze flicked to hers and she smiled.

Their plans had breathing room now. This was good.

"To the newlyweds and business prospects," Babette said.

Everyone lifted their glasses. "To a whole new unrecognizable life," Burke said forcefully. He emptied his glass and Babette lowered hers to the table, clinking it with a spoon.

"Come on, newlyweds," she coaxed, watching them expectantly.

"Jill isn't into public displays..." Burke began uneasily.

"This is so exciting," Jill said, trying to divert the topic. "I'm sure the two of you will have so much to talk about at the conference."

Tiffer was staring at Burke, and she could sense things shifting. Burke needed this deal. Jill needed this deal. But there was something going on under the surface, and if Burke didn't kiss her, who knew what might happen.

"Come on, newlyweds," Tiffer's wife repeated. "Let's celebrate!" She clinked her glass again.

It was just a kiss. A kiss that could solve and protect everything.

Jill hooked her hand around the back of Burke's neck and pulled his face close to hers. "Kiss me."

He stared at her, his whole body taunt with tension. For a moment she thought he was going to pull away, deny her, humiliate her with rejection.

"Fine. Brace yourself."

Jill's amused laugh was cut short by his lips landing on hers. His mouth was hungry, impatient and demanding. She gripped his face, forcing him to slow down and enjoy the moment, the contact. It could be their last kiss.

His mouth was hot, his hands moving to her waist, pulling her closer. She needed this. Desired this. She wanted to crawl into his lap and feel his body pressed to hers like a comforting presence.

What was this between them? They fought like they could barely stand each other, then the next moment were laughing, and then kissing so passionately they might burn the place down.

No wonder she'd married him.

She let out a moan of contentment as his tongue met hers. She edged closer. Someone cleared their throat, but Jill shut out the rest of the world so she could enjoy being lost in Burke's kiss.

She was fed up with trying to please lovers, walking away never quite satisfied, and this kiss...this kiss claimed that Burke was the type of man whose mouth made promises she knew his body could keep.

She remembered. Remembered a lot.

And it was all toe-curling good.

There was another loud throat clearing and a pleading voice said, "Sir. Madam. *Please.*"

Burke broke the kiss first, his eyes hazed with lust and longing, which Jill was certain was being reflected back at him full force. He looked as though he was struggling to place himself, like he was lost in some alternate universe. They were both breathing hard and it was difficult to resist the urge to draw him back into another life-altering, world-tipping kiss. To lose herself again.

"Sir? Madam?"

She'd crawled onto Burke's lap at some point, sitting sideways, completely absorbed in him. Her side was cold and wet, and she realized they'd spilled his water glass over the linen tablecloth.

Their waiter was awkwardly standing over them, trying to fix the tangled cloth.

"Oh! I'm so sorry." Jill jumped up, the tablecloth shifting with her movement as she tried to squeeze her larger frame into a gap between chairs she swore she would have fitted through a year ago. Another glass of ice water toppled over, spilling into Burke's lap. Jill exclaimed and snatched a napkin, swiping at his crotch. Realizing what she was doing, she straightened in horror, elbowing the waiter, who was trying to sop up the water on the table.

"I'm so sorry!"

Tiffer had a hand over his mouth and was barely holding back his guffaws, while his wife fussed about with the waiter. All around the restaurant, attention angled toward the growing mishap.

"I'm so sorry," Jill said yet again, tucking her elbows at her sides, her hands clenched together across her chest so she wouldn't cause any more harm. The borrowed suit jacket was gaping, revealing her open blouse with the missing buttons, and she quickly readjusted it. She dared a glance at Burke, who looked shell-shocked.

"It's fine," Tiffer's wife kept repeating, her face bright red. "It's fine."

There was no way this evening was being saved. Jill had acted inappropriately, spilled water everywhere while she made out with her accidental husband, misleading Burke's possible future business partners as well as completely humiliating herself.

She needed air. She needed to get away from this mess and the spontaneity and disaster that followed her whenever she was with Burke.

She needed to save everything before it was too late.

BURKE WAS STILL STRUGGLING with the shock of having made out with Jill in the middle of the posh restaurant. He hadn't expected the kiss or his intense reaction to it.

No wonder he'd married her. She was some sort of temptress that made him want her—badly.

Babette was gaping after Jill, who'd fled seconds ago. Tiffer was still laughing, every once in a while letting out an extra loud guffaw.

Burke clutched the edge of the table, trying to wrap his head around the situation and how he had obviously mortified his...his wife.

They might have an accidental marriage, but there was no reason he shouldn't still treat her with respect. And he wasn't so sure he had. It was like everything he knew about himself and how to behave went out the window when she was around.

"Please excuse us." He tossed his sodden napkin on the table along with what cash was in his wallet.

"No, please." Babette pushed the money back his way. "Go to her."

Burke turned, leaving the money, eyes averted to avoid seeing the mirth of the other patrons.

He caught up with Jill almost a block away. Despite her high heels, she could move like an Olympic speed walker.

"Jill..."

She went faster, her hands moving to her face as though dealing with tears.

Burke's shoulders sagged. "I'm sorry. But really...it's okay. It's not a big deal."

It was just a hot kiss, right? Spilled water. Worse things had happened, he was certain.

She didn't turn, didn't slow. "I'll see you at the meeting tomorrow." Her voice was tight with emotion.

This was usually where Burke would bail, have his assistant send a nice breakup gift and move on. He stopped walking and shoved his hands into his wet pants pockets, her winter jacket still tucked over his arm. She'd left it behind in her haste to leave and she had to be chilled—or soon would be once her mortification wore off.

"Are you okay?" he called.

"No," she shouted. "That was so...so *humiliating*." She turned, her expression so stricken it caused him to start walking again.

"So hot?" he murmured, when he was within a foot of her.

She let out a shuddery exhalation, her breath causing a cloud in the cold evening air, her fingertips going to her brow as she dropped her head. "Not helpful."

He held out her coat and she blinked at it before gratefully sliding her arms into the sleeves.

"It was also…" He cleared his throat, saw a brick building beside them and leaned against it. "…unexpected."

Act casual, man. It was just a kiss.

A kiss that had opened a floodgate of memories from them laughing in the bar, to him proposing, to waking up alone. Abandoned.

He rolled his stiff shoulders. Surely it wasn't true abandonment. She'd claimed she hadn't even remembered most of the night and, until recently, it wasn't as though he recalled many details, either.

Jill was looking up now, apparently worrying over something new. "I *lied* to them."

"Not really. We *are* married."

She sniffed once, twice. She kept tipping her head higher and higher, as if she might somehow rise above the emotion plaguing her and get it back under control.

"Come here," he said, lifting his hands out at his sides.

"I'm fine," she said quickly, shivering with the cold. Another sniff. She was losing the battle. Despite the way she could bust his balls, she was a woman on the brink. A woman with a wet skirt wearing a too-big suit jacket stuffed under her open winter coat, making her look like someone in need of a hug.

He eased to her side, checking to see if she was okay with him in her space before wrapping his arms around her, drawing her body against his, stroking her hair. She let out a shudder, her face tucked into the crook of his neck. She was the perfect height for a snuggle, and her soft curves felt…good. Really good. Comforting almost.

How did this mess they were in somehow feel so right?

Did he just need a hug, too? Was that all this was?

"I'm sorry," he said again.

Her arms snaked around his waist, squeezing him tight. They stayed that way for a long moment, a cold breeze gusting around them, sending discarded fliers up into the air, swirling before settling around them, the nearby streetlight brightening their piece of the earth.

She tipped her head back to study him, leaving the spot against his neck feeling chilled.

"Okay?" he asked.

"I'm not going back in there."

"Still hungry?" They hadn't gotten past salads.

Her gaze traveled to his mouth, and without thinking, he let nature do its thing, pulling her cold lips to his. But this time, knowing now how easy it was to get caught up in the power of kissing her, he left it at a gentle, sweet kiss before pulling back.

"What was that for?" she whispered.

"It just felt right."

"Just felt right?" Her brow furrowed. "That sounds familiar."

Her arms were still around him and he gave her another squeeze, not quite ready to let her go. He chuckled as a new memory weaved its way to the front of his mind, unfurling there. "I think that's what I said after I proposed to you."

"You proposed?"

"You don't remember? The biggest day of your life?" He grunted in disappointment. "I'm hurt."

She gave him a playful scowl and pushed him away. "Marrying you was not the biggest day of my life."

"Then what was?" he asked, snagging her chilled hand as they began walking, worried she'd leave him standing on the gusty street, his curiosity unfulfilled.

She shrugged. "I'm not sure it's happened yet. But marrying you is *so* not it." She laughed, her eyes crinkling. For a moment he felt a connection between them, and it made him want to find a way to share more moments like this with her.

"Again, I'm so hurt you don't remember our big night."

"*You* don't even remember it." She leaned closer, tagging him on the chest with a finger from her free hand. She didn't seem to mind that he was still holding her other hand and he wrapped his other hand around it as well, pressing his warmth into her. She had paused in her walking, looking thoughtful. "Or do you?"

"Some of it. Mostly just the beginning and the morning. But the past day has refreshed a few details, as well as placed a few things I thought were..." *Fantasies*. "...dreams."

They fell into step, moving again, and he readjusted their grip so they were palm to palm. It felt good, that connection. Solid and strong.

"So, tell me the story of how you proposed," Jill said. "If you remember." She was studying the sidewalk in front of them, her steps uneven as she avoided the cracks in the concrete.

"Afraid you'll break your mother's back?" he asked, referring to the old saying that if you stepped on a sidewalk crack it would have that result.

"The day I stomped on them all the way home from school my mom was in a car accident."

"I'm sorry, Jill."

She flashed him a bright smile. "Just kidding." She stepped on a crack, and he winced. "So? You proposed?"

"We were in that bar in the basement of the conference hotel. Remember it?"

She nodded.

He focused on the threads of memory he had, willing them to flesh out into a full story so he could enthrall her with its retelling.

"There was a wedding there that night. The place was packed."

She was squinting like an amnesiac struggling to pull up her own name. "Good music?"

"Yeah, it was very festive. There was a live band playing songs in Spanish." He backtracked to explain that the wedding had had a Mexican theme and there had been lots of fun traditions and that the partiers had drawn them into the celebrations. "At one point I turned to you at the bar and said, "Will you marry me?" You laughed like you were going to have a seizure, knocked back a shot, then said, "Sure. Why not?"

Her cheeks had been flushed, the night fun, full of unexpected moments of freedom blending into the next. He hadn't wanted it to end.

"Like I was going to have a seizure? So romantic," Jill teased. She'd been swinging their linked hands, and when she noticed, she dropped his, shoving her fists deep into the pockets of her coat, his borrowed suit jacket peeking out from under its hem. He suspected that if she truly had been planning to burn it she'd changed her mind.

"When you asked me later why I proposed I replied that it just felt right. You agreed, and then I'm not really sure what happened after that."

"We found a late night chapel."

"Yeah?" He turned to her, waiting for details. He knew this part—he'd searched the registries after seeing her yesterday and had tracked their marriage back to the chapel on Shalina Avenue. Just in case the certificate was a fraud. Which it wasn't.

"That's where we got married. I looked it up."

"Me, too." He shrugged at her inquiring look. "Just performing due diligence."

She sighed as they walked slowly, her steps measured. "So this thing with Tiffer... It's good for your business?"

"It could be a life changer if he accepts my proposal."

"I hope that... That I didn't..." She gestured vaguely toward the restaurant they'd left behind.

"I'm sure it didn't change a thing." The money part was going to be an issue, though. If Jill didn't repay her loan there was no way he could personally secure Tiffer's fee, let alone the increase. The company couldn't leverage that amount due to its expansion plans. In other words...stuck.

Jill let out a groan. "I can never go in there again. Nobody in the business world will take me seriously."

Burke was silent for a moment, then, realizing she was still fretting, said, "Are you kidding? Everyone was wondering how to get what we have."

"We have nothing but accidents, Burke."

He shrugged noncommittally, feeling strangely as though he'd failed her.

"If you want me to go to that conference with you—even though we'll be divorced..."

It still surprised Burke on some level that Tiffer had indeed previously denied a partnership because of his dating habits, and not the health or positioning of his company.

"Just...let me know whatever you need."

He nodded thoughtfully, considering her offer. She'd definitely put a kink in his plans, but a deal with Tiffer would help Burke forgive any damage she'd inadvertently done. Assuming he got the deal and could pay the fee.

Possibly if he shifted priorities for the next two months he could find a way. They could angle that momentum they'd been creating right into the global market.

Two months, though. That wasn't a lot of time.

"How about we cross that bridge when we come to it?" Burke said finally. "But pencil me in, seeing as Tiffer only seems to like me when I'm married."

He thought about the weight of that statement. The implications.

Burke glanced at the woman walking beside him. He could already see that divorcing Jill was going to be a problem for his bottom line in a way he hadn't quite anticipated.

CHAPTER 3

Overlooking the city of Dakota from his top floor apartment, Burke ran on his squeaking treadmill, which was set off to the side in his living room.

Thinking and thinking.

There had to be a way to raise enough money in time to work with Tiffer. Assuming the man accepted Burke's pitch in April.

Beyond his apartment windows Burke could see the mountains rising in the distance, hiding Jill's hometown of Blueberry Springs. They had to get a divorce. It was just too risky to let her stay tied to his life, business and finances.

How serious had Tiffer been about Burke bringing his wife to the Metro Conference pitch? Would it be an automatic "no" like in the past if he showed up single?

Burke's treadmill program decreased the incline, putting him into the cool-down zone, the squeaking quieting enough that the TV on the wall across from him could be heard. There was a news piece about the missing adult daughter of a British Mafia family, followed by a story on a murder-suicide. Burke hit the remote, turning off the television. Leave it to the news to put his life into perspective.

He stepped off the treadmill and wiped the sweat from his brow with a towel. He found his tablet on the coffee table and pulled up the order he'd placed last night for a new treadmill, then canceled it before sending a service request to a local repairman instead.

To raise the fee to work with Tiffer, he was going to need to save more than a few thousand on workout machinery. Maybe he should skip repairing the machine altogether and just use the office gym more regularly?

He thought back to Jill running on the treadmill beside him, decked out in her business attire. He smiled and shook his head at the memory of her persistence. There was something about that woman...

No, he was definitely repairing his treadmill, as the gym had too many distractions.

He swapped out his tablet for his cell phone, and with his sights locked on a sculpture his assistant had convinced him to buy, he took a photo. Two years ago he'd charged Gulliver with the job of finding a decorator. Instead, his assistant had personally taken up the task of turning the sleek apartment into a home. But the overpriced sculpture, like everything else in the place, meant nothing to Burke.

The little fur-ball of a kitten Burke had found in the building's trash bin came skittering across the floor. Nobody had claimed the little beast and it had been a fluke that the cat hadn't been crushed or carted away before Burke found him. Burke's aunt, however, thought it was all serendipitous, as she'd been trying to convince Burke to settle down, get a pet, and all that grown-up jazz.

She'd nicknamed the cat Serendipity, but out of protest, Burke had decided to dub him Fluke. It fit better, anyway. Plus it was a boy. A boy who'd just pounced on his shoelaces, sinking his claws through the mesh tops of Burke's sneakers.

"Ow!"

He peeled the cat off his foot, sticking the puss on his shoulder, where he liked to ride. The feline began to purr on his warm perch, rubbing the top of his head against Burke's five o'clock shadow.

"What else can go from this place, Fluke? Hmm? Other than your scrawny butt, of course."

The cat's claws sank in and Burke wasn't sure if it was for balance or in protest for the insensitive comment.

"Don't worry, your real owner will find you soon," he said, turning to snap another photo. "Then you can go home."

The cat made a flying leap to the nearby couch, his claws making a shredding noise as he slid out of view over its back, dropping onto an arrangement of blown glass vases Gulliver had insisted weren't girlie.

Burke heard the sound of breaking glass and swept the cat out of the mess.

"So...I guess I can't sell the couch, since you just ruined it. Or those one-of-a-kind collectible dust-catchers." Burke touched the thin cut in the couch's fabric. "Seriously. Common courtesy, cat." He cleaned up the glass while Fluke sat nearby, tailed tucked neatly around his body, looking innocent and slightly regal as he blinked at Burke. "It's okay, I never liked those, either."

Sighing, he toured the rest of the main floor, snapping a photo of a painting, his drum set, the leather massage chair he'd never used and Fluke had yet to destroy.

Burke took the open staircase to the bedroom loft, continuing his mission. Once done, he uploaded the folder of photos to his assistant's virtual to-do list, then showered and got dressed for work. He debated locking Fluke in his bedroom for safety and to narrow the feline's swath of destruction, but last time he'd done that, he'd come home to curtains that looked like a five-year-old's first macramé project. It was best the cat be left to roam the entire apartment, spreading out the mess so it didn't seem as bad.

Burke locked his apartment, checked to make sure the neighbor's kid was still okay to come by after school to play with Fluke for a bit, and forty-five minutes later walked into his office, to find a panicked Gulliver.

"Are we losing our jobs?" his assistant asked in a hushed tone, scurrying alongside Burke. His usually well groomed and perfect appearance was flawed by a shirt that hadn't been tucked in at the back, a sure sign the man was flustered.

"No. What do you have for me today?"

Gulliver handed Burke a steaming mug of coffee, and instead of digging into the plastic folder tucked under his arm, he pleaded, "You can't close the place. I know profits haven't been what we projected, but Declan's son needs surgery. He needs a good health plan. Andrea's about to go on maternity leave. You can't leave her unemployed with a new baby."

"Keep your voice down. Nobody's losing their jobs."

The office had quieted, and everyone was studiously trying not to look at Burke, and failing. The only movement was a leaf falling off a potted fig outside Andrea's office.

"Everyone back to work," Burke said, before striding into his own office, barely refraining from slamming the door. Within seconds, Gulliver was letting himself in.

"What is it?" Burke asked with a weary sigh.

"Emilio thinks he has HIV again—and no, he didn't have shingles, it was a spider bite, thanks for asking—so I really can't deal with trying to sell your personal possessions in the faint hope of keeping the company afloat. I have enough drama in my life, and if we're going down we need to just accept it. Not cling to the sinking lifeboat."

Burke took a second to unpack all of what Gulliver had said. He started from the top.

"Does it ever make you wonder why Emilio keeps thinking he has HIV when he's in a committed relationship with you?" he asked gently.

Gulliver tossed himself onto the low couch near the door. "He likes the attention. He's loyal."

"Have you tried focusing on him more when you're home? You know, put down your phone?"

"Will you fire me if it takes more than a few hours to reply to your emails?"

"Probably," Burke said with a teasing smile. He'd started the company with Gulliver at his side and couldn't imagine walking into the office without the man there, ready to help him tackle his jam-packed days. They hadn't grown this big, this fast by lollygagging or by being unfocused. Gulliver was so integral that he'd even named the company. A horrible name, but still. He was as much a part of the place as Burke was. "By the way, I want to talk to the marketing department about leveraging the uniqueness of our company name."

Gulliver nodded to acknowledge the additional task. "About time." He switched subjects with his usual speed. "He just can't seem to be happy."

"Emilio? Another brilliant reason to stay single. You never know if they're happy or about to leave you."

Gulliver was watching with his eyebrows raised. Obviously, his assistant had heard something and was waiting for Burke to mention it. Burke had a feeling that whatever it was, it was about Jill.

Burke took a sip of his coffee to buy himself time, then set it down, noting that Gulliver had chosen a plain black cup, which was a sure sign he was in a touchy mood and that Burke ought to tread carefully.

"You know if we're going down as a company I won't draw it out. You'll be the first person to know. And to stick with your analogy, I'll give everyone plenty of time to securely situate themselves in a lifeboat."

"I knew it," Gulliver moaned.

"Oh, stop already."

Gulliver pulled himself out of the funk. Well, mostly.

Burke pushed back his shirt cuffs, his attention catching on the stylized comma tattoo on his right wrist. It wasn't a bad tattoo, but he wasn't an editor or bookish type and the black mark made no sense to him. Although according to Gulliver, who had a degree in creative writing, he did tend to put too many commas in his memos. Maybe the tattoo was supposed to be ironic. He'd wanted to ask Jill, since the mark had appeared the night they'd married, but he was too embarrassed by the already large list of out-of-character things he couldn't recall having done that night. But apparently had.

He held up his wrist. "Make me an appointment to get this thing removed, would you?"

"I like it."

"It's ridiculous and has no meaning."

"Live the cliché with your drunken tattoo." Gulliver held up a hand that was blotchy and pink. "My eczema has gotten so bad there is no way I could ever get a tattoo."

"See your doctor."

"The medicated creams don't work because I'm so stressed. If we're going to try and remove something, let's focus on fixing my eczema rather than your perfectly fine tattoo."

"Did you send out any partnership letters? We need to raise funds in case Tiffer accepts our pitch."

"I literally *screamed* when I got your email. Emilio fell right out of bed. *How* did you manage to snag that pitch spot? Was he drunk? Did you offer him special favors?"

"There are still a lot of hurdles to get over before the pitch. Such as raising the funds for his contract fee." And showing up there with a wife. One whose name was Jill Armstrong. The very Jill Armstrong he was intent on divorcing.

Burke repositioned the cup sitting on his desk. There had to be an answer that solved everything.

"I sent them. But nobody can afford to work with you, so don't get your hopes up," Gulliver stated.

"You have to sell all that decor stuff. I don't need it."

"Sell it yourself."

Burke turned to look out the window behind him. Streams of traffic four stories down were choking each other with their exhaust fumes, visible in the icy air.

"Why can't this be easier, Gully?"

"Because then everyone would be doing it. There are more profits in choosing the environmentally destructive option. Our business is about *not* going that route, so please don't change for the sake of cash. We'd all make a Burke voodoo doll if you did." Gulliver gestured to the offices beyond the closed door. He lowered his voice. "Any luck with Autumn's father and the tax breaks?"

Burke shook his head. "The only thing I'm close to getting is an unwanted girlfriend."

He winced at the thought. He was *married*.

Gulliver stood up. "No pressure, but you're responsible for the world, Burke Carver. Our futures and fate rest in your hands."

Burke pursed his lips at the dramatic statement, giving Gulliver a look. "Thanks for the added weight on my shoulders."

"It's why we love you. We trust you with our lives because of those big broad shoulders of yours." Gulliver, with a sassy look, left the office, closing the door behind him.

"Gulliver!"

The door opened. "Yes?"

"The file?"

"Right." Gulliver handed him the folder made from recycled plastic, quickly outlining the day's "must-do" items.

When he let himself out again, Burke began on the starred task—the most important item. The door opened once again and Burke suppressed the urge to groan at the interruption. He had issues to mull over. Specifically, the fact that he couldn't seem to get Jill out of his mind. And not just because he needed both to divorce her *and* stay married to her.

Oh, right, and according to the starred item on his list, he also had to sort out a way to boost the profitability of their bamboo fiber T-shirt line.

"And," Gulliver stated dramatically, "just to reiterate, I'm not selling off your possessions. I lovingly chose each and every one of them specifically with you in mind." He closed the door again before Burke could reply.

Burke pressed the buzzer that went to Gulliver's desk. His assistant didn't answer. Burke began tapping the buzzer, knowing it would eventually annoy him into answering.

"Not selling a thing," Gulliver chirped through the speaker a few moments later.

"Yes you are, unless you come up with a better way to raise the capital."

Silence.

"And I have an appointment downtown at three. Clear my calendar."

"Hot new date with the new girlfriend?" Gulliver asked, without his usual gusto.

So he had heard about Jill.

"Something the opposite of that."

"Should I prepare one of the larger I'm-a-doofus breakup gifts so she might come back, since you went for one who wasn't cool and lifeless?"

"There is no girlfriend," Burke said, taking special care to emphasize each word.

"I heard about MacKenzie's. She seems frisky. Someone to keep you on your toes. And definitely better than that cold fish Autumn Martinez. When are you getting rid of her again? I can pencil her in for a formal dismissal so she gets the hint that you don't do real-ationships."

"Funny. Thought of that one yourself?"

"I did. And there's a very nice up-yours gift on sale at the shop around the corner that could have her name on it."

Burke silently shook his head, trying not to smile. There were both upsides and downsides to having an assistant such as Gulliver.

"So?" the man prompted. "What's going on with this new woman? Does Autumn know?"

"Jill and I are nothing," Burke said, feeling the lie. Whatever they had, it was certainly something. Unpredictable, too. He'd never gotten lost in a kiss like that before. Or married on a whim, either.

And his need to comfort her last night...what had that been about? That was putting the "real" in real-ationship.

But he didn't have time for someone who had 'big mess' written all over her. He needed to divorce her, move on. He could figure out Tiffer later. Right now he needed to focus on finding a new lead to chase.

"You're the world's worst liar, Burke Carver," Gulliver said. "So? What should I send this nice Jill—what's her last name?—so she doesn't cause you grief later? Or should I send her flowers so she keeps coming back?"

"She's already taken more than she should."

"Oh, do tell your friend Gully everything. I promise not to tell a soul—and did I mention everyone is soulless these days?"

Burke sighed, then put on his stern-boss voice. "I need a list of my personal assets, as well as those of the company, by two."

Gulliver said quietly, "Oh, boy. She got you *bad*."

"It's not like that," Burke said gruffly, even though, again, he felt like he was lying.

JILL SAT with Rebecca Walker in Mandy Mattson's small wraps

and sandwiches café in Blueberry Springs. Years ago, when Jill was a teen, the Ute elder had taught her how to make her natural soaps and creams, using ingredients that grew in the local alpine meadows. Since then she'd always been working on the products in one way or another, selling them first to family and friends, then in the stores and farmers markets around Blueberry Springs.

Rebecca, who had been watching Jill all through their meal, finally said, "You look tired."

"Long night," Jill replied. She'd been up fretting about Burke and how mixed up he made her feel, as well as the possible consequences of their spontaneous marriage. If only she hadn't accidentally thrown out their marriage certificate the next morning. If only she'd looked inside the envelope.

When she and Hayes had divorced it certainly hadn't been fun, gutting her inside for what felt like ages. With things between her and Burke being complicated and emotionally all over the place, she knew she wouldn't be gutted. But she was still worried over what she might face later that day. So much so that she almost broke her vow to keep her marriage a secret around town, and asked Rebecca to come along as moral support.

But soon it would be over, and she could focus once again on raising enough money through her traditional botanicals to rebuild the Ute friendship center, which had been destroyed in a forest fire years ago. Rebecca kept telling her she didn't need to, that it wasn't her responsibility. But Jill knew how much that community gathering place was missed. Not only was Rebecca's son becoming involved in drugs now that he and his friends wandered the town at night, but it had been like a welcoming second home to Jill as a teen. It had been a place where laughter and calming drums were the soundtrack instead of arguing parents and a twin sister who was too busy being popular with her boyfriend of the week in their shared bedroom.

It was time to get serious about earning enough to rebuild the center. Jill had kept the Ute waiting long enough.

"Man problems," Rebecca declared, guessing the reason for Jill's lack of sleep. Her big smile lit up her face.

"Sort of," Jill admitted.

"Not Devon?" Rebecca knew the whole sad story about Jill and Devon Mattson. How they'd happened to be on the same plane to Hawaii years ago, and staying in the same hotel. It had been a coincidence. One that had brought them home as a couple, much to everyone's surprise. But Devon was a free spirit, or had been until Olivia Carrington had come back into his life. He was adventure, fun and spontaneity. Jill was steady and reliable. He needed Band-Aids. She had them stocked.

It hadn't worked out. And she'd wasted years of her life focusing on a relationship that wasn't meant to be—even after it was over. A discount deal had brought them together, not fate.

It had been happenstance, plain and simple. Just like it had been happenstance that had led her parents to win a weeklong trip for two when Jill was thirteen. That had been followed by a "meant to be" gig, according to her father, that had resulted in them staying on board the cruise for an additional two-and-a-half months as the fill-in musicians, while Grandma Armstrong stepped in back home to take care of the girls.

It had seemed like fate until her father had fallen off the stage during a storm and damaged the tendons in his forearm, making it impossible for him to continue his career as a guitarist. Her parents had come home with no future, no income.

That, according to Jill, was hardly the serendipitous luck her father claimed it to be. Her parents' marriage had gone downhill after that, only recently stabilizing again.

She'd learned about believing in happy coincidences leading to success. The only luck out there was the kind you made on your own.

"Not Devon," Jill confirmed to Rebecca, shaking the past from her thoughts.

"Good. He wasn't the right man for you."

"You could have told me," Jill said lightly.

"Did I not tell you every day? I said, 'Jill, this is not the man for you.'"

Jill gave her a rueful smile. "I didn't want to listen."

"You didn't want to listen," Rebecca confirmed. "You wanted to believe in love, like every young woman. Just wait. I will find the right man for you—and before your sister's tenth wedding anniversary party in May."

Jill straightened. "Actually, I found a dating site that has a very scientific algorithm which will sort through the site's most eligible men and find the perfect one for me."

"Oh, I love dating sites. So many juicy options."

Jill laughed. Rebecca was a grandmother. A *married* grandmother, but she had a cheeky spirit that kept her young.

"You'd never stray," Jill stated.

Rebecca's eyes danced.

"I had the site recommend someone to me last night," Jill went on.

"And he's the reason you're tired today?"

"No." She laughed. "I haven't contacted him yet." Eager to share what had been a secret up to this point, she turned her phone to Rebecca and showed her the man's profile.

Her nose scrunched.

"I know," Jill said quickly. "He's not handsome, but look. He already owns a house. That shows stability. He has a ten-year plan. He's investing for his retirement. My life's well organized and even I don't do that."

She couldn't help but wonder if Burke had all those things. He had the handsomeness in spades.

"You should invest," Rebecca said.

"I plan on investing in a friendship center." She continued on quickly before her friend could say they had Mandy's café to gather in, where they didn't have to do the baking or clean the coffeepot. "He's also very well organized." Jill tapped on the man's profile photo to show the bookcase behind him. "See? No dust and the books are in alphabetical order. By author."

Rebecca Walker didn't look impressed.

"We're a 98 percent match."

"But is there love? Chemistry? Sexual passion? Being too much alike is boring. It's like being alone, except there's always an annoying version of yourself hanging around all the time."

Jill giggled and put her phone in her purse. "I've been swept away by the idea of love before and it didn't work out. I'm planning it this time. I'm getting too old for wild-goose chases."

The older woman shrugged. "But that's the true beauty of love."

BACK AT WORK, Jill parked her SUV outside All You's brand-new two-story, log-and-river-stone headquarters. The commissioned building fitted perfectly into the mountain town. It was modern yet rustic, and utilized solar power in its green build for the all-natural cosmetics' home. A nice little full-circle moment, as the products had prevented a massive hydroelectric dam from being built adjacent to the picturesque little community.

She headed to her office to pick up a stack of spreadsheets, then went to Emma Carrington's office. Her boss was sitting near one of the peaked two-story windows at her massive mahogany antique desk, wearing a silk blouse and fitted black slacks, her pixie cut looking adorably chic as always.

"I have an appointment in the city again this afternoon," Jill said, walking across the large room. Jill kept her focus on the papers as though organizing them, hoping Emma wouldn't ask for details about needing more time off. She feared the woman would see right through her and read the truth. And not just because she'd had her own secret marriage last year to Luke Cohen, the man she now worked alongside.

Emma took the spreadsheets and flipped through them. "How are the orders?"

"Holding steady." Jill toyed with the wide leather bracelet she'd taken to wearing on her left wrist.

"Everything okay?" Emma asked when she was done, setting the orders aside.

"Yes, thanks." Or it soon would be, anyway. "I'll be back by six and then work until nine or so, and tomorrow to make up for the rest of the lost time."

Emma was watching her, and worried she might see through her artful dodging, Jill snatched a binder off her boss's desk. It had papers shoved in willy-nilly. "Let me organize this for you."

"Are you sure everything's okay?"

"Just fine, thanks."

"Do you need a friend to go with you? I can clear my schedule. I wouldn't mind doing a little shopping at a real mall."

"No," Jill said quickly, just as Ginger McGinty, the local bridal shop owner, entered the office, her reddish curls bouncing jauntily. "Really. But thanks."

Ginger took one look at Jill's expression and said, "You've got a secret."

"What? No." Jill cringed. She'd protested too fast. *Way* too fast.

Both women were watching her, and Jill sighed, giving in. "I'm meeting with Burke Carver." She stopped, unsure what else to say. Emma would assume Jill's ancient business proposal was being considered. Ginger would assume it was a hot date.

It was neither. How did you explain it was a meeting to dissolve a marriage you forgot had even happened? One's wedding day was not something most women didn't remember. Especially not someone like Ginger, whose whole life revolved around celebrating the big day.

Emma squealed. "I knew you two would strike a deal. Is he playing hardball? Do you need advice?"

Jill ducked her nose into the messy binder, straightening the sheets.

"Are you blushing?" Ginger asked. "You have a crush. This is personal, not business."

"What?" Emma sounded startled. "Like a date?"

"No, no," Jill said, impressed with how casual she sounded.

"Oh. Well, he *is* cute," Emma stated.

Jill felt herself blushing even more. Burke wasn't cute. He was handsome. Very handsome. And he kissed like... She'd better not think about it or Ginger would totally read the situation the wrong way.

"Well," Emma said, "I can't believe it's taken almost a year for him to get his butt in gear and see what your products have to offer." She leaned back in her office chair, arms crossed, looking indignant on Jill's behalf. "Your businesses are perfect for a partnership."

"I doubt anything like that will come from this meeting," Jill muttered. "But I appreciate your optimism."

"Let me know if you need me to give him a nudge," Ginger said with a mischievous wink. She was a well-known matchmaker whose shop attracted customers from miles and miles away, even more so now that Emma's sister, Olivia, was designing one-of-a-kind dresses for her. But it was Ginger and her matchmaking skills that truly seemed to be boosting her business these days. She leaned against Emma's desk, giving their short-haired friend a pointed look. "I hear mixing business and pleasure is the way to go in this town these days."

Emma laughed. "Hey, it worked for me!"

"And Ethan and Lily," Ginger added.

"I don't anticipate needing your services in the near future," Jill said. "At least not with Burke. I'd rather keep things professional."

"Like Amy and Moe." Ginger tapped her chin. "That's professional, but they totally have a thing for each other. How long until they succumb, do you think?"

"They tried being more than friends," Jill said, referring to the two long-time friends who ran the town's brew pub together.

"They have a marriage pledge," Emma stated. "Marry each other at thirty—and Amy is only months away."

"But neither of them will actually go through with it," Jill declared.

"I think they will..." Ginger had a wicked glint in her eye.

"Yeah, if you have any say," Emma teased.

"You know me well, my dear," Ginger said. "Jill, if you change your mind, you know where to find me." She headed for the door, then, remembering why she'd popped by in the first place, said, "Are we on for that late lunch, Emma?"

"You bet. But I have to be back by two for a conference call."

Ginger flashed her a thumbs-up, her green-and-gold wedding band winking in the sunshine that streamed through the room's windows. "Meet you at Mandy's then. Tell us how it goes with Mr. Dream," she added, waggling her eyebrows at Jill. "I'll be sure to tell Cupid to meet you there."

"Not funny."

After finishing up a few tasks, Jill made the two-hour drive to Dakota, the closest city to Blueberry Springs, glad the roads had been plowed since the previous night's snowfall. It was just beyond the mountains, at the base of the foothills. Dakota always seemed like a different world, and Jill felt odd without the peaks surrounding her in a protective ring. But even though the geography had opened up, she somehow felt closed in today. Was it the impending divorce? When her ex had run off she'd found it embarrassing. Humiliating. The gossip had been the worst of it, especially after everyone found out Hayes had been stealing from the café right in front of her. This time it would be an unemotional, private divorce, but she still felt apprehensive, as if something wasn't quite right. Wasn't going according to plan.

She found a parking spot a few buildings down from the law office, and met Burke on the sidewalk. He nodded hello and hit his remote, locking his sedan. Under his arm was a thick, expandable folder that she presumed had lists of his sizable assets.

She had a one-page printout.

"Hi," she said nervously.

Burke was wearing a blue ski jacket that brought out the color of his eyes. He'd had his hair cut since yesterday, and as he moved to open the door for her she could see a faint tan line where it had been longer in the back. She longed to touch the skin, see if it was warm.

"No suit jacket for me?" he asked.

"I told you I was going to burn it. You didn't believe me?" In truth, in Blueberry Springs everyone dropped their dry-cleaning off at a depot which then sent the laundry off to the city, meaning his jacket wouldn't be back for at least a week.

"Nope. You're too sweet."

"Did I fail to mention my dad owns a gun range?"

"Then remind me never to mess with him."

"I'm the one who hits the bull's-eye on a regular basis," she said as she walked through the door he was holding for her. She hated to admit just how much she loved seeing his smile falter.

Their meeting with the lawyer was fairly straightforward, other than Burke spending a fair amount of time assuring that the way things were laid out, Jill wouldn't get a dime belonging to him.

"Burke, it's okay," she said calmly. "I don't want anything of yours. We're ending this like it never even happened."

"Except you owe me a pile of cash."

"Except that," she added quietly.

As much as she wanted his opinion to not matter, his lack of trust stung. She understood he had to protect himself, but he kept acting as though she was angling to steal everything, through a loophole in the divorce agreement. Although, after snatching a peek at his company's numbers and putting two and two together, she understood why he wanted the loan paid back ASAP. He'd earmarked his own available credit to complete a major expansion project. By claiming it unknowingly, she'd basically chained him to a concrete block, cut a hole in the ice over Blueberry Lake in the middle of winter and tossed him in. Goodbye, Burke.

She shivered, imagining how he must feel.

"That's it." The lawyer stood, ushering them out. "My assistant will call you when the papers are ready. Typically in about a week. Two at most."

As they left the office, Jill asked Burke, "Do you have business partners you can appeal to? For the funds you need?"

He slid her a sidelong look, and she felt as though she'd overstepped, asking about his business.

"They're tapped out," he said. "I need funds for both my expansion project and for Tiffer's fee if he likes our pitch in April."

"Your business was one of the up-and-coming, most-profitable new businesses featured in the *Esquire Daily Business News*. I'm sure he'll say yes."

"You need to pay me back," Burke said tightly.

"You need more than what I borrowed."

"We also need as much capital as possible so we have skin in the game, so others will have faith in us. We can only raise that if we've made a significant investment."

"Maybe you could stretch out your expansion? Like, do it in stages? Look into crowd funding?"

It felt overwhelmingly impossible that her business was directly accountable for the success of his. The more she thought about it, the more she felt as though her world was slipping out of her grip.

Burke turned to her on the street, his expression somber. "We *are* doing it in stages, except you just removed the ability for us to complete stages five through eight. You threw a tornado at my house of cards."

Jill nodded, trying to stay cool.

House of cards. House of cards.

Nothing about this situation was anywhere near cool-inducing.

"This loan? It's your problem, Jill. Jobs depend upon you paying it back."

She couldn't repay it in less than five years. And for the first time, she realized why Wini, the manager of the Blueberry Springs bank, had continually refused her loan applications. It wasn't just because the local branch had been swept downstream during a flood last spring and had some hefty rebuilding costs, but because Jill had no collateral. She had big dreams and a five-year plan, but nothing to back it up.

She sucked in a deep breath, then another, struggling for calm.

It wasn't helping.

Burke's employees depended on her. Burke depended on her.

She bent over, trying to encourage the dizziness to pass.

"Jill?" Burke said, his tone lacking concern.

"Trying to breathe."

"Jill. Please stand up."

There was a hint of urgency in his voice, and she straightened in time to see an alarmed looking woman in her fifties hurry up to them. She was wearing warm Inuit-styled mukluk boots, and an ankle-length down jacket, her gray hair tied in a ponytail.

"I'm okay. Just lightheaded," Jill said quickly.

Burke hugged the woman warmly as she reached them. "What brings you to this part of town?" he asked her.

"Gulliver said you were acting odd, so I tracked your phone."

Oh, boy. It was his mother, Jill realized. A highly overreacting, overprotective mom who would chain Jill to the train tracks if she found out what she'd just accidentally done to her son.

"I should never have given you access," Burke was muttering affectionately.

The woman turned to Jill. "Who have we got here?" She glanced up at the red sign above them, her eyes narrowing. "What should I know that you're not telling me, Burke Bartholomew Carver?"

Any moment she'd realize Jill had ruined her son's dreams.

Jill had to bend over again so she didn't pass out.

"Jill?" Burke said, clearly unimpressed by her behavior.

"I can't pay it back fast enough. I'm sorry. I don't mean to ruin everything. I want to fix it, but I just…I can't."

How had she so quickly and easily screwed up everything again? She even had a plan! A good one.

"I know." Burke sounded as though he couldn't unclamp his jaw. He was furious. He was going to sue her. She would never build the friendship center, never earn enough to move out of the suite in her perfect twin sister's garage. She'd be the piteous unlucky-in-love Auntie Jill forever.

"I promise I'll think of something," she whispered. She *had* to. Absolutely had to. She just didn't know what that something was, and that very fact freaked her out a tremendous amount.

"Jill, please stand up."

"Are you okay?" The woman's voice was so kind it made Jill's heart hurt.

"Yes. No. I'm trying to be. It's really hard right now."

"Burke," the woman said, when Jill dared take a peek at her, "I think you'd better take us for coffee and explain yourself."

BURKE NEEDED Jill to pull it together. Otherwise his aunt Maggie was going to kick his butt so hard his teeth would need replacing. She was already piecing things together—thanks to Gulliver saying Burke was acting strangely. And why would he think that? Burke wasn't acting that odd. Just because he'd been seen kissing a woman who wasn't his usual tough-as-nails businesswoman type, had asked for a printed list of his personal assets and had told Gulliver to sell a few trinkets...

Burke sighed. Yeah, that looked kind of bad, didn't it?

No wonder Maggie was here to bust his chops until she got to the bottom of it—especially after seeing Jill all but hyperventilate on the street outside a divorce lawyer's office.

Maggie had marched Burke and Jill straight to a little bistro just down the street and ordered them all black coffees, sitting them down in a quiet corner.

"I'm Maggie Carver, Burke's aunt," Maggie said, reaching across the table to shake Jill's hand. She paused to give Burke, who she'd seated right beside her, as though she might have to reach over to yank on his ear, a stern look.

"Pleased to meet you," Jill said, before introducing herself.

The bistro was cold, the walls a blaring white, the lighting harsh and unforgiving, making Jill's face look pale and delicate framed by her long black hair. It felt as though Burke was in an operating room. Or an interrogation room.

"Sorry, I should have introduced you," he said.

"I raised you better," Maggie told him in a gentle, but chiding tone. She turned to Jill. "Am I to presume you're Burke's wife, seeing the two of you were outside a divorce lawyer's office?"

Burke cringed. Jill was wide-eyed, looking at him for direction.

"We're getting a divorce," he said, a familiar pressure building in his temples.

This time he wasn't losing everything. This time things were going to be different.

"You two got married?" Maggie asked. She shifted in her seat to face him more fully. "Burke?"

He was unable to meet her eye. As difficult as he'd been over the years, he didn't keep secrets from her. Never had. She'd taken him in, kept him from becoming a true orphan, and when she'd fallen ill after he'd graduated from high school, he'd passed up college to care for her. A decision he knew she regretted, but he didn't. Never would. That time together had been sacred to him, even though difficult, and it had helped him forge a strength and determination he knew he wouldn't have otherwise.

He nodded silently.

"It was an accident," Jill said quickly.

"There are no such thing as accidents." Maggie was starting to smile despite the flash of concern she was trying to hide. She knew what he'd faced with his previous marriage. Knew he hadn't wanted to marry again. Ever.

"Neither of us remember it," Burke said simply. "Drunken night. We're divorcing."

"It was a temporary lapse in judgment and the parting is mutual and friendly," Jill added supportively, and he shot her a grateful look.

"Exactly. Neither of us want to…"

"Talk about it. To anyone."

"Right. Or—"

"Be married."

"And do married things." He caught Jill's eye, his voice automatically dropping an octave. "Although maybe some of the funner stuff would be okay."

Those kisses at MacKenzie's had been out of this world. The kind where the top of your head blew off like in the cartoons and you walked around with your tongue lolling out the side of your mouth and little hearts floated in the air for hours afterward.

Jill choked on a surprised laugh, looking embarrassed by the way he'd shot that one straight from the hip. To his delight, she played along. "Try and make it memorable this time."

"Try and keep your hands off me."

"Try and keep it rated for public consumption." Jill covered her face as if she was mortified, but her shoulders were shaking with laughter. She dropped her hands after a moment and groaned, head tilted to the side, her long hair fanning over her shoulder. "That was so embarrassing."

"You two acted like newlyweds, I heard," Maggie said, her own hands clasped on the tabletop, her coffee untouched.

"You heard about MacKenzie's?" Burke asked in surprise. If she'd heard...then Gulliver had. If he had, the public likely had. Would that mean Autumn and her father had, too? He had a feeling the governor was hoping Burke would take his spoiled, twenty-four-year-old daughter off his hands for him, and he would not be impressed that Burke hadn't mentioned this aspect of his personal life.

Maggie was studying them thoughtfully, not answering Burke's question. "I don't understand. You two seem good together."

"We're not a match," Jill said uneasily. "He goes for my sister's type."

"You have a sister?"

"Identical twin."

Burke smiled and Jill rolled her eyes. "See? You're ridiculous. I don't go for ridiculous." She pushed her coffee away and crossed her arms.

"Come on, for all your planning, I bet you love the adventure of hanging out with a man like me," he teased, cradling his coffee cup in his hand.

"How do you know I'm a planner?"

He finished his coffee, setting down the cup. "I've never seen a more detailed business proposal."

"Oh. Well, you're not husband material. As fun as you might claim to be."

"You heard her," Burke said, turning to his aunt. He was not husband material. Never would be. He lifted his palms as if to say *"Present me with a better argument than that."*

"You need to let go of the past," Maggie warned.

"I have, and I learned from it, too." He could feel his earlier humor slipping away.

Jill collected her purse as she stood, her smile pinched. She said to Maggie, "It was lovely meeting you. I'll let you two talk." She gave Burke a teasing, more relaxed smile as she added, "I'm sorry our meeting couldn't have been under more pleasant circumstances."

"Ouch," Burke said, acting wounded. "Are you implying I'm an unpleasant circumstance?"

She turned serious, her playful banter gone. "I'll pay back that loan. I'll figure this out. Everything'll be fine. I promise."

There was fear in her eyes and he hated to believe he was the one who'd put it there. But he nodded, acknowledging her promise.

Maggie tipped her head to the side as she studied Jill's pained expression. The pounding in Burke's temples returned full force. It didn't matter what he did, he was going to hurt or disappoint someone.

"Jill..." He stood, starting to reach for her, then changed his mind. He wanted to tell her everything would be all right, but at the same time, from a business perspective, he couldn't let her off the hook, as everything would most definitely *not* be all right.

She flashed a smile. "I'm sorry I can't stay. Thank you for the coffee."

Once she was gone, Burke slowly sat again. Maggie turned to him, silently watching. Finally she said, "I think this is the right thing."

"The divorce should be finalized within a week or two. And no, I don't want to talk about it."

"I meant this...accidental marriage, as you two are calling it."

"We're not calling it anything." The idea of the two of them having a "thing" got under his skin in a way he couldn't explain. He wanted that with her—a something. And wanting something from women always led to pain.

"You were always a romantic," Maggie said, digging through her purse for chewing gum. "Normally it causes you to throw too much into it or chase off after the wrong women."

"I don't do that."

"Your ex-wife? You wanted that to work and I admired your persistence and effort, but wanting something badly doesn't make up for the other person not wanting it. You can't make someone else love you."

"I know that," he said gruffly. She made it sound so bad. When you were married, you tried. End of story. He'd just tried harder than Neila, who'd been taking advantage of their union. She'd taught him a very valuable lesson about love. She'd pretended—convincingly. And when she'd decided she was done, she'd cleared out their joint accounts as well as the house, even taken their dog, Misty. He'd come home with a bouquet of flowers to celebrate their six-month anniversary and found a For Sale sign out front and a Dear John letter on the mantel, like some horrible cliché.

The worst part was that she wasn't the first woman to up and leave him after he'd offered everything he had.

He wasn't the kind of man women kept. It was that simple.

"You two have something." Maggie waggled her finger between Burke and Jill's empty seat, chewing on her fresh piece of gum. "And maybe being thrown together takes the pressure off, so you don't mess it up with idealized dreams."

Burke checked his phone, wishing something urgent would come up and let him escape. "Don't read too much into it—we're getting divorced. She has nothing to lose and everything to gain from this marriage."

Maggie was silent.

"I, meanwhile," he said, with a touch of self-righteousness, "have everything to lose."

"Do you?"

"Yes. As do my employees. I need to protect them."

"Burke, can I ask you something?"

"No."

He sighed when she continued, anyway. "Why, do you believe, you have a new woman each month? And don't think I haven't noticed."

"I like to have fun. They do, too. It's mutual. And it's not every month." Lately it had been more like every six months. It was just too much work trying to do the dance. Don't get too close, don't get involved. Don't create too many common experiences that will make you believe it's actually real.

It was never real.

"Know what I think?" Maggie asked.

Burke leaned back in his chair, staring at the white wall in front of him, knowing she was going to tell him no matter what he said.

"You're afraid of being truly and deeply loved. You either sabotage the relationship by falling too soon for someone who just needs someone to lean on, and hold it against some ideal you have in your head. Or you keep the woman at arm's length and don't let her in."

Burke took her untouched cup. "Want a warm-up, Dr. Ruth?"

"Honey," she said gently, placing a hand over his forearm so he couldn't slip away. "You can't say your mother's death, followed by Fiona's indifference to stepping up to raise you, hasn't had an impact on your relationships. And growing up without a male role model, or seeing a healthy heterosexual relationship—"

He shifted, shaking her hand off his arm, not wanting to have this conversation again. Yeah, Fiona, his mother's wife of nine years, didn't want him after the car accident that had taken his mom's life. He'd broken an arm and a leg in the collision and needed some surgeries insurance would almost cover. That wasn't the big deal. She simply hadn't wanted him.

And so he'd fallen on Aunt Maggie, who was too good to send him off to live in an orphanage.

"I'm happy." Burke stood. "Happy enough, okay? I tried marriage. It didn't work out. Jill and I are getting a divorce. It's what's best. I can't give her what she wants and I need her to stay out of my life." His heart was pounding and his mouth was dry. His urge to run and never stop was incredibly compelling.

"Oh, Burke." Maggie's eyes were sad. "I wish I'd done better by you. I thought I was doing the right thing giving you my undivided attention instead of accepting Kurt's proposal. But maybe if we'd married it would have been good for you."

Burke shut his own eyes for a second, softened by her morose, and gutted by the guilt he felt at her sacrifice. "You did better than anyone else would have, and if it weren't for you, I'd probably be in jail."

"Don't let her go," Maggie pleaded, standing, holding him close. "Not yet."

"There's nothing there." He felt as though he was lying to her. It was the same feeling he'd had when he was fourteen and had boldly lied to her—the only time he ever had—about stealing the running shoes he needed for ninth grade gym class. She'd been between jobs due to illness and he'd been at a stage where his feet seemed to be a new size every week. He'd known it was wrong, but hadn't known what else to do. The guilt had kept him up all night and the next day after school he'd gone out and found a job. Two weeks later, he'd paid the store back for the shoes that had fit him for only three weeks. Five, if he ignored the pain in his toes.

"Don't give up on her, Burke. But most of all, don't give up on yourself and your ability to give and receive love."

"Maggie..." He gave her an exasperated look.

"Please. For me."

"Love has nothing to do with this marriage."

"Don't let your fears get in the way of what's best. Don't close your eyes to reality. There's a way to make this happen. I can feel it."

Burke paused. A reluctant plan was beginning to form. It wasn't ideal, and it went against what he wanted in the short-term, but long-term it was exactly what he and his business needed. He just had to find a way to make it happen.

He bent to give his aunt a kiss on the cheek. "Thanks."

"Invite me to the real wedding!"

"There won't be one," he said cheerfully as he headed for the door.

He ignored how she muttered, "Famous last words."

CHAPTER 4

*J*ill pushed away from her desk. It had been a long day of trying to catch up on her work for Emma, but the offices at All You were now abandoned until tomorrow. With the building empty she turned up her music and grabbed some labels from her printer.

She stretched out her back and yawned, pausing to flip open one of her magazines on organizing spaces. Katie Leham had once asked her to work as a contractor for her decorating company, when she'd seen how Jill had helped Mary Alice organize her purse. Not that the woman actually kept the system; she still preferred to keep items in her bra rather than in her handbag. But the idea of becoming a home organizer for the wealthy, instead of working for Emma as well as trying to run her own botanicals business in the evenings and weekends, was appealing to Jill. Everything would have its place. No chaos. No stressful juggling of life. Just systems. Easy.

She closed the magazine and went to work labeling folders, her stomach growling. She reached into her desk drawer, pulling out her plastic snack bin. Microwave popcorn. Perfect. That would tide her over before she went home around nine.

Her cell rang on her desk and her heart leaped with anticipation.

Was it Burke?

Whoa. Where had that come from? Of course it wasn't. And if it was, he would only harp about her paying back that loan.

She answered the call.

"Hi. Jill Armstrong?"

"Yes."

"This is Zebadiah from WWYL."

"From where?"

"We Win Your Love."

"Oh, right." The dating company she'd hired to find her a suitable date—or even better, boyfriend—in time for her sister's tenth wedding anniversary, which was in early May. She'd gone to them and their fine-tuned system so she wouldn't look sad and pathetic as the divorcée twin with absolutely no hope at love.

Yup. Lame. That's what Jill was. But she had come to terms with that fact eons ago and appreciated that Zeb called her every so often to chat about their matches.

"We have a man for you! He's very interested in your profile and the two of you score well in the compatibility department."

"I'm not sure this is the best time for me..." Jill began. She probably should put her subscription on hold or something until she was officially divorced.

"You won't want to drag your feet or he'll be snapped up. He's a catch." Zebadiah lowered his voice. "He's got a five-year plan."

A five-year plan was her weakness. Like a man's six-pack abs were to her sister.

"I'll shoot his profile over to you via email."

Jill put Zeb on speaker and tapped into her email. She winced. "Um...he's not quite my type."

"He puts a checkmark in all the boxes."

"Maybe there should be one for hygiene. He didn't even wash or comb his hair for his profile photo, Zeb." She sighed. "I know

I'm being finicky, but..." Her mind shot to Burke. He was the kind of man with a five-year plan—as well as one for the next ten years, and maybe even twenty—despite his spontaneous whimsical nature, and he managed to do more than simply roll out of bed each morning and smile for a camera.

Keep your standards high. Your next husband is forever.

Well, the one after Burke, she thought with a sigh.

"No, no problem," Zeb said smoothly. "I get ya. I'll keep looking. Just remember—you're not getting any younger, and these men aren't, either."

"Thanks for the reminder." She hung up and gave herself a moment. Why was this so difficult? She'd filled out personality profiles, taken their matchmaking tests and so far they'd found nobody.

She was one step away from letting Blueberry Springs find her next man.

Her stomach growled again, reminding her of her interrupted task of preparing a snack. She began reading a text from her dad as she walked to the break room.

I put Tay-Tay in your car. He said he misses you.

Jill peeked out the window, spying her SUV parked alongside the building. Her dad had taken Taylor, her Great Pyrenees, for a walk, as he did almost daily since his heart attack a year and a half ago. He'd given her the pup when things had finally fallen through with Devon Mattson and she'd been down and out. He'd handed over the stray and told her to "shake it off." At first Jill had thought he was talking to the dog about the dirt matted into his white fur. Turned out he was talking to her and the funk that had settled like a cloud. She'd ended up with the Taylor Swift song "Shake It Off" stuck in her head and had named the dog Taylor, which her dad jokingly changed to Tay-Tay.

Really? Jill typed back. *Taylor misses me?*

Yup.

Not a chance.

Sure you weren't out to sneak a burger and couldn't take Taylor inside the restaurant?

Maybe.

Jill chuckled to herself. The March evening was unseasonably warm, but still chilly, and she knew Taylor, a massively furry hundred-pound beast, would be comfortable sleeping in the cozy vehicle until she was ready to head home.

The microwave dinged and Jill broke open the bag of popcorn, inhaling deeply. Best supper ever and it smelled divine.

She definitely needed to leave Taylor outside. The dog would practically smother her trying to get at his favorite food, popcorn. And who could say no to those big brown eyes?

Jill squeaked when she exited the break room, her popcorn flying into the air as she delivered a chop to the intruder's gut.

"Oomph!"

Jill jumped back as she processed the fact that the intruder was actually her boss's husband, Luke Cohen, the man in charge of practically half the company. "Oh, Luke! I'm so sorry." She fluttered around him, feeling horrible. "Are you okay?"

He groaned and placed a hand against the doorjamb. "You pack a bit of a wallop."

Jill moved from foot to foot, adrenaline still flowing through her veins. "My dad taught me self-defense."

"He did well." Luke winced as he straightened.

"I thought I had the building to myself."

"Sorry. I came in to dig out the contract for the new greenhouse conveyor. It's acting up and the overseas support team should be just coming in to work about now."

"I have the contract in my filing cabinet if you need to reference it."

"Thanks. That would be helpful."

Jill crunched over the spilled popcorn, heading to her office.

"I'll grab a broom," Luke said.

"Nah, I'll just let my dog in. He makes an awesome cleanup

crew." Jill walked to her filing cabinet, pulled out the contract and handed it over.

Luke let out a low whistle as he took in the color-coded binders lining the shelf above her computer, and just below it, the perfect row of sticky notes detailing her next workday. As she completed each task, the note came down.

"I should hire you to organize my desk."

"That would be so much fun."

"And my car. And my closet."

"Do you have a tie rack? I love tie racks."

"Yes," he said with a smile. He turned to the door, the contract in hand. "I think you missed your calling. You should be a professional organizer."

"Thanks. You know, your office isn't that bad," she called after him. He didn't spend much time in there, which helped.

"It's because I spread things out, so you don't notice as much."

"It sounds like you're making excuses for not being a slob," she joked.

"You know it."

"Hey, Luke?"

"Yeah?" He came back a step or two.

"I, um..." Jill suddenly felt nervous. "I'm wondering if you would be willing to fund my project."

"You have something new?" he asked.

"Well, no." She'd already talked to Luke before he turned over the CEO reins of Cohen's Blissful Body Care to his cousin Cash Campbell. She'd been hoping Luke's company would like to partner with hers. But hers was too small, their needs too great. It had been the same with Emma's business, only a little less of a match in terms of product and market.

Luke was waiting for her to explain herself.

"I revamped my business plan." And she had. She'd spent her lunch restructuring her proposal so it was easier to see what she had to offer.

"Oh?" Luke took a step toward her office.

Excited, she pulled out the glossy-covered package.

Luke took it and asked, "What's new?"

"I honed it."

"It was already quite honed."

"I highlighted my priorities, my purpose. How to be more productive with my growth."

Luke had flipped to the final page. "But your projections are still the same, and still very conservative."

"I don't want to be a flash in the pan. I've got a financial advisor and accountant already taking care of everything on the money side. Taxes. Paying bills. Everything." Nothing would be missed. No bills slipping through the cracks and going unpaid. No charming scallywags "helping her out" and stealing everything instead.

"You're still too conservative," Luke said. "You need to stretch, reach and challenge yourself. Take some risks, relinquish some control and leave room for the unexpected. That's the only way. There isn't room for growth in here."

"The unexpected is unreliable."

"This is how to make a hobby cover its costs," he said gently, handing back the packet. "Unfortunately, I can't afford to finance hobbies."

Jill clutched the papers, crestfallen. "I know it's not as aggressive as it was before, but I'm working full-time now and I don't want to miss anything by overtaxing myself."

"Have you considered that maybe being an entrepreneur isn't the right fit for you?"

She nodded, her throat thick. She'd made promises to Burke as well as to Rebecca.

She was going to keep them.

She just couldn't quite figure out how.

BURKE STRAIGHTENED HIS SUIT JACKET, thinking of Jill. She still hadn't returned the one he'd loaned her—his favorite—when her blouse buttons had exploded. There was something about the jacket's cut that always made him feel capable of taking on anything when he wore it. Including the governor, who'd asked him to meet for dinner to discuss taxation.

But tonight there was no lucky jacket to prop him up. It was just himself and his favorite crisp, white shirt and a subpar jacket.

From the doorway of the restaurant overlooking the city's small lake, he scanned the patrons, keeping an eye out for Governor Martinez. After talking to his aunt yesterday, Burke had thought he was going to have to keep Jill despite the risks associated in doing so. But then, like the all-clear after having firefighters crawling all over your smoking home, the governor's assistant had called, asking him to meet the man for dinner.

At long last, it was time to usher in tax breaks and financial incentives for green companies. The government was finally going to help those who were trying to make a change that would benefit the environment. The breaks likely wouldn't come into effect immediately, but they'd be something his company could bank on. The first foothold in the wall he was trying to scale without a harness.

"Mr. Carver, right this way," said the maître d'.

Burke followed the man, spotting Autumn Martinez's signature French twist from across the room. Why was she here? Had the Martinez family found out about his wife and were they going to confront him for never mentioning it? But why couldn't he see her father—was he glad-handing the room?

Speaking of which, Burke stopped as he passed the mayor's table.

"Any tax breaks on the horizon?" he asked lightly. The question had become a bit of a joke between the two of them.

"Is that all you talk about?" the mayor retorted, eyes dancing as he ribbed him.

Burke smiled, his next line ready, as per their informal script. "Until you put some through to help support green initiatives, yes."

The mayor laughed good-naturedly. "I'll ask to have it put on the agenda again, but you know how it is. Times are tight and tax breaks cost money."

Burke went off script. "You know...they could actually pay off in the long run for the city's economy. Bring in more businesses such as mine. More jobs, more spending. We'd all still be paying taxes, just at an incentivized rate. We could shoulder some of those parks and recreation expansion plans around town, too."

The mayor nodded in a way that left Burke uncertain whether he'd been heard or whether he was just being humored. Then the man gestured toward Autumn, who was sitting a few tables over. "Don't keep your woman waiting. She's been here at least ten minutes."

Your woman?

Burke saluted him casually before making his way to Autumn's table, the maître d' pulling a chair out for him upon arrival.

"Hello," Burke said, sliding into the seat across from Autumn. "I presume you'll be joining your father and me tonight?"

Her smile lit up her eyes, and she shifted the linen napkin over her lap. He found the wine bottle, when he pulled it out of the ice bucket beside their table, was rather light.

"Silly man," Autumn said coyly, one expertly curled tendril of jet-black hair curving along her high-boned features as she tipped her head to the side. "This is a date. Just you and me."

Burke gripped the edge of the table, pushing back in his chair. There was a rushing sound in his ears. He'd been suckered into thinking he had a lifeline, and had told Andrea, his overly pregnant financial officer, to stay late prepping possible new tax scenarios so he could approach potential partners first thing in the morning with updated financial proposals.

And for what? A setup? Andrea should be at home with her feet up and a heating pad on her aching back.

"I planned this for us," Autumn cooed as she snagged his right hand, pulling it across the table toward her. "You've been so busy. I hardly see you."

"I've been working on an expansion, beating the streets trying to find ways to keep our company in-state." He tried to squirrel his hand away from hers. "It's very intensive."

"Oh, sweetie. You work too hard."

"It would be easier and more financially viable to move everything overseas, where labor and business costs are cheaper."

She gave a disinterested "hmm." So much for that tidbit making its way back to the governor, to light a fire under him.

Autumn frowned at Burke's wrist, which she'd barely relinquished and was now yanking her way again. She pushed up his shirtsleeve.

"What's this? A tattoo?" She scowled at the black ink. "What is it? A hook? A comma? What's it supposed to mean?"

He gripped the edge of the fabric, jerking the cuff back over the inch-long, off-centered mark.

"Why did you get it?" Autumn asked.

"I don't know."

"Burke, this is the problem with you. It's hard to have a boyfriend who doesn't talk. Who doesn't open up." She was using a soft expression. As if conversing with a wounded kitten. Speaking of which, there was a good chance Fluke was trashing his place as a thanks for being abandoned for the evening. They had a routine. Burke came home, ate, then worked with the cat curled at his side on the couch. When he broke the routine, he often came home to find the cat had eaten a houseplant.

From the corner of his eye, Burke saw Tiffer Garbanzo frowning at him from across the restaurant. Didn't that man ever eat at home? He was the last person Burke wanted to see right now.

"I should probably go," he said uneasily.

Autumn pouted. "But you just got here." Her eyes sharpened. "You have time to dine with my father, but not me?"

"Your father and I were to discuss business. If he's unable to be here, then I need to get back to work." He stood. "I'm sorry, Autumn. You're a lovely woman, but I don't want to lead you on. I simply don't have time for a girlfriend right now."

"You make me sound needy."

"That's not my intention." He bent to place a kiss on her cheek, just missing her lips as she turned to try and make it something other than a polite, chaste goodbye.

"Is this about the other woman?" Autumn said, as Burke stepped away from the table, her voice level.

Burke stopped in his tracks, turned back. "I'm sorry?"

"The woman from last week." She was staring at her wineglass, her face expressionless.

Woman. Not wife.

Burke let out a sigh of relief.

He could only imagine how she would feel if she found out he'd been married while attending events with her.

"You kissed her in MacKenzie's."

"I did," Burke admitted.

"I saw the pictures."

Wincing at the way he had undoubtedly hurt Autumn's feelings, Burke decided it was best to sit and hopefully avoid a scene.

He glanced at Tiffer, who was, as expected, subtly watching things play out.

Burke hated that he could so easily be painted as a two-timing good-for-nothing. He'd always tried to be better than that.

"It's me or her."

"What?" Burke turned his focus to Autumn.

"Me. Or her." Her expression was stony. "I don't share my men."

Burke gaped at her. They'd cut a few ribbons at grand openings, had a few laughs and maybe one or two chaste good-night kisses. She couldn't possibly think things were that...*real*. Heck, things were more real with Jill—and not just because they were legally married.

Autumn stood, towering over the table in her five-inch heels. "I'm telling Daddy."

"Autumn..."

"I don't like being used, and he told me you were nice. I chose you even though you're not rich, because you'd make a good husband."

Whoa! Husband?

"I'm sorry if I made you feel like we were more than—than..." He was at a loss for words. "Friends."

"Friends? *Friends?*"

Burke searched desperately for a way to save this. Not just because of the tax implications of being on Autumn's bad side, but because he really couldn't afford to have Tiffer thinking he was the awful man that events were lining up to make him appear.

"I'm the kind of man women leave," he said calmly. "Women don't marry men like me." He drew up short. Not the best thing to say when he was, in fact, married.

Secretly.

Secrets never stayed secret though, did they?

"I'm sorry," he said. "I really am."

"No. Don't you *dare* tell me you're incapable of love as some excuse to shake me. I know what we have and it's special. I will not tolerate you running away."

"Autumn..." He summoned patience and strength.

She lifted her glass of red wine, flinging its liquid in his direction, her mouth twisted as she had her temper tantrum at his expense. But the rim of the glass curved the liquid upward, creating an arc over the table and splattering them both instead of landing in his face.

Burke could feel Tiffer smirking from across the room, and practically see their potential deal flying out the window.

When he looked up, Autumn was already storming away, leaving him at the table with white shirt cuffs splattered with what looked like blood.

"We need to stay married."

"I'm sorry, what?" Jill asked, staring at Burke. He had been waiting for her in the parking lot outside of All You in Blueberry Springs. How had he known she was working late?

"We need to stay married," he repeated.

"Let's move to my car," Jill said, shivering in what had been a lovely pre-spring wind rolling off the mountains earlier, and was now starting to nip with a bone-chilling ferocity. A sure sign they were in for some interesting weather tomorrow.

Taylor woke up as she unlocked the car, letting out a low woof of hello before seeing Burke, which sent him into a barking frenzy. One hundred pounds of fur and loyalty jumped into the front seat, spraying spittle across the windshield.

"Easy, easy." Jill reached in, settling the dog and sending him into the backseat. "Say it, don't spray it," she muttered, using her sweater's sleeve to wipe the steering wheel as she sat down.

"Am I okay to get in?" Burke asked from the passenger's side.

"He had popcorn earlier. He probably won't chew your face off."

"Reassuring." Burke eased himself into the seat beside her. Taylor craned his neck to sniff Burke's face before giving it a sneak-attack lick.

"No lick," Jill said, half expecting an innuendo from Burke.

Taylor sighed as if he'd been hard done by with Jill's refusal to let him maul Burke, and curled up on the backseat.

"I need this deal with Tiffer," Burke stated.

And Jill needed the divorce that would surely impede his ability to close said deal. She was still hoping they could divorce before the word leaked out that she'd married on a whim and then forgotten about it. And him being in Blueberry Springs wouldn't help her keep that secret.

She'd asked Wini, the bank manager, to stay quiet, of course, but even with client confidentiality it was a small town where nothing remained secret for longer than about five seconds. Not even news of Amber Thompson's—now Malone's—adult sister had stayed quiet for that long. Although...that one had stayed under wraps for a few decades, giving Jill hope that her marriage could, too.

"Here's the thing," Burke said, his palms together as he carefully chose his words. She caught a glimpse of his white shirt cuffs, which were dotted with red.

"Are you bleeding?" She shifted in her seat to inspect his shirt, trying not to recoil. "What happened?" Taylor tried to squeeze his way between them, but Jill gave him the command to stay.

Burke squinted at her in the dim glow of the parking lot lights. He looked at his cuffs when she pointed to them. "It's wine."

Taylor tried to make his way into the front seat again and Jill opened her door, getting out, the dog scrambling to follow despite the way his large body barely fit between the two front seats. Jill quickly shut herself in the car again, gaining a loud *woof!* from her betrayed four-legged friend.

"Someone threw wine at you?" she asked.

Burke didn't say anything, just scratched his forehead.

"Who was she?"

Taylor hefted his front paws onto the window beside Jill. He whined, then lowered himself, claws scraping against the vehicle's paint. "Seriously, dog."

"He's like my kitten."

"You have a kitten as well as a girlfriend? I didn't picture *that*."

"Of course I have a kitten. Who doesn't enjoy having their home destroyed while they're out? And as for the girlfriend? If I had one, she'd likely do the same if she found out I've been married for the past several months."

When it looked like Taylor was going to jump up again, Jill opened the door once more, letting the chilly breeze into their warm haven. The dog nudged his head under her arm, pressing close to her side.

"I need to seal this deal with Tiffer," Burke was saying. "I also need to remain married to you in order to do so." He let out a defeated sigh. "I've tried, but I honestly can't see any other way."

"I don't want to stay married. No offense."

"My plan—"

"If it involves staying married or telling people, then I'm out. I'm signing those papers as soon as they're ready next week."

Burke slumped in his seat, staring out the windshield, his large hands resting loosely in his lap. Peeking out from under the edge of his right cuff was a black mark. A black mark that looked a lot like the one under Jill's two-inch-wide leather bracelet.

"What's that?" she asked quietly, her heart pounding.

Burke glanced over to see what she was referring to. He turned his right wrist upward, then slipped the cuff over the mark. "Nothing."

Jill slowly unsnapped the bracelet covering her left wrist, feeling a cascade of chills running down her spine. She revealed the inch-long apostrophe that was at the edge of her wrist, mirroring Burke's.

He stared at it, his expression unreadable.

"When did you get that?" he finally asked, clearing his throat.

"Woke up with it." Almost a year ago. Her heart was pounding so hard she could feel it all the way down to her toes. "And you?"

His eyes met hers in the dim light, and the gravity of that night hit her once again. "Same."

"What do you think it means?"

Burke shrugged.

He had his hand out in front of him, the sleeve pushed up now. His tattoo was off-centered as well. His to the left, where hers was to the right. She reached across the cab, lining her wrist against his. When holding hands, their tattoos fitted together, forming a heart.

BURKE COULDN'T STOP STARING at their matching, interlinked ink. His comma or apostrophe or whatever it was met with Jill's, forming a heart. A freaking heart.

Maggie's words circled in his mind. *You were always a romantic.*

This tattoo was definitely something a romantic would get. A drunk one who'd lost his mind.

Normally it causes you to throw too much into it or chase off after the wrong women.

He'd thrown too much into this one, obviously. Marriage and matching tattoos. But why?

Was Maggie right about him? Did he put too much into the wrong kind of relationship, or else kept it loose and easy so it would never become anything real?

"Are these supposed to be ironic?" he asked, covering his tattoo again, his voice tight with an emotion he couldn't identify. He had a feeling the tattoos were an in-joke neither of them remembered.

He was never drinking again. At least not enough to mess with his memory. Or judgment.

Jill let out a derisive snort. "I think couples' tattoos are a bit…"

"Tacky? Cheesy?"

"Yeah. They're like matching jackets. We all know you're together, you don't have to be matchy-matchy."

"Do I detect bitterness?"

"There's no need to show off that you found your partner." She gestured to his tattoo. "Why do you still have yours?"

"My assistant refuses to make the appointment for me to get it lasered off. He's a lit major and likes that I have punctuation permanently inked on me."

"Ah. And you're so special and spoiled you can't make the appointment yourself?"

"You still have yours," he pointed out. "You like it?"

She didn't reply, just snapped the leather bracelet back over it, and for some reason, it bothered him that she felt the need to hide it. Not that he tended to flaunt his own.

"Then let's get them removed together. It'll be like a divorce party. A divorce *present*."

Her lips curved upward, but she said nothing.

"No?" he asked.

"We *are* getting divorced, but let's skip the parting gift. I can pay to get it done on my own."

"I wasn't offering to pay."

She was petting her dog, which was sitting outside, head resting in Jill's lap. "We can't stay married," she said. "You do know that, right?"

For the first time Burke considered the fact that she might have a love life that didn't jive with her being married. "Does he know?"

"Who?" She looked down at her dog with a frown. "I don't think dogs—"

"No, I mean your boyfriend." Wow. It felt awkward saying that.

"My *boy*friend?" She was giving him a look, and he really hoped she'd say she didn't have one.

"You could be in a serious relationship for all I know. I didn't want to sound like I was trying to pick you up."

She laughed. "Well, I *am* in a relationship." She said it quickly, authoritatively, and he wasn't sure whether to believe her or not.

"We share a bed and care for each other deeply. We like long walks through the meadow and spend weekends together. He's always waiting for me when I get off work because he clears his schedule for me. He's very devoted."

"You're talking about your dog, aren't you?"

Her eyes twinkled.

"Okay, so you're not in a serious relationship with a human," he clarified. "So why can't we stay married? Just until we get what we want."

"And what do we want?" There was a huskiness, a hunger skimming the surface of her words like a water beetle dancing over the water.

He had to have imagined that.

"To resolve all of our mistakes, fill the potholes and come out ahead," he said uncertainly.

Did that even make any sense?

Jill let out a heavy sigh. "Marriage isn't going to solve anything in my life. Quite the opposite." She got out and opened the rear door, letting Taylor back inside the vehicle.

She wanted out of this marriage, something Burke knew he should respect. He'd dodged a bullet with Autumn tonight, but he might not a second time. And with Autumn, there was certain to be a second approach. Especially with her father getting tired of supporting her.

A quiet divorce would likely protect him and his reputation. And the fact that he was trying to hold on to Jill made him wonder if it was due to some messed-up reason he didn't fully understand. A reason Maggie did.

"What can I do to make this work?" he found himself asking.

He felt old emotions clamp down on his lungs. He'd said the same exact thing to Neila the first time he'd seen her after the Dear John letter.

She'd laughed. Told him he couldn't charm his way out of it.

She needed someone who was capable of loving her, and he was never around, so how did he think that was going to work?

He'd replied that if she loved him she'd support him. He was making something of himself and creating a business, a life for them.

She'd laughed at that, too.

Jill got back into the driver's seat, her dog secured. She studied Burke for a moment before saying, "You want to make this work?"

"Not in a romantic sense, but there are benefits to us remaining married." He thought of how Tiffer's smirk had smarted, all the way across the restaurant earlier. Meeting up with Autumn may have ruined everything. But showing up at the Metro Conference with a strong-looking marriage could possibly save it.

Somehow.

Either way, getting divorced certainly wouldn't alleviate the problems that were currently cinching him to the proverbial railway tracks.

"You want to make this work?" Jill repeated. She leaned closer, her body almost touching his shoulder.

He nodded.

"Then become someone else." She shifted back in her seat and started the engine.

"Besides that," he said sharply, redirecting a vent that blew cold air in his face.

"Besides becoming the man of my dreams?"

"Oh, how you wound me, my lovely wife." He'd meant the comment to be flippant, offhand, but it came out cutting.

"I'm divorcing you. Getting married was a mistake, and I'm not going to let it grow into a bigger one by dragging things out."

He knew if he got out of her car, it was over. Done. It didn't matter that they'd had some laughs, some moments. "I have a proposal you'll want to say yes to."

"Just because I said yes to the last one doesn't mean I will again."

"We're good together."

"If you were outside right now, I'd be trying to run you over. It's difficult to do that when you're sitting beside me. Please get out."

In the backseat, Taylor let out a sigh, impatient to go.

"What if I helped you?" Burke insisted. He knew she was eager to grow her botanicals business. He'd said no to her first proposal, but that was a different time, where helping her grow wasn't what he needed—wasn't what he had time for. Now anything that could bring in cash and ensure she paid back her loan—and quickly—was worth a shot. Anything that could help him prove to potential investors that STH was stable, and looking for other ways to diversify, strengthen and grow.

He felt that if he and Jill were married he'd have more control over how things went down. It was a tie to bind them, another layer of commitment, so she couldn't pull out and leave him high and dry on a whim.

"Remember that business proposal you brought to me at the Metro Conference?"

"The one you said no to? The one where I'm too small and insignificant, with no vision and no potential for exponential growth?"

He winced. "I didn't say that."

"And now you've changed your mind because we're married?" She was cynical, pragmatic, and even though it was making his life difficult, he found he appreciated that about her. She wasn't going to get taken by a con man, that was for certain. "What's your angle?"

"You want to expand your business. I want to expand mine. I need to establish diversity and stability. You could be part of that."

"I don't mix business and pleasure." She looked scared.

"It won't be like that. Just say yes."

"Does it matter what I want? Does it matter that I don't want a husband I don't recall marrying?" Her voice was high now, panicked. She yanked off her bracelet again. "What if I don't want this embarrassing tattoo, but I'm too scared it's going to hurt having it removed? What if I need to spend the money somewhere smarter than tattoo removal and divorcing you? Have you thought of that? Have you thought past yourself and considered the wake of destruction you've left in my life?"

Burke sat back. He hadn't.

"We make mistakes when we're together. We do crazy stuff like making out in the middle of a restaurant, and you blow up my five-year plan with an exhale and a wink."

He knew that feeling. He had a plan, then she walked in and everything skewed. He still wasn't sure if it was a good thing or not. But that restaurant kiss had been a real head-turner. And not just for those observing them, but for himself, too. He'd never kissed or been kissed like that before. Ever.

Jill continued, "I'm not that person and I don't *want* to be that person. I've made promises to people and I lose control when I'm around you, but that can't happen. I can't miss reaching my goals. Not this time."

"You lose control?" Burke asked softly.

"Restaurant, Burke," she snapped. "Tattoo. Marriage. The list isn't getting shorter. I don't have the time or energy or resources or knowledge to expand at the rate you want to." Her voice was small, her gaze way too focused on her wrist. "I can't."

"Are you afraid of failing?" He could help ensure that she didn't.

"I'm not ready. It's not what I want."

"But you took out a loan so you could. Did you lie to the bank?"

"Burke, let it go." Her voice was thick, as if she was fighting tears.

"I can't. It's my money, and what you're saying and doing doesn't line up."

Her dog was pushing his head between the seats, nuzzling Jill's arm.

"Let me help your business," he said. "It won't fail. I promise. We'll grow it. You'll reach your goals and pay back the loan in record time." And create another revenue stream he could present to his potential partners. If they were married it tied them together on another level, making everything that much more secure for him.

"I'm not afraid of failure." She wouldn't meet his gaze. "I've started working for Emma Carrington since then, and so I've created a more gradual growth plan."

The vehicle was silent other than the sound of the dog panting.

"Did you know I live in fear every day?" he said. "You know how many employees count on me for their livelihoods?"

He waited for her to speak, but she didn't.

"Twenty-five in my office alone. My financial advisor is about to have a baby. The marketing manager's son needs major medical care. They count on me. Ralph's just about at retirement. Gulliver finally bought a house." Burke let out a sigh. "I can't let them down and I won't. It's not an option. And I won't let you down, either."

"So you think selling copious amounts of my products on your site is going to save everything?"

"Yes." That had been her ambitious proposal. She would use his platform. He'd take a nice share of the profits. He'd known then that her business was too small to keep up, but that was before he'd decided to step in and take control. He'd hire someone if need be. He just had to show that viable income and growth to potential future partners.

She shook her head and started the engine. "When?"

"I want all of this established as soon as possible so I can have contracts in place with potential partners to cover Tiffer's fee."

"That's two months," she said in disbelief.

"I know there's a lot to do, and I'm not saying we're creating a money miracle. I just have to be able to prove to investors that we're able to make it work, and that there's strong potential in us working together."

"There's a lot to do..."

Add her items to the website, boost her production. Boom. Done.

"It's feasible. When I know what I need to do, I can move fast."

"Would it really work?" She was tempted. Time to close the deal.

"It will," he said.

"You paused."

"I know how much we need to sell to get that loan paid off. It's not beyond the realm of reality to cut your five-year plan down significantly with the right kind of platform and marketing. And I can provide that."

"I have a full-time job." Her expression was pinched again.

"I'm an expert in this area."

"An expert on the brink of losing everything. Do you really think it's wise to take a risk right now?"

His heart was pounding, but he knew the right answer. Knew the truth he had to live by. "Would you rather try and fail, or would you rather die knowing you could have maybe done something? Could have possibly made it all work out if you'd just stepped outside your fear and tried?"

She fiddled with her bracelet, her face lowered.

She was tempted. Tempted to trust him, believe in him and his plan.

"What would you do with a successful company? What's your dream?" Burke asked.

Her gaze was soft, out of focus, as she stared out the windshield. He knew she could see it, even if she wasn't ready to share it.

"I've been stalking a deal with Tiffer for a long time," he said. "We're this close, Jill. But I need you. I have staff who know how to sell stuff."

"What if I say no?" She turned to him. She was breathing faster, considering his offer. So close.

"Why would you?"

"Because…" Her gaze drifted down his torso. "Because…."

"Then it's a deal." He took her hand, shaking it.

"Burke…"

"Consider it," he said quickly, opening his door. "We'll meet in my office tomorrow to iron out details."

"I have a job to go to, you know!"

And before she could outright refuse, he let himself out of the car, knowing that even though it might not be today, soon she was going to say yes.

CHAPTER 5

𝓑urke handed Andrea a gift bag overflowing with tissue paper. Balloons were strung up on the staff room walls and a yet-to-be-cut cake was waiting on a side table. New cloth diapers were stacked up beside the company's very pregnant financial officer, who was watching him with curiosity.

"Burke," she said with a judgmental frown, "tissue paper?"

"I thought we were better than killing the planet with excess paper products," Gulliver chirped. "What's next? Leaving all the office lights on overnight?"

"The store did that for me and it's reusable—unlike most wrapping paper." Burke bent to place a kiss on the mother-to-be's cheek. He'd completely blanked out about the baby shower for Andrea, his mind caught up in business and the fact that it had been a week since he'd last heard from Jill, who was set to sign their prepared divorce papers in less than two hours.

"And you didn't tell them no?" Andrea asked. "Normally you would." She arched a brow at him and placed a hand to support her back as she eased into the chair behind her. "What's got you so distracted?"

Burke waved off the comment. He couldn't talk about Jill, that was for certain. Or the fact that he still didn't have a way to leverage money for their expansion plan or for working with Tiffer, should he offer a deal.

"Is this because the company's going under?" Gulliver asked, his cup of purplish-red punch at the ready, as if he might need to splash it on someone. Namely Burke, who automatically took a step back. His shirt had never recovered from Autumn's merlot, and Jill hadn't returned his suit jacket. His wardrobe was feeling the loss of his two favorite garments. He didn't need to add a third.

And things happened in threes, they said.

Burke took another step back.

"Chill out, Gull," Andrea said affectionately. "We're in the black and always have been since day one. We're just stretched with the expansion—which I still argue we don't truly need."

"A global market will help keep us stable through downturns," Burke reminded her.

"True, but..."

"It's fine," he insisted.

"Is it?" Gulliver pressed forward. The staff had moved past Gully's drama from almost two weeks ago, no longer regarding his "sky is falling" attitude with any seriousness. Thankfully. Nevertheless, Burke gave his assistant a stern frown. He didn't need everyone worrying again.

"Well, whatever you do, you'd better keep up on my maternity leave payments, buster." Andrea shook a fist at Burke.

"Gulliver is selling off all the kitsch in my place so your baby can have the best there is."

"Am not," Gulliver said hotly.

"Don't sell your kitsch, you big goof." Andrea was still whisking pieces of colored tissue paper from the bag. "Is there even anything in here?"

"Careful. Don't rip the paper. We can reuse it," Gulliver said, shooting Burke a look of disapproval as he plucked the discarded pieces from the table, smoothing each one before carefully folding it.

Burke checked the clock on the wall. Maybe if this party wrapped up soon he could meet Jill downtown and make one last plea before she signed.

There had to be a way. He'd seen her hesitation. She wanted to work together. If he talked to her, he was certain he could change her mind. Everyone wanted money and success, and he was confident he could provide both. He just had to get her to trust him. And seeing as he'd managed to get her to trust him long enough to marry him, a simple business deal shouldn't be an issue.

"Burke?" Andrea said.

"Hmm?" He tried to focus on the party, lifting his shoulders and placing a smile on his face.

"You still with us?"

"Yeah, yeah, of course. I have a proposal out that's caught my attention. It may pull me from the office a bit over the next few months."

"The place won't be here when you return," Gulliver said sadly to Andrea. "I bet he's already doing contract work for others." He glared.

"Gulliver, don't be such a downer," Burke said with a sigh.

Behind him he heard one of the techs whisper to someone, "Where's the best place to post a résumé these days? Do you think Ethan Mattson would hire me to work for him?"

Ethan was STH's website contractor who did most of the site's heavy lifting from his home office in Blueberry Springs.

"If we go under," came the quiet reply, "he'll have less work, too."

The tech heaved a tremendous sigh, causing the pounding in Burke's temples to pick up. "Maybe we could have a résumé workshop and help each other polish ours up."

"Would everyone just stop?" Burke said a bit too loudly as he turned around to confront the doomsayers. The room silenced at his outburst. "Sorry. I'm sorry. But come on, you guys, we're going to be okay, so can we try and be optimistic and positive? Create some good energy in here? We've got this."

"Let's have some cake," someone suggested.

"Is it gluten free?" the tech asked.

Gulliver scolded, "It's cake! What do you expect? Of course it has gluten. And sugar. And butter. And milk. And eggs. I was up all night making this, so don't you dare complain."

"It's beautiful, Gull," Andrea said.

Burke gently directed Gulliver away from the group, putting him on the other side of Andrea.

"How about nuts?" someone teased, and Burke shot him a look. *Not helping.*

"I hate you all." Gulliver threw up his hands, then crossed them over his chest with a huff, in what Burke was fairly sure was a fake sulk. "Next time I'm putting laxative in the icing." He turned to the mom-to-be. "Well, except yours. It wouldn't be a nice thing to do to the unborn, who has yet to wound me."

Andrea opened Burke's gift at long last, a pack of organic baby wipes, along with an amber teething necklace, several minuscule organic cotton outfits, and gentle natural baby soaps to go with the large stroller the office had chipped in to purchase. She pulled him down so she could give him a half hug from her chair.

Gulliver, grumbling about a lack of gratitude and everyone's sense of entitlement, began cutting the cake, serving slices to all but the offending parties. "You funny boys can serve yourselves."

"Why can't he get it through his head that this is only a hiccup and that we're not going under?" Burke whispered, taking the chair next to Andrea.

She shrugged. "I think he wants to marry Emilio. But summoning the courage to ask is killing him."

"Why would he want to do that?"

"Because he loves him."

"Emilio is a hypochondriac mooch," Burke declared. "Gully could do better."

"Don't you tell him that. Be supportive."

"He deserves better."

"Of course he does. But he loves Emilio and so he overlooks his faults. We all do that when we're in love."

"Just another reason to stay single," Burke said.

"Nobody's perfect. Not even you."

"I never said I was. Which is even more reason to stay single. Save the women of the world from all that I am." He winked at Andrea before realizing the room had quieted, with everyone's focus on something behind him. He turned to see a woman in the doorway. She was a tall, voluptuous drink of sex appeal in a fitted red sweater and jeans that did something to his brain that caused an elevated heart rate, and smoke to pour from his ears.

"Hello," Gulliver called. "Are you a friend of Burke's? You look familiar."

It was Burke's wife.

Jill.

The one who planned to sign divorce papers that very afternoon. How could she possibly be even more captivating than he'd remembered? And why was he drinking her in?

Jill was about business, a means to an end. Nothing else.

That's why she was captivating—he needed her business to help his grow. And natural medicinal creams? Who didn't love that? He had the market; she had the product.

"What are you doing here?" he asked, his throat suddenly dry.

His dry-cleaned suit jacket was in a clear bag slung over Jill's shoulder. Her confidence faltered and a flash of uncertainty clouded her expression.

"You wanted to talk to me about a...proposal?" she said.

"This is the out-of-town business deal?" Gulliver's entire being had lit up, and he floated across the room, placing both his hands over Jill's. "I'm Gulliver. STH is a sustainable, stable company and we absolutely love that you've come in to talk to us today."

"Thank you." Jill introduced herself.

"Oh, you are all woman." Gulliver stepped back, appraising her. "Are you the one Burke—"

"Let's talk in my office," Burke interrupted. He was at Jill's side in a flash, plucking her from Gulliver's grasp.

"I don't want to take you from your party," Jill said, her dark ponytail swinging as she refused to allow him to push her from the room. One of her cool hands wrapped around his as he tried to direct her away from Gulliver. Her touch was gentle and it sapped his will to protest, even though he knew it wasn't wise to have her join the party. "I can come back later."

Gulliver had angled his way closer again, scooping up the dry-cleaned jacket. "Is this Burke's?"

Jill said calmly, "I had a wardrobe malfunction and he was kind enough to lend me his jacket."

Gulliver turned to Burke and lifted a hand, clawing the air with a quiet *"Rrrowr."*

"Sorry, everyone, but I need to have this meeting with Ms. Armstrong," Burke announced sternly. "Enjoy the party and cake."

He escorted her to his office, very aware that he wanted to give this gorgeous woman whatever she wanted, even if it ended up being beyond his best interests. Which meant he needed to be tough, play hardball. No emotion. Nothing but business.

Right. He was pretty certain he could do that.

If, say, he stayed on his own side of the desk.

JILL FOLLOWED Burke into his office. He smelled amazing and his office felt warm and inviting, thanks in part to the potted plants he had growing along the tall window behind his desk. He shut the door behind them, turning his steady gaze upon her. Suddenly the room felt too close, her sweater too tight, his tempting proximity much too real.

"Hi," she whispered.

"Hi."

They stood facing each other for a long moment before remembering themselves. Burke cleared his throat and moved to the other side of his desk.

"Sorry for interrupting," she said.

"It's fine. I'm glad you came."

"I wanted to talk to you before I sign the papers."

"It's better for both of us if you don't sign," Burke said.

"I like your proposal, but I'd prefer to grow my business at a slower rate than you've stated. I came here because I want to make sure you understand this isn't personal, and that I plan to uphold my promise to pay back the loan."

"I was genuine in my offer to help."

"You mean take over." Take risks. Leave too much to chance. She'd done that with the café by letting Hayes take care of all the financials, believing his words about growing the business and earning her a bonus from the owners. She'd fallen for it, practically choosing the flooring for the friendship center then and there.

But Burke was different, she reminded herself. He had a reputation that preceded him and had offered to help. She was being a chicken, plain and simple. Working with Burke would be the fast track, and the unknown aspects of that left her with heart palpitations.

"Hacking growth to suddenly break out as the next It Thing is methodical," Burke was saying. "Growing this way is faster because you build precious momentum, which shoots you forward in a way that moving slowly just doesn't allow."

"Thank you for your proposal. I appreciate—"

"You're never going to get the growth you're hoping for with your current plan. It's stifling. You've bound your own hands. There's no room for chance and opportunity."

"It's important to me that I maintain the integrity of my products."

"That's practically my brand. You need to loosen up so you can succeed." He was standing now, hands on the desk, leaning forward. "Stay married to me. Just until I meet with Tiffer."

"Can you meet with him tomorrow?"

"He only accepts pitches from potential clients twice a year. I'm lucky he said yes at all, and I'm not going to push it by asking him to make an exception."

"Then he'll have to deal with you being divorced."

Burke sighed, sitting back with such a haggard look of defeat that Jill hesitated. Now was the time to leave his office, but she found she couldn't.

But she couldn't stay, either.

If word got out about her accidental marriage, she'd never be able to show her face in Blueberry Springs. Yes, Ginger had married someone she didn't know very well last year, but she was in love. It had worked out for her and Logan. Whereas Jill had gotten drunk, married a man and forgotten about it by morning. That was embarrassing.

"Goodbye, Burke."

"A partnership could be very lucrative for us both."

"We don't have to remain married for that." She reached for the doorknob.

"You borrowed against my personal credit, which I was planning to use to expand STH. You used me—even if accidentally—and I think it's only fair that I get to use you in return."

"You can't be serious. That's not how marriage works."

"So in our case what's mine becomes yours, but not the other way around? How's that fair?"

Jill shifted from foot to foot, wary of where he was going with this conversation.

He was calm. Too calm.

"In small towns marriages aren't segmented and individualized," she explained. "The bank manager sees what's in the union by way of assets and liabilities and makes her decision based on that."

"I'm desperate, Jill. You threw a giant wrench in my company's plans. You saw Andrea out there. She's having a baby any day. These people *need* me. I risked it all with that expansion plan. The one you tanked. They think we're in the black, but when you count the chips...we can't afford to lose even one at this point."

"You shouldn't have taken the risk," Jill said, feeling the uncertainty of wrongdoing edging up inside her. He'd taken the risks, not her. This wasn't her fault.

But she *had* borrowed that money against his credit. Credit he'd planned on using...

"Please, Jill. I *had* a plan."

"Have you paused to consider how this looks?" she asked, buying for time. "Our marriage makes me seem foolish. Like I'm not in control of my own life."

"We can fix this problem. We can fix it together."

Her hand drifted from the door.

"You owe me."

That tight feeling in her chest and the lightheadedness from the other day returned, and for the first time in a long while she wasn't sure what was right.

All she knew were the facts, and she did indeed seem to owe Burke Carver for accidentally messing up his plans.

BURKE HELD HIS BREATH. Jill had hesitated. A precious moment in time where her indecision sat on a precipitous. Where a puff of wind could send it down either side. Yes or no.

She'd moved from the door and was hovering near the chair across from him.

"Say I was to help you..." She wasn't looking up from the floor, and he forced himself to remain silent while she chose her next words. "I don't want to tell anyone we're married." She looked up, an apology in her gentle expression, already seeking forgiveness in case her words had stung.

"Okay," he said slowly. "I won't tell anyone if that's what you want, but these things tend to not stay secret. You've already told Tiffer, for example. And my aunt knows."

As well, Autumn knew Jill was something to him—she just wasn't quite sure what, exactly. The odds of them keeping this all quiet for the next few months weren't ones he'd bet upon.

Jill raked her fingers through her ponytail, looking thoughtful.

"I don't care if the world knows I'm married," Burke said.

"Well, I care. We were married for almost a year and didn't know. I *dated* people, Burke. And so did you. It looks like we *cheated* on each other."

He was silent for a beat, feeling as though he'd done something wrong, even though he'd been just as unaware as she had been. "I'm sorry."

She hadn't seemed to expect the apology and it took the fire out of her. "Me, too, I guess."

"I'm sorry that it might look bad for you, too."

"Because you move from woman to woman?" She shifted, jutting out a hip. "Don't give me that hurt look. See it from my perspective. I married a man who doesn't commit. This is my life. My reputation. I'm not the kind of woman who..." She blinked hard.

"Okay," he said gently, understanding that she was upset with appearances in regards to their marriage. "I'll do my utmost to keep it secret. We'll stay together until I can pitch to Tiffer. I'll help you with your company. We'll both reach our goals."

He pulled out the agreement he'd had his lawyer do up on the off chance Jill decided to work with him rather than divorce him.

"What are you doing? I didn't say yes."

"I want you to read this," he said, "and amend it so the terms work for you." With slow, measured moves, he slid the paper to the edge of the desk.

Jill's shoulders dropped a notch, and she tentatively took the stapled document. She flipped to the second page, her bright eyes flicking over the paragraphs of text.

"It's a package. Contract and marriage. You get your loan paid off faster than you'd planned, get free marketing and a partnership with a strong company with reach. You boost my product diversity and store's profits, while I also get to prove to Tiffer that I'm a stable human being worthy of receiving his agency's global marketing contract. We both win."

Jill was considering his words, a frown in place. "I have a full-time job."

"I promise to support you in whatever way you and your business need."

She watched him for a long time. Finally, she nodded.

"Okay?" He felt his spirits lift. "You'll sign?"

"Let's grow my business and hopefully save yours."

"Our partnership will provide a—"

He didn't get to finish his spiel before Jill interrupted, saying, "Do whatever business mumbo jumbo you need to do to make your life better again, then step back out of mine."

"First chance to leave, and you're already looking forward to it."

"Why wouldn't I?" she challenged, hand on her hip, the dare in her eyes waking a fire within him.

"Because you need a man like me." What was he doing? He had her ready to help him and he felt the need to make a point?

For what? To make her look at him with that spark of interest most women shot his way?

Why did he have to keep reminding himself that this was *not* personal?

It had to be that fitted red sweater messing with his mind and bringing up memories from their wedding night.

"Don't act so full of yourself," she said, her voice level. She scooted her chair to his desk, grabbed a pen and began scratching things on page three, initialing her modifications. He craned his neck to see what she'd changed.

It was something he could live with.

Her scent was sweet, like strawberry ice cream.

She looked up, pointing the pen at him. "When I mean don't tell anyone we're married that also includes my family. Everyone. And tell your aunt not to mention it to a soul." She continued working on the document. "And don't take over my business. You get a say, and can be helpful, but I make all the big decisions. I'm the one in control."

She scrawled a few extra terms at the bottom, and was about to sign when Burke stopped her.

"We need a notary."

"Oh."

"My assistant is one." He texted Gulliver, who was likely still in the staff room.

Within moments Gully came marching in. "Everything all right? You said you needed me." He caught Jill's tense expression and gave Burke a scowl. "Do I need to put laxative in your coffee? You've obviously upset this nice woman." He shot Jill a supportive look of sympathy.

Traitor.

Jill let out a soft huff of laughter as Burke grumbled, "We need a notary."

"Are you signing under duress?" Gulliver asked, looking at her over his shoulder as Burke inked his name onto the documents.

Jill giggled in surprise. "No."

"Good."

She signed as well, then Gulliver completed the papers with a flourish. As he backed toward the door, he made a fist, extending his thumb and pinkie to represent a phone, and held it to his ear while saying to Jill, "If you need anything, sweetie, you just give me a call."

"Remember who signs your paychecks," Burke said, before his assistant disappeared, contract in hand.

Burke let out a long sigh of relief. It was over. He'd done it.

Now the real work began.

DONE. She'd done it. Jill had agreed to stay married to Burke for another two months. She could do that, right? She'd get a friendship center out of it, thanks to a quick boost in sales. He'd get a deal.

Easy. He lived hours away and her family would never need to know about the accidental marriage.

"Just out of curiosity," she asked, as they moved toward his office door, "why do you think I need a man like you?"

"To fix your business," he said quickly.

"And?" She hated that she was fishing, hoping that there was a more personal reason.

"You want me to tell you that your sweater is enough to give a man a heart attack, and that every time you fight with me I forget who I am? I should avoid you, but instead I can't stop thinking about you."

Jill felt shaky inside, thanks to the intensity in his gaze. "I agreed to stay married. You don't need to start making things up to try and flatter me."

"It's not a lie." He was standing so close the air grew still around them. She'd shifted without noticing, their lips merely inches apart.

He gently took her by the waist. "I want to make you smile and let go." He eyed her face, ensuring she wasn't about to slug him, then took advantage of her indecision by pressing his mouth to hers. Her fists landed gently against his collarbone without vindication as their kiss deepened, their bodies softening as they got caught up in each other.

He broke the kiss. "You need spontaneity, fewer plans." He angled his head to kiss her again, but she stepped back just as she heard a loud gasp that sounded too feminine to be his. Jill looked to the door to find a gorgeous, midtwenties Latino woman glaring at them.

"Burke!" the woman scolded.

He jumped away from Jill, hands lifted in the air like someone accused.

The woman came roaring in, her mouth moving fast as she swore at him in both English and Spanish.

"Autumn," Burke protested, "What are you doing here?"

"I came to tell you I won't be shaken off." She staggered on her high hells as if she'd had too much to drink. "You can run, you can hide, you can be hurtful and aloof, but I know the truth about you. You're capable of love—you have a *kitten*! If that's not a cry for love, then I don't know what is! I am not going to let you run after the next skirt that comes along because you're afraid of what we have. We have a connection, Burke. You and I are meant to be."

"Autumn, we are not meant to be," Burke said patiently.

Jill made her way to the door, sidestepping quietly, hoping to escape unnoticed.

This was exactly what she'd been talking about when it came to their marriage. A big mess. And she'd just been wooed into signing on for more. What was it about Burke Carver that made her unable to side with reason?

Just as she reached the door, Autumn beat her there, her large dark eyes locked onto Jill's. "This one's mine. My daddy's a very powerful man, so don't even think about sneaking around with him behind my back or I'll make you sorry."

"Excuse me? Are you threatening me?" Jill asked, giving him tone. Her competitive edge reared up and she barely bit down in time before she told Autumn to back off because he was *her* husband.

"Come on, Autumn, I think you've had a bit too much to drink at the country club this afternoon," Burke said, stepping between them. "Let's get you a ride home and maybe something to eat."

Autumn whirled on him. "I know what you're trying to do. Sweep me off to my daddy so you can be together. He doesn't love me and now neither do you." She let out a wail as Burke shuffled her over the room's threshold. She whirled, stepping back into the room. She pointed at Jill. "You're not even that pretty!"

She shook off Burke and left, and Jill called halfheartedly after her, "At least I'm not a spoiled brat!"

Gulliver stuck his head in the door the second after Autumn stormed off. "Well, that should get interesting. Do you need me to send her a—"

"Not now." Burke rushed past Gulliver in pursuit of the tipsy socialite, who, by the sounds of it, had just cleared everything off Gulliver's desk outside Burke's office.

"Tomorrow? When she's had a chance to cool down?" Gulliver called. "Good plan."

"Was that the governor's daughter?" Jill squeaked, already knowing the answer.

Gulliver nodded. "For the record, I've never offered to put a laxative in my boss's coffee for her." And then he was off.

Jill stood in the suddenly quiet office, gathering herself. Autumn was going to make Burke pay, meaning things were going to get complicated. Jill stared at Burke's desk where she'd just signed the contract.

Could she find it, rip it up, and escape this giant mess before it completely unearthed itself? Legally, wasn't there a five-minute back-out clause where if you changed your mind within five minutes of signing the contract became null?

She didn't think so. Which meant she was stuck with it.

But why had Burke run after Autumn? Was he just being a nice guy or were they actually involved? Was that why he'd agreed to not tell anyone about the marriage?

And if so, why did that hurt?

Jill heard voices outside the office and the ticking of a bicycle's pedals as someone pushed one past the open door. She slipped out of the office. Gulliver was whispering with someone while picking up his desk items that had been strewn across the floor by Autumn, and Jill hurried past, gaze averted. Within moments she was racing down the stairs she'd come up just two weeks ago with Burke.

She should have asked more questions before signing. Should have paused to *think*. She'd felt a strange sense of obligation and responsibility for Burke, his employees and the business, and as a result had thrown her own plans out the window. Now she was staying married to a man with a woman on the side. There was no way this would remain secret—just like he'd warned.

Her shoes slipped on the last step and she grabbed the railing, narrowly avoiding cracking her head on the concrete steps. She righted herself and pushed open the emergency exit door, gulping in the cold March air. She needed the privacy of her car. She needed to get away from the city so she could think.

To her left, just outside the office building's tall glass doors, she heard Autumn shouting at Burke, and saw him reach for her while she flagged down a passing cab.

When would Jill ever learn? Burke made her head a mess and she did stupid things without thinking through all the possible implications. She was ready to rip his throat out one moment, then ready to flip up her skirt for him the next.

Not cool.

Burke Carver.

Hot. Irresistible.

And a big, pushy you-know-what who thought he could sweet-talk his way into getting what he wanted from women. She'd tossed out her plan for him. Her quite possibly two-timing husband.

A giant, painful bubble formed in her lungs, making it difficult to swallow, breathe.

She got in her car and dropped the keys while trying to fit them into the ignition, and fought the need to cry. She snatched them off the floor and tried again, shoving them into the slot. The car started as her cell rang. Despite knowing better, she picked it up.

"Where are you?" Burke demanded immediately.

"I have a date," she said primly.

"You're married."

"So are you!"

"Autumn and I *aren't* a thing."

"She obviously didn't get the text message. Or was it an email? Candy gram via your well-trained assistant? You misrepresented yourself."

"We still have things to discuss."

"I'm busy. Maybe next time if you want to talk you can hold off kissing me, and tell your girlfriend to stay home." Jill hung up, then stared at her phone in shock. She felt panicked.

She needed to work with him, stay civil. But he made her lose control, forget herself. He made her feel alive, wanted, and it made her crazy in the head.

But it wasn't real. It never would be. She was just a business problem he wanted to have go away, and he was willing to say whatever he needed to in order to make that happen.

Her phone rang and she answered, snapping, "What is it about you that makes me feel and act like a crazy woman?"

There was silence before Burke said quietly, "Cancel your date."

"No."

There was no date. That had been a lie to give her space, to make him back off, to feel that maybe she wasn't as easy as he believed.

Even though it felt as though she was.

"Are you free tomorrow?"

"I'll have to check my calendar."

"Don't make this harder than it has to be."

"What's that supposed to mean?"

"We're business partners. Don't play hard to get."

"It's called giving you the cold shoulder so you'll take the hint and leave me alone so I don't have to drop a piano on your head." She turned off her SUV, fuming. "How long until she tells the world? How long until..."

She gulped as her throat tightened.

She should have divorced Burke and moved on. How long until she heard the odd rumbling about her having a secret husband, despite swearing Wini to silence? How long until she was avoiding text messages and ditching half-eaten brownies in Mandy's little café when she saw the gossips heading her way?

She didn't want to deal with the embarrassing fallout of her drunken actions. She just wanted it all to go away.

"Autumn won't talk."

"She's going to blab." Most people would fear the embarrassment, but Autumn was different. She wouldn't sit in the dark, licking her wounds. No, she craved attention and would milk this situation for all it was worth.

"Then we'll take the wind out of her sails," Burke said decisively. "We'll...spin it. Turn it into a way to promote our businesses. We'll tell your family and friends. But I won't play doting husband," he warned. "I don't do kissy commitment stuff."

"We're not *telling* anyone."

"It's still best to work together."

"I haven't gone back on my word—or the contract."

"Where are you? Is that your car down the street?"

In the distance she could see him through her rearview mirror, standing on the sidewalk, craning his neck, searching for her.

"I've got to go."

She hung up and pulled away before he could catch up and convince her to do something rash, such as tell the world she'd married him in secret months and months ago.

Then forgotten about it.

With her heart beating fast enough to rival the RPMs in her SUV's engine, she tore home, realizing the truth. If they were going to have a chance with Tiffer, they were going to have to publicly reveal their secret.

They were going to have to own it.

CHAPTER 6

Burke stretched as he got out of his compact hybrid car and took in the gas-guzzling pickup trucks lining Main Street in Blueberry Springs. Most of them were so big his car could ride in their back.

There was more snow here than in the city and he moved through the slushy stuff as he enjoyed the sunshine, heading toward the Wrap It Up sandwich shop where Jill had requested he meet her. It was in an old, narrow brick building that had been revitalized, giving it a new lease on life. The place had character and charm and he liked it and the owner already. Especially if she was responsible for the amazing chocolaty aroma wafting onto the street.

A few hikers decked out in renewable hemp and bamboo hiking pants walked past, laughing and chatting, thumbs hooked under their backpacks' shoulder straps. His wandering gaze caught the looming mountains, the trees arching over the street. The town had a beauty and uniqueness that he could get used to.

He reached for the glass door, but before he could push it open a swell of apprehension washed over him. Inside, waiting, was his wife.

Wife.

He exhaled slowly. He had thought he'd never call anyone by that title ever again.

He pushed his way through the door.

It would all work out. He'd been through worse. And he'd told Jill he wasn't going to act like a real husband. He was here in town to beat everyone to the punch as part of his and Jill's plan to head off the inevitable Autumn fallout. He'd allow everyone to put a face to his title as Jill's husband, then move on with business.

They would have a modern marriage or whatever she'd called it when she'd phoned him late in the night. Not open or casual, but not live-together, happily ever after, either.

But now, being here, looking for her among those having coffee in the packed little place, it all felt a bit too close, too real.

Burke scanned the tables, spotting Jill sitting toward the back, her fingers running through her dark ponytail like a comb, her eyes cast downward. As he approached, he discovered she was fully absorbed by her e-reader.

He slipped into the chair across from her, asking, "What are you reading?"

She flipped the screen toward her chest, hiding it. "Nothing."

"Erotica?"

"Just a sweet romance, thank you very much." She held the device closer.

"Why?"

"What do you mean, why?" She narrowed her eyes.

"You believe in that stuff?" He pointed to her e-reader. His aunt Maggie loved romances and read at least one a week. He kind of figured it was her way of vicariously having what he'd denied her—the opportunity to marry the man she'd loved. "True love and happy endings for everyone?"

"You don't?"

"I don't." It took all his conviction not to explain himself to her.

Jill studied him for a beat before tucking her e-reader into her bag and asking, "Did you find the place okay?"

"No."

She inhaled as though about to speak, giving him a thoughtful look.

"It doesn't say 'Mandy's' on the sign out front," he pointed out. She'd asked him to meet her at Mandy's café. After passing down Main Street enough times to start collecting stares, he'd finally stopped for directions. Turned out Mandy's was actually part of the chain sandwich shop Wrap It Up which had gone independent a few years back. But because it was owned by local waitress-turned-business-owner Mandy, everyone called it that.

Go figure. Small towns.

Directions around here probably sounded a lot like, "Turn left where Polk's barn used to be, then go down almost as far as you can, then turn at the big rock. You'll know it when you see it."

"Sorry," Jill said. "Do you want some coffee?"

The place smelled like fresh baked brownies and Burke glanced toward the front counter. "It smells like something delicious was just made."

"Those would be Mandy's whiskey-and-gumdrop brownies. I don't recommend them."

Burke quirked an eyebrow. "Why's that?" They smelled incredible.

"They're highly addictive."

"In that case—" he patted his flat stomach "—I'll pass. I got your spreadsheet for your products and prices this morning before I left. I think we need to charge more."

"There is no 'we,' remember?"

"They're specialty, handmade formulas, not just small things to add into your cart to reach the free shipping threshold. You can charge a lot more for that. Especially since Gulliver tried that eczema cream sample and is over the moon about it."

"I sell more at a lower price, and make more money overall."

"My market isn't about volume, it's about people feeling as though they're making a difference and doing the right thing with their purchasing choices. They don't mind paying more."

"Is that why you have cash flow problems?"

"I don't have cash flow issues." He crossed his arms over his chest. When she continued to give him a questioning look, he reminded her, "I need money for that expansion you mucked up."

"Here they are!" A woman with a white-streaked bob came over, hands clenched together.

Jill stiffened like a rabbit trying to blend into her surroundings so she wouldn't be spotted. Burke would suggest it was too late for that. And seeing as his whole purpose of being here was to put a face to the "new husband," he turned, playing his role.

"Burke Carver," he said, standing to shake the woman's hand.

"I'm Wini, the manager at the bank here in town. What a surprise to find that Jill—" She glanced at her, her mouth snapping shut.

"It's okay," Jill said quietly. She looked up, trying to act casual and failing spectacularly. "Our marriage is no longer a secret."

Seriously, did she have to cringe while saying that?

"So you're the woman who gave my lovely wife a loan without me having to cosign?" Burke asked.

Wini smiled warmly. "We keep things easy out here! I'm so excited for the two of you. Congratulations."

"In the city it's customary for both parties to sign."

She waved a hand, still smiling. "Small towns are much more personal, Burke, sweetie." She gave his arm a friendly squeeze. "I can't believe she's kept you hidden away for so long. You'll love living here."

"His business keeps him in the city," Jill said, remaining in her seat, "and he'll be keeping his home there, as well. We have an independent partnership. A marriage that allows us to—"

"You're leaving town?" Wini asked, so aghast that Burke found it amusing.

"No, we have a modern marriage where we are independent from each other," Jill said patiently. She was delivering her lines awkwardly, like an actor performing live for the first time and slightly freaked out by having a real audience.

"Long distance won't work." Wini tsked as she took the seat across from Jill. Burke took the one beside Jill, wondering if he was supposed to sling his arm across the back of her chair. What type of man did she go for? Possessive? Indifferent?

Wait, why did it matter? He was in town for five minutes, to give everyone a smile and a wave before sailing out, never to be seen again.

"We thought our Jill was *never* going to find someone again," a woman cooed as she hustled over, eyes dancing. She shook Burke's hand, then took the seat across from him. "I'm her mother, Jenilee Armstrong. Jill's sister, Jodi, is the one who gets all the men."

"Is that so?" he said, when it seemed as though she expected him to comment.

Jenilee reached over to pat Jill's clenched hand. "With her teenaged years full of shooting competitions, then the boxing and lifting weights with her father… Well, we thought she might be *more* than a tomboy, if you know what I mean. We're so pleased you've come along and married her. It's so difficult to find a soulmate when you're living in a small town and prefer women."

"I'm not gay," Jill said.

"Well, we know that now."

"There's nothing wrong with being a lesbian," Wini added supportively.

"I assure you, Jill is not a lesbian," Burke said, making certain his voice was extra deep, rough and manly. He shot Jill a smile that made her cheeks grow pink.

Jenilee cleared her throat. "Well, dear, I'm glad you found someone who accepts you for who you are. Especially after pining after Devon for all those years. That was so horrible to watch." She glanced at Wini as though seeking support.

"Who's Devon?" Burke asked, curiosity getting the better of him. He couldn't imagine Jill pining over anyone.

"Mom," Jill warned, standing up.

"Her ex-boyfriend. He lives here in town."

"He does?"

"She'd get this sad look, as though wishing he'd notice her." Jenilee turned to her daughter. "You deserve a man who adores you. Especially after the whole café thing with that no-good—"

"Mom," she said sharply. Jill looked as if she didn't know whether to grab Burke and run or stand her ground. Maybe stand her ground while tackling her mother to the ground with a cloth soaked in chloroform.

Burke could kind of see that last one playing out. Jenilee had a way about her that made him want to stay in town and be the best husband for Jill just to get the woman to shut up and quit putting her gorgeous daughter down.

"Oh, honey," Jenilee said. "Worrying is what moms do. Just ask your sister."

Wow. Ouch.

"Well, we have to run along," Burke said, standing up, taking Jill's pleading, darted glances his way as a hint.

Mrs. Armstrong stood, coming around the table, clutching Burke's arms as she sized him up. "You are so handsome. Jill has done well." She released him so she could give her daughter a quick squeeze. Jill stood like a statue, not moving to reciprocate as her mother whispered, just loud enough that Burke could make out what she was saying, "Try a bit harder with this one. Ask your sister for advice on how to keep a man. Maybe lose some weight and leave your hair loose. I have curlers if you need them."

She released her dejected-looking daughter, and Wini squeezed Jill's arm in sympathy.

"We don't have that kind of marriage," Jill said weakly. "It's a modern, professional partnership that allows us independence so we can focus on our careers."

For all her preparedness, Burke could see it wasn't working despite what he was certain was a color-coded, multistage war plan. He stood, taking a step forward so he was shoulder to shoulder with Jill, and gave the other women his most winning smile, hoping it didn't look like a grimace.

"Did you know how long I had to chase Jill and these dangerous curves of hers?"

He pulled her so they were hip to hip.

"At conferences all the men want to talk to her. And why not? She's gorgeous, intelligent and articulate. She can talk sports or business." He allowed his gaze to linger on her. "Not only that, but she has products she's obviously put her heart and soul into. My company is excited to be partnering with hers. We're going to put her products on the map just like they deserve." His arm was around Jill's shoulders and he pulled her closer. "Aren't we, honey?"

Her expression said *Oh puh-lease*. Yeah, yeah, he was breaking his own rule. But it was for a worthwhile cause. Her.

"Oh, Burke, darling, that's just a fun hobby," Jill's mom said, giving him a serious look. "Now that she has a husband she can focus on other things."

"A so-called hobby that will soon make her rich." He let that sink in for a moment. "I fully support Jill and her dreams."

"We support Jill," Jenilee said quickly.

"Good. Because anyone who doesn't will be speaking to me."

Jill's eyes widened and Jenilee tucked her chin in, shooting Wini a look of surprise.

"Right, honey?" he said.

Jill was uncharacteristically silent, and he wasn't sure if she was dreaming of running him down with her SUV, or considering keeping him.

He kind of hoped for the latter.

JILL HURRIED her problem husband from Mandy's café. He was being sweet and supportive and acting like the real deal—a catch. The kind of man she could fall for in a way that, if he ever left her, would shatter her heart and trust forever.

"Why did you defend me?" she demanded, once they were on the street. He could *not* stick to the plan, could he? There was no room for improvisation. They were supposed to act as though they'd intended to get married all along. Eloped. But not in a romantic way. No "honey," no love. Just business. Dry, boring and problem-free, making it possible for the town to forget he even existed.

Instead he'd stood up for her and tugged on her heartstrings like he'd been snuggling a puppy.

She sighed, torn. She *wanted* what he'd pretended they had. But they weren't going to have that, and the embarrassment of another failed marriage was going to hurt.

The gossips would offer their sympathy and support—all the while trying not to act too excited over the speculation going on behind her back. What had she done this time to lose her man? How had she been wronged? Why did she keep choosing the wrong fella?

"What are we going to do?" she asked.

"Relax. We'll figure it out." Burke appeared unaffected by her concern, as well as pleased with himself.

"Burke..."

"Seriously. Life always has a way of working out."

She rolled her head to the side, tired of arguing. It was too late to change the way he'd acted, anyway.

She rubbed her temples. Why did it seem as though she was always having to change course when he was around?

"Boxing?" Burke asked, his eyes twinkling with mischief.

She felt as though he was two steps away from laughing at her and her hobbies. She rested her hands on her hips. "Do you have a problem with that?"

"Did you compete?"

"In boxing? No."

"Show me." Burke had begun walking backward down the sidewalk, palms open as though he expected her to punch them.

"I'm not going to hit you."

"You said your dad owns a gun range, and your mom mentioned shooting. Do you prefer guns?"

Jill summoned a dirty look, but she secretly appreciated that he remembered that tidbit.

"Did you compete in shooting?" he asked.

She sighed. "Why the sudden interest in me and my life?" She really didn't want to talk about her old competitions or she'd find herself telling him about how it had all ended when she'd lost the scholarship for riflery. Lost everything, it felt like. All because her dad, who was also her coach, was still on his "once in a lifetime" trip that had turned into a several-months-long gig. Jill had shown up for the biggest competition of the year with her grandmother as her stand-in coach, naively thinking she was prepared. She hadn't been.

Everything had gone wrong from not having a back-up rifle in case hers jammed—which it did—to arriving late for the first heat, to her period starting three days before she'd expected it, and staining the white shorts her grandmother had insisted she wear as they were more feminine than the usual track pants she wore to meets. That had been the last time Jill had ever competed. It was soon after that that she'd met Rebecca and begun hanging out with the Ute instead of at home where the pressure to be someone other than herself felt like it was always mounting.

"You're interesting," Burke said.

"We have business to attend to. Business you messed up by breaking our 'no lovey-dovey' deal."

"Are you a sharpshooter?" He gave a small bounce and began walking beside her again. "You were good, weren't you?"

"Does that intimidate you if I was?"

"Are we talking skeet shooting or biathlon or to-the-death combat?"

"Why are you so excited about this?" Most men didn't think her skills were cool unless they were from deep in the woods and figured she might be able to bag an elusive mountain lion.

"I love hard core."

"It's not very feminine."

"I happen to admire strong women. It doesn't matter if your favorite hobby isn't one you do in a skirt and full makeup."

"Maybe I shoot better in high heels."

He bit back a grin. "That's a sexy image."

Jill sighed. "Can we talk about business and how you rerouted our whole entire strategy for dealing with our messy lives back there?"

"I thought you liked talking about the personal side of things?"

"Don't act like that around my family and friends."

"You want me to act unsupportive?"

"No. Yes. No." It would look worse if she'd married some guy who didn't stand up for her—that would be like Hayes all over again. "Just…you're complicating things."

He'd stopped walking. "How does supporting you complicate things?"

"This isn't for forever."

"You don't need to keep reminding me that you aren't keeping me."

She rolled her head again, feeling its weight. "Burke…"

"*You're* complicated. You know that?" He looked miffed. "I did what was right back there."

"And I appreciate the sentiment, just maybe not the timing and the 'honey' part."

"Why can't this be easy?"

"Because we had a plan and you deviated from it. That makes things complicated and messy."

"Let's talk about something else."

"Fine. How's Autumn?"

"Seriously?"

"Okay. Then how soon will my products be on your site? How soon do I need to start filling orders?"

"I'm planning to talk to Ethan Mattson today even though he usually doesn't work Sundays. He's my tech guy. You know him? He lives in town."

"I used to throw sour cherries at him when we were kids. This is Blueberry Springs. Of course I know him. In fact, he's probably already heard that you and I are married and that you're all lovesick over me, *honey*."

Burke smirked at her dig and said, "Well, hopefully he doesn't hold a grudge, because he's going to be adding your products as a pop-up add-on when consumers check out from my site." He rubbed his hands together. "Any more family for me to meet today?"

"You're liking this, aren't you?"

"Live in the moment, *honey*. I'm an expert at putting too much into relationships like this one—doomed from the start."

"Nice."

"What? It's true."

"I think we've done enough damage for the day," Jill said with a sigh.

They'd inadvertently stopped one block off Main, where the closed, abandoned Johnson's small café still sat, its windows thick with years of accumulated grime, the newspaper lining them yellowed and falling down.

Just like Jill's current plans involving keeping her life together and Burke at bay.

BURKE WAS STILL SURPRISED by how they'd ended up at Jill's father's shooting range after his meeting with Ethan. He'd been pretty certain Jill was going to run him out of town after meeting her mother. With Jenilee he'd gone a bit off script, acting like a real husband. They were supposed to keep it light and easy—his specialty—so that when they divorced things would just keep ticking along like they'd simply taken out the week's trash. Nothing more.

But her mom was a real piece of work and no man worth his salt—fake husband or not—would have stood by and let her keep talking to her daughter like that.

When he'd finished meeting with Ethan over at the techie's home office, Jill had been waiting out on the driveway, hands shoved into the pockets of her jacket to keep them warm, the late afternoon sun streaming over her dark hair. For a moment he'd wondered if he should have invited her into the meeting, even though it was about the structure of his online store.

She'd stood awkwardly, surrounded by the melting snowdrifts edging the driveway, looking like a schoolgirl waiting for her crush.

Okay, maybe that was him projecting his hope a little bit.

"I'm sorry about earlier," she said.

"There's nothing to apologize for. I'm the one who muddied the waters for you."

"Still, I shouldn't have been so hard on you. I overreacted, and I do appreciate you standing up for me."

"I stepped out of line by acting so..." He had studied her as he searched for the right word "...dedicated."

Their eyes had met and a flash of something indescribable had rippled through him.

She'd held out her hand. "Truce?"

"I was never mad," he'd replied, taking her hand and feeling that same warm wave move through him again.

"Let's try and keep it lighter from here on out, okay?"

He'd nodded. "Ethan offers his congratulations, by the way." He'd gestured to the house behind him. A black cat was sitting in the window, watching them.

"Told you he'd have heard already," she'd replied with a teasing lilt. "Blueberry Springs is small, and marriage and babies are usually the biggest things to happen to people."

"He didn't call me lovesick, though," Burke had replied, referring to her earlier comment. "And he loved that I stood up to your mom."

Jill had sighed, looking less the schoolgirl and more the peeved wife. "And did he say I'm lucky to have you?"

"That's implied," Burke had said with a teasing grin. "And I was thinking—you can divorce me for being too protective. Win-win, right?" He'd winked and she'd laughed.

"Yeah, that might work."

And just like that things had settled, that small barb of tension between them melting away.

"And you know, even so-called modern marriages have a bit of I-have-your-back-honey built into them."

The next thing he'd known they were hanging out at the range, Jill arranging for weapons and ammo.

Armed and dangerous. Just how every man liked his wife to be after he blew her plans to pieces.

At least there were a lot of witnesses around in case she decided to take care of him, so to speak.

While Burke waited for Jill to finish chatting with the guy behind the counter about the weather, her marriage—she was still trying for the modern marriage of independence angle, he noted—the man's mother's health and pretty much the state of the entire town of Blueberry Springs, he checked emails on his phone. As he replied to Gulliver about Andrea's impending leave, a text popped up from Autumn. She had tickets to a hockey game tomorrow and was hoping he could join her. Box seats. His favorite team.

He ignored the message and returned his cell to his back pocket.

Moments later the phone vibrated and, unable to resist, he checked it.

A scantily clad selfie from Autumn.

Oh, boy.

He deleted the image and returned the device to his pocket once again, wondering how he was going to get her to take it down a notch—or ten—and move along to someone else.

He didn't even want to think about how she was going to react when she found out he was married. Maybe he should let her hear it from him instead of from the world?

"Ready?" Jill was carrying their weapons, as well as ear protection. "We're over here."

Burke brought his mind to his present problem. His wife, and the town that now thought he was real.

She handed him a revolver that was surprisingly heavy, as well as solid. He'd shot a gun twice, but he'd forgotten how serious they felt.

"Go first," he said.

She nodded, securing her ear protection as she stepped to the counter, her feet spread. She wore an expressionless game face, a dimple appearing in her cheek as she concentrated on the paper target strung up at the other end of the building. The gun kicked as she shot off three quick rounds, all of them hitting the middle of the sheet.

"Nice job." His voice sounded slightly hollow from hearing himself through the earmuffs.

While keeping the muzzle of the gun pointed down, she lifted the muffler from her left ear and he echoed the move.

"Sorry?" she asked.

He could hear a phone ringing and he glanced at his own. It was quiet.

"Nice job."

"Thanks. It's mine." She waved her cell as she lifted it to her ear. "Hello?" She returned it to her pocket. "That's the fourth time this week I've had someone hang up when I answer. It's getting annoying."

She scowled and they covered their ears again as she pushed the button beside her, sending the target farther back. It went back and back and back until Burke wasn't even sure he could see the inner circle on the man-shaped silhouette any longer. She shot three more times, then brought the paper forward.

There was one large hole where every single bullet had gone through the center.

"That's sexy," he said, rubbing his chest with his free hand. He felt a bit intimidated—which she'd predicted earlier—but not so much he was going to worry about his manhood when he didn't measure up to her skills.

She flipped her earmuffs off one ear again and he did the same. "Your turn."

"Hit the paper, right?"

She smirked. "If you can."

The smirk didn't help his ego. Not at all.

She prepped a new target for him and he managed to knock the corner of the large paper from about ten yards.

"Remind me not to expect you to ever save me in a gunfight," she said loud enough for him to hear through the earmuffs.

"Don't worry. I'll be hiding behind you."

She laughed and he wanted to kiss her. All that shining confidence was sexy.

He also liked the way her jeans hugged her hips, and the way that laugh had lightened her entire demeanor.

They finished shooting, then made their way to the lobby,

where Jill called people by name, selecting a bag of chips from the concession. The man behind the counter waved her money away.

Jill was a whole different person here. She was relaxed, smiling, at ease and happy, not wound up and stressed. This was her haven, her safe place where she blew off steam—apparently a fair amount, judging by how well the other regulars knew her.

Burke found himself once again wishing to kiss her.

He remembered the one from the restaurant. It had been two weeks ago, but yeah, he definitely wanted to kiss her again. Just like that. Maybe he could convince her that since he'd messed up being the "indifferent husband," they could do "whirlwind mistake" instead. That could be fun.

She shared the chips with him and they walked through the building, bumping shoulders and laughing about inane things like friends who've known each other forever often do.

"This is nice," he said as they moved toward the parking lot. "Thanks for not shooting me."

"Oh, there's still time," Jill said, darting a playful glance at him.

There was a stack of bales in the distance and the popping of paint guns. Kids covered in paint were making their way out, smiling and laughing.

"Paintball, too?" he asked. He liked paintball. The fact that everyone was running and ducking usually leveled the playing field and made him look a bit more skilled.

"My dad added it after Nicola and I created a paintball course for an event. It's been really popular."

"Who's Nicola? Your sister?"

"No, she's a friend. My sister's too girlie. We used to work for the town together."

"You and your sister, or you and Nicola?" He took the last chip and popped it into her mouth.

"Nicola," she mumbled as she chewed. "My sister and I did work together once, though."

"How was that?"

She made a face, her earlier tension returning.

"That good, huh?"

"It didn't end well."

"Do you two still talk?"

"I live in her converted garage, so yes. It wasn't about us, it was...complicated."

"There's that word again."

"Fine. It's a long story then. Better?"

He nodded and took the empty chip package from her, tossing it in a large barrel meant for trash. As he did, Jill called out to a tall, broad man who resembled a lumberjack.

"Hey, Jillycakes. Who's this?" The man was watching Burke as though he knew exactly who he was. Intrigued and smiling, but there was a hint of paternal protective wariness that straightened Burke's spine.

"Her husband, Burke Carver," he said gamely, shaking the man's hand. "You must be Argo Armstrong." His father-in-law crushed pretty much every bone in his hand without even cracking a satisfied smile.

"So you're the guy who eloped with my baby girl, and are just showing your face now?"

"*Daddy!*"

Argo crossed his arms, rolling back on his heels. Burke was fairly certain the man was considering where to start disemboweling him. Start high or start low?

"Yes, sir," he replied bravely. "That's me."

"You must be quite the man to get my girl to drop that fancy algorithmic dating service and run off with you in an uncharacteristic moment of spontaneity."

"Dad," Jill warned again.

Algorithmic dating service? Yeah, that sounded like Jill.

Argo broke the tough-guy act in a flash and beamed, clapping Burke on the shoulder. He said, "Aw, come on in here, son." He brought him in for a quick man-hug. "You're family now."

"Thanks," Burke said, feeling stunned by the sudden turnaround.

"But you take good care of her or you'll have her daddy—that would be your father-in-law—to answer to. You understand?"

"I do, sir."

"Good. Because if you hurt her I'll have you strung up so fast you won't even have time to holler for help, you understand?" The man looked ready to go Thor on him and bring down the hammer if he stepped out of line.

"Dad," Jill stated firmly.

Wow. This was all feeling pretty real. Neila's dad hadn't given him a speech like that. In fact, nobody ever had. No wonder Jill was still single. Her father had likely scared off any potential suitors.

Burke nodded crisply. "Understood."

"I like this one," Argo said to Jill. He slung an arm around Burke's shoulder, walking and talking. "We're going to have to get to know you better. Take a men's trip. Do you like fishing? Bowling? Do you play an instrument? Did Jill tell you I used to be in a band? What about—"

Jill said with a laugh, "There's plenty of time to get to know Burke."

Burke shot her a look. There was? And why was she smiling?

"And no," she added quickly, "he doesn't play an instrument, so you can just stop that pipe dream in its tracks."

"I do, actually," he said.

"Get out of town," Argo said, smacking Burke on the chest as he stopped walking so he could face him more fully. "What do you play?"

"Drums."

"You do?" Jill was watching him with a look so skeptical it could have been in the dictionary as a visual definition of the very word.

"Right on, right on," Argo said. "I play bass guitar. We have a band that could use a drummer. We practice every Tuesday night unless Alvin's feeling crotchety and won't play sax for us. So pretty much all the time, actually."

"Dad, he's not joining your band."

"Fine, fine." He pulled Jill into a one-armed half hug, kissing her on the forehead. "There's time to work on that. I'm excited for the two of you." He turned to face Burke again, releasing his daughter. "So? When do you move to town? I've heard you've been married for some time? Why the big secret?"

"It's a long story," Jill said, walking on her father's other side.

"I happen to like long stories."

"I'll tell you later," she said.

"It's no longer *I*, it's *we*. You're married now." He stopped and placed a hand on each of their shoulders, addressing them both. "You two understand that? You're a team. No secrets. You have each other's backs. Always." When he seemed to feel they had it through their heads, he dropped his hold. "Now, when are you moving, Burke? I have a truck you can borrow, and I'll round up a bunch of guys to get your stuff out here. Name the date."

"He has work in the city," Jill said quickly.

"And?"

"We haven't figured things out yet."

"Jill without a plan?" Argo's eyebrows shot high and he turned to Burke. "*Jill* without a plan?"

"Yes, sir," Burke replied, feeling uneasy, like he was letting his own dad down, and as though he should have an ironclad plan at the ready. Not that Burke knew his father, but he kind of imagined this was what it would be like if he did. That tough-love thing he got from Maggie—only more extreme. You knew they were on your side, but you also knew that they'd kick your butt across town and back if you let them down.

For some reason, Burke really didn't want to let Argo down.

CHAPTER 7

*J*ill sat at the bar beside Burke in the local pub, Brew Babies, sighing into her pale ale. He'd met her dad. Her hands were shaking as she lifted the glass to her lips. She'd thought her father would think the spontaneity of her marriage to be fun, and he had. What she hadn't counted on was how enthused he'd been. It was going to break his heart when Burke didn't come around again, didn't move to Blueberry Springs, didn't join his band, didn't go on his man-trip.

Her father had been disappointed by Jodi's husband, Gareth, for years and had been counting on Jill to find a man to fill the vacant son role. And Hayes, for the record, had been a disappointment as well. In fact, her dad had left him in the fishing shack in the middle of Blueberry Lake on their first and only man-trip, stating he couldn't spend another minute with him.

She hadn't meant for things to progress with Burke's visit from a casual "hello, this is my husband" to whatever had happened today. Everyone was so thrilled for her. And Burke was so perfect he was making things impossible.

This was not what a casual, businesslike marriage looked like.

It felt *real*. And even worse, she liked spending time with Burke. Liked it a lot.

She moaned internally. What was she going to do? Divorcing Burke was going to create such a stir.

Amy Carrick, one of the bartenders, set a fragrant pizza in front of Jill and Burke.

Pizza, then send Burke back to the city and spend weeks fielding questions on where Mr. Perfect was hiding out. She'd have to figure out a way to downplay their perfect little marriage.

As they dished pieces of pizza onto their plates, Jill couldn't help but feel a bit as though they were on a date.

"I like the addition of the feta," she called to Amy, who was responsible for the pub's menu.

"Thanks." Amy turned to Moe Harper, the manager, who was also her best friend. "Told you!"

Moe shrugged in his wrinkled shirt, giving his colleague a soft smile. "You're usually right."

Amy raised her hands in the air. "You all heard that? Triumphant at long last." She bowed grandly.

Jill high-fived her when she righted herself again, and turned to Burke, who had downed his beer, no doubt unsettled from the way her father had adopted him on the spot—after a little protective fatherly what-for, of course.

"I'm sorry about my dad. He's been waiting for a real son-in-law for a while."

"A real one?"

She shrugged, feeling her cheeks flush at how from Burke's point of view it likely sounded as though she was falling for their own act. "One that's interested in the same things as him."

Burke wiped his hands on a napkin. "Ah."

"I didn't know you played the drums."

"There's a lot you don't know." When Amy gestured to Burke's empty glass, he shook his head, refusing a second. "I have to drive."

"He was a little over-the-top," Jill said.

"Don't apologize or be embarrassed by him. I think it's wonderful how kind and welcoming he was. It's obvious how much he cares for you and you're lucky to have that." Burke fell silent for a moment, his whole demeanor seeming to flatten somehow.

"Family is special," he said, as he tipped up his glass to retrieve the last trickle of beer.

Burke took another slice of pizza and bit into it, leaving a string of cheese sticking to his chin. Jill reached over and wiped it away.

"Is this him?" asked an excited voice from behind her.

Jill twisted on her stool to find Emma and Ginger standing behind them at the bar.

Burke turned, confirming his identity, causing Emma to squeal and hug Jill, just about pulling her off her seat. "I *cannot* believe you two snuck off and got married! Why didn't you tell me!"

"And you didn't even get a dress from me," Ginger scolded. "I would have given you a special deal."

"Sorry."

"Tell us everything," Emma demanded.

"We got married," Burke said simply when Jill looked at him uncertainly. "Emma Carrington" He shook her hand. "It's been a while."

"It has. Good to see you. This is Ginger McGinty. She owns the bridal shop in town and you denied her the chance to make Jill look amazing."

It was Burke's turn to apologize.

Amy came down the bar with more napkins. "You got married?"

Jill nodded.

"Sweet. I didn't know that. Congratulations."

"Whenever you see a woman in town who looks like Jill, make sure you turn and give Jill a giant kiss, okay?" Emma told Burke.

"Emma!" Jill laughed, pleased by her friend's loyalty.

"Why?" Burke asked, frowning.

"Her identical twin sister, Jodi, thinks she wrote the book on men, and she's always rubbing it in that Jill's still single and unlucky in love."

"But no more!" Ginger crowed.

Burke nodded. "I can do that." He sent Jill a simmering look full of promise.

"Really, it's not necessary," she said, her mind all too ready and willing to imagine what his giant kiss might feel like.

Burke addressed Emma. "Something like this?" He slipped to the edge of his stool, cupping one hand behind Jill's head.

She met his eyes. No. Nope. Surely he was *not* going to demonstrate here. Just because the modern marriage plan wasn't working out so well, it didn't mean they were going to act like newlyweds and *really* give the town something to talk about. He was just playing a form of Truth or Dare. He'd *promised*.

But he tipped his head toward hers, their lips meeting.

He was such a big, fat promise breaker.

He kissed her slowly and sweetly, bringing her to the edge of her seat as he threatened to break the kiss. She wanted more. She didn't want it to end.

No doubt sensing that, he leaned into her, his lips firm on hers as she swept her arms around his shoulders, her fingers slipping into his short hair. They broke the kiss to inhale before diving in for more.

The bar erupted in cheers and catcalls.

"Hello!" Ginger called. "We have a live one."

Jill broke the kiss at long last, feeling dazed. "Wow."

"Yeah. Just like that, Burke," Emma said, her voice dripping with satisfaction.

"Are you two going to have a reception?" Ginger asked. "I have some very nice gowns that would be appropriate."

Amy was propped against the bar, her chin resting in her hand. "I wish I could find love like that."

"Amy, you shush," someone a few stools down said. "You have Moe." It was Katie Reiter, a local interior designer who used to work as a nurse with Amy—back when they'd both thought it might be their career of choice. Amy had hopped jobs a lot, but she always seemed to settle back at Brew Babies with Moe.

"We're not in love," Amy replied.

"Um, hello?" Ginger said. "He promised to marry you on your birthday if you don't find someone by then." She lifted an eyebrow. "I also have the perfect gown chosen for you, by the way."

"I was just wishing someone would sweep me off my feet," Amy muttered.

Moe, his shaggy hair falling over his forehead, was watching her from the end of the bar where he was filling a pint. And letting it overflow, by the looks of things.

"Her birthday is in June," Jill added for Burke's benefit.

"Nice. A deadline marriage," he said. He checked his watch. "Speaking of deadlines, I should head back to the city."

The women around them groaned. "Do you have to?"

"I live and work there," he said.

"When are you moving to Blueberry Springs?" Amy asked. "Moe has a truck you can borrow if you need one."

Burke had stood, fishing in his wallet for his debit card. He paused to glance at Jill, who knew they couldn't dodge that question forever.

"We haven't really planned anything," she said, hoping to defer the conversation to a ways down the line when Burke hadn't been around for a few weeks and it seemed less odd that he was staying in the city. Right now, their plan of doing the fake long-distance thing would just strike everyone as odd and draw more attention to their less-than-conventional arrangement.

"How can you not plan living together?" Ginger exclaimed. "You're married!"

"Hey, you married a man you didn't know was a spy, *and* I know for a fact neither of you had a plan on where you were going to live," Jill said.

"Well, that was different." Ginger sat in Burke's spot.

"You will move here, though, right?" Amy asked. She turned to Jill with big eyes. "*You're* not moving, are you?"

"She can't. She needs to be here for her products," Emma said firmly. "Plus her organizational skills keep my life from falling in. Burke, you have to move here. But you guys have to move out of Jodi's garage. I'll ask Luke to talk to the Realtor for you. He *loves* working with Blueberry Springs Realty."

Jill chuckled, knowing Luke found the Realtors slash accounting office slash stationary store to be infuriating after the exclusive salespeople he'd once dealt with on primo properties back home in South Carolina.

"I'll see you ladies later," Burke said, slipping into his coat and ignoring the Realtor offer. "Nice meeting you."

"I'll walk you out," Jill said. Maybe if she did, she'd get another one of those steamy kisses of his.

As she exited the pub, her friends all gave her a thumbs-up and grins. They were going to ride her for a long time to find out what went wrong when her marriage "failed" in a few months.

Burke's car was angle parked on the street between two pickups instead of in the gravel lot.

"I'm sorry," he said, gesturing to the pub. "I didn't mean to make things complicated for you."

Jill waved it off. "Nah, don't worry about it."

He played with the keys to his car.

"I had fun shooting stuff with you," she said. She loved that he hadn't acted hurt that she was a better aim than he was. If he wasn't her accidental husband, she'd think about keeping him.

Night had settled in around the mountain town while they'd been inside, and the snow that had melted during the day was turning to chunky ice. The Sunday night traffic was starting to pick up around the pub, tires crunching across the gravel lot as they entered or exited the street, depending on if they were part of the dinner or drink crowd.

"Well, I guess I'd better head home," Burke said, stepping to his compact car. The way it was tucked between the much bigger trucks made it look ridiculously adorable.

She wasn't ready for Burke to go home. She'd had a surprisingly fun day—despite her parents—and a nice supper, too.

"I guess I'll see you around?" Jill asked, unable to keep the hope from her voice. He'd gone over everything for the site with Ethan, and now it was simply a matter of keeping things ticking along in terms of sales, so she could pay back the loan ASAP. Anything else they had left to do could likely be done by phone or email.

Burke didn't move for a moment, then slowly glanced back at her. "Thank you for the fun afternoon. I needed that."

"Anytime you want to shoot something up, I'm your gal."

He chuckled and nodded, then climbed in and closed his car door. He put down the window. "We should get together next week and see what we can maximize. You know, once things start rolling."

Jill felt a thrill zip through her at the prospect of seeing him again. "It's a date."

She reached through the window to shake his hand, and immediately felt foolish for doing so—not just because she looked eager, but if anyone was watching it would look formal and stupid. But Burke's grip felt warm, firm and sure, and she soon forgot about worrying about appearances. She let her grip linger, her gaze locking with his. She wanted to stick her head inside the car and kiss him.

Instead, she stepped back, tucking her palms flat in the back pockets of her jeans.

"Bye," she said softly.

Burke nodded, putting the car into Reverse. He smiled at her, and her own grin grew.

If she wasn't careful she'd lose focus on the fact that this wasn't real.

Burke was watching her as he pulled out, and a passing pickup clipped the back end of his small car, sending him skidding sideways, the air bags deploying as the vehicle bounced off a neighboring truck.

Jill squealed and ran to him. His window was still down, and she asked, "Are you okay?"

He looked like he was being smothered by marshmallows with the air bags surrounding him. He was trying to push them away while sputtering, "I'm fine. I'm fine."

The driver of the truck climbed out. It was Alvin Lasota, one of the biggest curmudgeons of Blueberry Springs. "He all right? I don't think I've ever seen a car that small before. Is that toy even street legal? I don't want to get him into trouble with the law, but I ain't up for lying to the insurance company again."

Jill managed to free Burke, temporarily ignoring the rancher, who was inspecting the very limited damage to the front of his truck. Burke stood on the asphalt and stared at his crumpled car.

"It's not a toy," he said gruffly.

"If you insist," Alvin said skeptically, thumbs hooked into the front belt loops of his jeans.

"It's better for the environment than that old beater you're driving."

"You couldn't even fit my sheep dog in that little thing. How am I supposed to ranch in an enclosed golf cart? A man needs a truck."

"Well, you just ruined my car."

"You ever tried looking before you pull off a curb, or were you too busy looking doe-eyed at your new wife?"

Burke's face flushed as he squared off with Alvin, and Jill pressed her hands between the two of them. "Boys…"

"Who are you calling boys?" both men asked, turning to her.

"I am, because you're acting like it."

"You'd better phone Scott," Alvin said. "This boy's insurance company is going to need to buy him a real car and it's best to have the police involved."

They all turned to look at the affected vehicle. It wasn't too bad other than the deflated air bags and the flat back tire that was bent at a weird angle. And the dents. There were some of those. And broken lights. Actually, quite a few pieces had fallen on the ground as the car did what it was supposed to in order to protect Burke.

So it was bad.

But both trucks looked like they were still in decent shape.

"*Your* insurance company," Burke muttered.

"You cut me off."

"You were driving too fast!"

"Boys!" snapped Jill once again. "Cool it."

She texted Scott Malone, the local police officer, and he arrived on foot less than a minute later, a ceramic coffee cup from Mandy's café in hand. "Sorry, wanted to finish my coffee so it didn't go cold."

He quickly settled the two men, taking statements and all pertinent details before promising to contact the owner of the truck Burke's car had bounced off after being hit. Then he returned to the café to finish supper with his wife, Amber.

"Sorry for the loss of your toy car," the rancher said, not quite looking at Burke as he got back into his truck. "You must be quite the man to drive something so small. Nothing to overcompensate for when it comes to your manhood."

Jill choked on a laugh.

"Sorry you didn't even get a scratch on your overcompensating environment killer," Burke grumbled.

The man scowled at having his comment twisted and thrown back in his face.

"You're not very good at making friends, are you?" she asked, as she quickly steered him away from Alvin, who was looking as though he was about to step back out of his truck and settle things once and for all. "Come on, I'll give you a ride to the city."

Burke sighed and rubbed his forehead. "I can rent something—my insurance company'll cover it."

"The local dealer provides rentals, but they're closed Sundays," she said. "I could call the owner, though, and see if he can get you something."

"Thanks."

Jill made the call and had an answer within a minute. She gave Burke the bad news. "He won't have anything until tomorrow morning at ten. Do you want me to give you a ride home?"

"That's four hours of driving for you," Burke said. "Two there, two back. I don't want to put you out. I'll grab a hotel and take the rental in the morning."

"Are you sure?"

"Yeah. It's almost eight already and you have work tomorrow. You wouldn't be home until after midnight."

A few hours with Burke in a car wasn't exactly a hardship. At least not when they were playing nice. Which seemed to be a more common occurrence today. One she found she quite liked.

"Where should I book a room?" he asked, as Frankie Smith came along with a tow truck for his car.

"Why don't you stay at my place?" Jill suggested quietly, as the amber lights of the truck lit up the night. She lifted her voice to call to Frankie, "I didn't know you were working for Gus."

"Just helping out. His gout's bugging him again. And Axel likes to ride along," he said, smiling at his son, who was ensconced in his car seat, toying with his feet and gurgling happily.

While Frankie worked, loading the damaged car onto the flatbed, Jill turned back to Burke.

"I don't want to be a bother," he said, picking up their earlier conversation about accommodations.

"Burke?"

"Hmm?"

"Please stay at my place."

He gave her a sly smile, and she quickly added, "It'll look weird if my husband is staying in a hotel, don't you think?"

His gaze slipped to her bare ring finger. "Think I need to carry you over the threshold?"

"Think you can?"

"I think I can do a lot more than that."

Suddenly the idea of him staying at a hotel felt a lot safer.

Jill's home was a detached garage in the back of her sister's yard that had been renovated into a small apartment. It was cute and had a surprisingly open feel to it, overlooking the river that wound through the town.

Jill hadn't stopped talking since they'd arrived, explaining, as she let her dog out into his gated run, how Taylor had been named. Before he could ask what her father had suggested she "shake off" with the ownership of the rescued pup, she changed topics with a swiftness that told him there was a story there. She then mentioned how the animal spent a lot of time with her parents, and that she often babysat for her sister, who had two girls. She also mentioned that last year her little home had flooded when the river rose, destroying some of her product supplies. Hence part of her need for the loan.

Jill was preparing the guest room for him, tossing boxes

around and making the perfectly organized space, which obviously doubled as her office, look almost cluttered. While she fussed, he took in the labeled containers of natural ingredients sitting on the shelf that ran above a long table to the right of the door. To the left was a bed where the boxes had been lined up. Near the door a bookshelf held marble pestles and mortars in various colors and sizes, and below that was a row of binders. He pulled one down and flipped it open, finding colored tabs, neatly labeled, with recipes inside plastic page protectors.

Jill reached across him, snatching the binder and just about tripping over her dog, which had stretched out on the floor, in the process. She placed the binder in a cardboard box along with a few others and used her foot to slide the entire box out of the room.

"Those are proprietary. Top secret. No snooping."

"You don't trust me?"

"Should I?" Her tone was slightly flirtatious, and he resisted the urge to grab her around the waist and drag her close enough for another kiss like that one they'd shared in the pub. He was kind of getting into this whole husband act.

She twisted out of his grip and surveyed the room with pink cheeks. "I think this should do. I'll put out a towel and facecloth for you in the bathroom."

"What if I'm not warm enough in here all alone?"

She picked up a folded wool blanket and chucked it at his chest.

He grinned, knowing he should let her be, but a part of him couldn't resist poking at her, dropping a few innuendos she took so well. He knew he was unsettling her, but she was so worried about what others thought that he wanted to shift her attention to herself so she thought about herself instead. Her pleasures, her wants.

"I'll also put out a new toothbrush on the counter."

"Wow, we're moving pretty fast. I get my own toothbrush?"

Burke tossed the blanket onto the bed and rubbed a spot on his chest that felt bruised from the air bag deployment. It had been a shock, finding himself in a daze, with Jill smiling at him, and then pow! knocked four feet sideways by a speeding truck.

But those little cars were built to keep people safe and that's what his had done. Even though it was now quite likely a total write-off.

Burke tested the mattress, depressing its surface with his fist. "I sleep naked," he said, angling his gaze Jill's way. "Is that a problem?"

She dragged her attention to the bedding as though imagining him there in the buff, then lifted her eyes to his. "Knock yourself out. So do I." She sent him a sly smile that torqued his interest as she waved the wrist that shared the same tattoo as his.

Yes. He was fairly confident he wasn't getting a wink of sleep tonight.

She left the room, and he listened to her move around the small apartment while he checked emails on his phone. When it seemed as though she must have gone to bed, he went to the bathroom, finding the new toothbrush she'd promised.

While he brushed his teeth he bent to check out the line of creams under her vanity, all sporting her Jill's Botanicals labels. He lifted each one in turn, reading their contents before unscrewing the caps and giving them a sniff, his toothbrush hanging from his mouth.

Burke spit out the paste, feeling as though he was snooping. He pulled off his T-shirt and inspected his chest. Sure enough, there was a bruise forming. Nothing bad, and if that was his only injury he'd consider himself lucky. He returned to the guest room, shirt in hand.

He jumped when he saw Jill sitting at the kitchen table, cradling a cup, her dog sleeping at her feet.

"Can't sleep?" he asked, feeling inexplicably nervous.

"I haven't tried yet. It's still fairly early for me. Normally I work for a few hours."

"But I'm in your office."

She nodded. He liked that she wasn't apologizing, simply stating reality. It didn't make him feel unwelcome, surprisingly enough. Quite the contrary.

He pulled out a chair, joining her at the table. There was something about being with Jill that felt so natural. No uneasy, awkward silences like there had been with Neila. Jill tested him, taking him from gentle arguing to laughing in a matter of moments. She kept him on his toes, and he liked it.

"So?" he said, not quite knowing his role. He and his past girlfriends had rarely ever spent a full night together, and had definitely never had any sort of bedtime ritual other than tearing each other's clothes off and then saying goodbye a satisfying hour or two later.

This...this was domestic. Or maybe it was just companionable. Whatever it was, it was different than anything he'd ever had with his first wife.

First wife. He now had a second.

He found himself rubbing the tender spot on his chest.

"Are you an early riser?" he asked.

"Usually. How about you?"

"I like the quiet of 5:00 a.m."

She had a pot of tea in front of her and she lifted it in question. He shrugged. He wasn't normally a tea drinker, but he may as well be polite.

She stood, getting a cup for him. She was wearing a loose sweatshirt and a pair of shorts.

"You have nice legs."

"That's true," she said, placing the cup in front of him with a soft smile, then filling it.

The mug had a stick man being chased by a bear, and said "Running Wild in Blueberry Springs."

He chuckled and inhaled the tea's aroma. Chamomile. That brought back memories of Maggie drinking the same brew while waiting up for him when he was a teenager. It made him think of nights on the town and pushing boundaries. And then feeling bad afterward for making his aunt worry. That phase hadn't lasted very long.

"Want to watch a movie?" Jill asked.

"I don't want to watch a romantic comedy."

She snorted in disgust. "This isn't a date. I watch those on my own, when I won't have a man scoffing at me, thank you very much."

He laughed. "What did you have in mind?"

"Die Hard."

Burke had taken a sip of the awful tea and laughed again, spraying warm liquid over the table. Underneath it, the dog sighed.

"What?" Jill protested, handing him a damp dishrag. "I happen to be a Bruce Willis fan."

"Have I ever mentioned that I like you, Ms. Tough Girl?" He wiped the splatters of tea and went to the sink to rinse out the rag, then hang it to dry.

"No, not specifically," she said, her back to him as she sipped her beverage, both elbows on the table. "However, you did marry me, which implies a certain level of like."

"Well played." He went to sit again, but a part of him felt anxious. If he sat he'd have nothing to focus on other than Jill. "Where's your TV?" He glanced around the small room before spotting the flat screen on the wall. In front of it wasn't a couch, just a love seat. No additional furniture such as an armchair.

It looked as though they might be cuddling.

He could handle cuddling.

Maybe.

Yeah, probably not.

"A love seat so you can snuggle with your dates?" he asked, setting their cups on the coffee table.

"I think we've already established this isn't a date," she said, slightly breathless as she took her spot on the love seat.

He sat down beside her, letting his thigh rest against hers. She looked as unsettled as he felt, and it pleased him to have her off guard.

She cleared her throat, that unaffected-tough-girl attitude coming out once again.

"You can hold my hand during the scary parts if you want to." She smirked, cranking the heat that was building inside him. "Since you thought I was going to choose a romantic comedy."

She was much more interesting than any movie Hollywood ever produced.

JILL COULDN'T CONCENTRATE on the movie. Burke kept pressing his thigh, warm and strong, against hers, and there was no way for her to shift away on the small love seat. She should have just read in bed. Or chosen a horror so she could play-act at being the frightened female and hide her face behind his shoulder.

She could practically hear her sister scolding her for missing the opportunity.

No, what was she even thinking? She didn't want to get involved with Burke. And she didn't want to pretend to be someone she wasn't, either. She'd tried that. The relationships failed and she felt stupid.

They had businesses to run and she needed, more than ever, to concentrate and ensure things didn't suddenly go off the rails. He was just so...easy to be with. She liked the way he made her feel—despite messing with her plans all the time. Somehow, it didn't seem to matter as much when he did, and she wasn't sure why.

She should probably be worried about that, shouldn't she? And yet she couldn't quite seem to summon the power to get there.

Sure, they kissed with a heat and energy that kept building between them, but she was fooling herself if she believed that energy was going to become a real marriage and a happily ever after. She might as well break her own heart now and save herself the trouble later.

Jill's cell phone rang on the coffee table and she ignored it.

"Are you going to get that?" Burke asked.

She shook her head. She was fairly confident there'd be nobody at the other end of the line, like earlier. Caller ID came up with nothing and a part of her had a feeling it was Autumn Martinez harassing her. Jill was one step away from asking Ginger's husband, Logan Stone, a man who ran his own personal security business, for advice on how to block someone whose number didn't even come up on her screen.

Burke was watching her curiously, but she didn't want to talk about Autumn. Instead she wanted to enjoy the way he had shifted so he was angled toward her, his arm slung over the back of the love seat, his body warm and wonderful.

The movie ended a while later and Jill realized she had zoned out for almost the entire last half, stuck in her own thoughts. She turned to Burke on the tight little love seat just as he turned to her. He was so close. If she shifted her shoulder and leaned in a little she could kiss him. Or maybe he could kiss her.

"Feeling tired yet?" he asked.

"Not really."

"So… We're married?" Burke asked, his focus locked directly on her bottom lip.

"That's what vital records keep telling us."

"We're going to stick it out until this financial business is all settled, right?"

"What are you suggesting?" She was leaning in, a slow tipping motion. She straightened suddenly, catching herself.

Burke didn't reply, but his focus softened from that intense one he often had when discussing business, to something more intimate. He took a strand of her hair, tucking it back, pausing to run his thumb down her ear.

She shivered and he sank his lips onto hers, his hand gently guiding her head to the perfect angle so they could kiss more deeply. As always with him, she found herself losing control.

He wanted her.

Her. Jill Armstrong. Too pointed. Too direct. Overbearing with detailed plans. Sharpshooter.

But when he woke up and realized she wasn't the one he'd been waiting for, he'd go running. And she needed him to stay. Just a little longer. Play the game, put on the show.

She couldn't ruin everything. Not yet.

What was she even thinking? Getting involved would only complicate things.

Oh, but he was such a good kisser... Couldn't she have it both ways?

She gently pushed him away. "I don't think this is going to help matters."

"Don't use the word *complicated*," he said quickly.

"Fine. Tangled. Thorny. Problematic."

"That sounds worse."

"I know." She stood, sorely tempted to stay in the cocoon of his body's warmth, reveling in the gentle freedom of kissing him. The corner of his lips turned up slightly, even though she was shutting him down.

Somehow, somewhere along the line they had moved past the awkwardness of an early relationship and built some sort of trust between them. And as a result, her not-quite-real marriage had begun to feel like the beginning of something real. Something special.

CHAPTER 8

"Wha..." Burke stared at the printout from Andrea. She had to have significant pregnancy-brain going on, the added hormones messing with her math, to come up with these numbers. There was no way they were correct.

"Andrea?" he called out of his office. He could see into hers from his doorway. Vacant.

"She's walking through a contraction," Gulliver said, barely looking away from his monitor.

"She's *what?*"

"You heard me."

"Why isn't she going to the hospital?"

"She's afraid."

"It's safer than having it here."

"She's developed an 'irrational' fear..." Gulliver made sure he looked up, placing air quotes with his fingers around *irrational*—a direct dig at the way Burke had suggested he was behaving for thinking the business was in the midst of dying a slow death. "...that this place will go up in flames as soon as she leaves, and she wants to earn as much at full pay as possible."

As Burke marched off toward the break room, Gulliver called

out, "Autumn came by. She was saddened greatly that you missed the hockey game, and said she'll organize a meeting with her father about taxes if you come to Saturday's gala with her."

Burke waved that away as though it would wave away Autumn's unwanted attention, too. He had a feeling any contact with her would be perceived as encouragement at this point.

He found Andrea pacing along the counter in the break room, the earthy smell of the small compost bin surely making her nauseated, as it had for the past nine months. Her contractions had to be bad if she was choosing to be near it.

"Hey," she said, her voice strained. "Nice day out, isn't it?"

Burke gave her a quick visual assessment. She was freaking out, all right. Time for a decent distraction. Work. He held up her printed projections. "Are these numbers right?"

"Can you check to see how dilated I am?"

"Absolutely not."

"Then no, I made them up, because I'm…eeaah-h-h…having a baby."

"Has anyone called Luther?" Her husband needed to come and strong-arm her out of here. Immediately.

"He's on his way."

Burke rolled the spreadsheet in his hands, at a loss. "Can I do anything? Other than check dilation." He shuddered involuntarily.

"Leave me…here to…die," she panted.

"You know the business is okay, right?"

"You saw the spreadsheet. It's doing great. As long as you don't mess things up with that woman. Her test stuff is selling hotter than our own add-ons. And purchasing her products boosts our own by 23 percent." She paused to pant. "It's symbiotic awesometastic fluffernutter. Oh! Sweet baby hopscotch, give me a hand to squeeze." She frantically batted at him.

Burke grabbed a banana from the fruit bowl beside him and handed it over instead of his much-needed digits. She squeezed the fruit right out the end of the peel on her next contraction, causing him to wince.

"Don't let that woman go," Andrea said, once the pain had lessened its grip. "Don't be yourself. Don't lose her. The business needs her."

"Jill and I are just—" What were they, actually?

Well, he was kind of avoiding her. And he had been for the four long days since he'd grappled with his unwanted desire for her back in Blueberry Springs—and barely won. Spending the day with her had twisted his mind into thinking…well, he wasn't sure what. Only that it was dangerous and brought all sorts of old warnings from Maggie to mind.

Thank goodness Jill had shot him down or he would have blown everything by listening to his libido.

But he'd promised to talk shop with her in a day or two. In person.

What was he going to do?

"You could get that deal with Tiffer," Andrea said. "Even without a loan. Just keep this up. Expand on it. This is the ticket."

"So the numbers are correct?" Burke unfurled the sheets, walking to Andrea so they could look at them together. She grabbed the printout, crumpling it in her hands before dropping it onto the floor.

"Get Luther. Now. And don't. Don't take her to bed. You hear?" She clutched her belly. "This baby needs to go to college."

"Plenty of time to mess up, then," he joked.

She growled in a way that had him scooting for the door and speed-dialing her husband to tell him to hurry.

Jill gaped at Burke, then at the spreadsheet. She pushed her beer and onion ring double burger away so she wouldn't stain the pages with Amy and Moe's Friday special.

"No way," she said, not believing her eyes. Ethan had set up a test site that diverted a fraction of STH's online customers toward her products during the checkout process. The number of orders that had come in over the past three days was thrilling. This was exactly what she was looking for.

Burke was grinning as though he wanted to lift her into his arms and swing her around. It was quite distracting. Maybe even more than the figures in her hand.

Jill clamped down on the hope that bubbled inside her. She'd been way too thrilled when his phone number had popped up on her caller ID—as promised—to chat about business. And way too happy to see him pull into town in his fuel-efficient replacement car.

"Ethan's setting up a system," Burke said, "where the prior day's orders will be emailed to you at seven each morning."

She nodded, performing calculations in her head. If they stayed at this test level for a month it would give her time to settle in, expand, prepare for going wide.

It was doable. She'd have to revamp her system a bit, of course, as this was an uptick in the number of orders she typically had to fill.

She took a sip of her beer, satisfied with the way things were shaping up.

"Hey, congratulations to the newlyweds," Scott Malone said, coming over and shaking hands with Burke. "Why didn't you tell me when I was dealing with your fender bender the other day?"

The two of them gave noncommittal shrugs.

"Get a new car?"

Burke nodded.

"Something bigger?"

"Scott," Jill warned.

"Oh, I heard the news!" Mary Alice Bernfield called. She ditched her coat at the vacant table just behind where Jill and Burke were sitting at the bar. "When's the baby due?"

"Seriously, Jill," Scott continued, ignoring the town gossip. "I wouldn't even fit in that thing." He gestured to Burke's similar broad build. "How does this guy?"

"It's not that bad," Jill said.

"Your mother must be so delighted to finally have you squared away," Liz Moss-Brady said, standing beside her sister. She and Mary Alice could spread gossip faster than a pyromaniac could send a house up in smoke. And while Jill felt her back involuntarily stiffen, she continued to ignore the women standing behind her. It wouldn't be long before they came right up to the bar, likely blocking her in so she couldn't escape until they'd sufficiently pried everything they wanted to know from her.

Scott winked at Jill. "Rounds on me." He subtly pointed to the sisters. "Think you'll need it."

As soon as he stepped away, they took over the vacant spot, blocking Jill against the bar as she'd predicted.

"When's the baby due?" Liz asked.

"The baby?" Burke asked, his beer halfway to his mouth.

"They're having a baby!" Amy called to Moe. He came down the bar, amicably putting an arm around Amy's shoulder.

"Babies are fun," he said. "Amy wants a whole herd. Make sure you tell her every gory bit about your birth horror story."

Amy pretended to punch Moe in the gut and he hammed it up, acting like she'd made contact. "You want kids, too. And you promised you'd give them to me if I marry you."

"I'm an abused man! She's forcing me to marry her against my will. Help! She's going to make me her sex slave."

Amy tackled him and they wrestled playfully behind the bar. It escalated until Mandy, who'd come in looking hungry and tired, reached over, grabbed the drink dispenser and shot club soda at the two of them.

"Hey!" Amy laughed, water dripping from her curly hair.

"You're cleaning that up," Moe said to Mandy.

"Keep the foreplay for after hours," she retorted, sidling up to the bar. "I'm so hungry I could eat a horse. Feed me."

"We don't serve horse." Moe crossed his arms. A dribble of club soda dripped from his shaggy hair, landing on his lip. He licked it off. "We also don't serve patrons who spray us with soda. Besides, you own a whole sandwich shop. Go there to cause your chaos."

Amy reached over with a bar towel, wiping Moe's face. She took extra time rubbing his cheeks and being especially annoying. Within seconds he had her wrists pinned, spinning her so she was against the counter, his mouth inches from hers.

For a second Jill thought they were going to kiss. When they broke apart, laughing, she found she'd been holding her breath.

Yeah, those two were totally getting married—but for real. She should place her bet with the gossips. Speaking of which, they were still hovering, distracted by the bartenders' display.

"If you two are done," Mandy said, "I'm craving something big and juicy. I don't care what it is, just make sure it has one of those big homemade pickle wedges Amy makes. No, make it two."

"Are you pregnant?" Mary Alice asked.

"Two babies?" Liz squealed. She eyed Jill. "Seven months from today for Jill. And about the same for Mandy."

"I'm not pregnant," Jill said. "For anyone who wants to concern themselves with reality and save their bet money."

"And I have a toddler at home. That's enough," Mandy said. She'd recently adopted a baby boy after years of secret fertility issues. Well, not so secret, seeing as even though she didn't talk about them, everyone knew.

"For now it's enough," Amy and Moe said in unison. They turned to each other with a grin and a "Jinx!"

The sisters, given plenty to gossip about with Mandy's order and Moe and Amy's flirting, drifted away, chattering madly. Jill gave a silent thanks to the powers that be for the diversion.

"When can you start filling orders?" Burke asked. "We aim to have all orders in the mail within forty-eight hours of them being placed."

Right. That meant she had significantly less than forty-eight hours, since she had to courier her products to his shipping center in the city and the courier left Blueberry Springs at ten each morning.

"Jill?" Burke pressed.

"Yeah, no problem. Mandy and I are sharing a courier."

"Did you say my name?" Mandy asked, perking up.

"Just telling Burke about our shipping deal." Her friend nodded and Jill explained to Burke that her orders would be riding with the thousands of brownies Mandy baked and shipped from her distribution center each week.

"So every day you'll fill the orders and send them over?" Burke confirmed.

"Five days a week. There's no weekend courier."

A full-time job and orders to fill. Every day.

She could do this, she reminded herself. She was good at organizing things and that's all this was—an organizational problem. She also had Burke and Ethan watching over things, making sure everything was good. She could handle this. She wouldn't fail Rebecca. She'd get her that friendship center, and sooner rather than later.

Burke grinned. "So? Are we ready to open this up?"

"What do you mean?"

"This was a beta test to one-tenth of our customers."

"One-tenth?" Jill said weakly, looking at the numbers again. She had erroneously believed the test had been served to *half* the customers.

"Expect ten times this. More once the word gets out and some reviews start popping up."

Jill stared blankly at the bottles of liquor lined up against the mirror behind the bar. The blue bottle of gin was out of place. Kind of like her sanity.

This was going to be a full-time job and she already had one of those at All You.

"Ten times?" She turned back to Burke. "Are you certain?"

"From Scott," Amy said, placing two bottles of beer in front of Jill and Burke.

"Thanks," they said, lifting the beer in a toast to the cop, who was over by the jukebox, trying to get it to take his money.

"This was a sample of one-tenth, so yes. I'm sure. Can you handle it?"

She'd be out of stock within a week. She needed help, but could she afford it?

"What?" Burke looked bemused. "I've rendered you mute?"

"You're sure these are accurate?" Jill demanded, checking the pages of numbers again.

Burke laughed. "Isn't it amazing? If customers like your creams as much as Gully did, you'll be up to your eyeballs in orders once we get some word-of-mouth going."

"There might be a slight problem with that."

Burke took a long pull on his beer, watching her, waiting for her to explain.

"I...handcraft these. From ingredients *I* pick. I'm not a factory."

But if she and a new staff of a few helpers could become one...kind of like what she'd originally envisioned with her more aggressive growth proposal last year, she could soon have it all. The loan paid off, the friendship center built at long last.

She was just going to have to let go of some of her control and hire help.

She inhaled slowly. She could let go, right? Letting go didn't mean sticking her head in the sand like she had with Hayes and the café.

"Can you fill the orders?"

"I can. I just..." She closed her eyes, hands bunched. "I need help."

"Okay." He began rolling up his shirtsleeves, revealing his wrist tattoo. Seeing it made her feel like freaking out, and she found herself curling her fingers around her own wrist.

"Okay," she said softly.

"Well?" He looked like he was ready to push away from the counter and take care of business. Just like he'd promised he would.

She felt the edge of panic. She needed assistance, guidance on how to quickly but reliably expand. But could she let go of some of her control without everything spinning away on her?

"You're going to help me?" she asked.

"I promised I would." He was staring at her. "Is that a problem?"

Only in that he was highly distracting. But otherwise, she was certain it would be spectacular.

"I trust you, Burke. So, no. It's not a problem at all."

BURKE FOLLOWED Jill out of the pub after she asked Amy to have their meals put on her tab.

"My wife has a tab at the local pub," Burke said. "I like it."

"It's a small town. People do that, you know."

From the back of her SUV she took a basket and backpack from the hatch.

"What's in the pack?" he asked.

"Water, trail mix, a rain jacket, extra socks, matches, first aid kit, and bear spray."

"You're always prepared, like a—"

"Don't say it," she said with a grimace.

"Boy Scout?"

She sighed. "Yeah. That."

He watched her for a second. "I would have joined the organization if I'd known you were going to be there."

She shot him a dark look and pushed the pack into his arms. "Come on, we're losing the warmth of the day as well as the light. This sap I need won't tap itself."

"You have a problem being called sexy, don't you?"

"You didn't call me sexy," she said, climbing into her car. He took the passenger seat, and within few minutes they were parking partway up a mountain and tromping along a snowy trail, the pack on his back.

"I like watching your hips sway from back here," he called to her.

She turned, looking like she wanted to smack him. Well, if you missed the fact that her eyes were shining with gratitude and pleasure. "We're business partners, buster."

"Married business partners." It was fun getting under her skin. It also distracted him from the fact that she'd looked downright panicked at the idea of filling all those orders. That panicked look could pack a lot of implications for his bottom line, as well as his reputation in the business, if he didn't keep an eye on where it was coming from.

"We need to collect sap for a cream. There's a nice grove just to the south side of where we are now."

"Are you trying to distract me?" he asked.

"Yes."

"What if the sap won't come out of the tree?"

"I know how to do this." She looked over her shoulder. "Are you stressing out?"

"Yes."

"There's this thing called the internet. I can order what I need and have it arrive within a week."

"Then why don't you?"

"It's not as fresh, and it's expensive."

"What are you going to do on the days when I can't come and help you?" he asked.

"I'm going to ask Rebecca and her family. They're already experts on all of this."

"Sounds smart."

They continued on in silence as she led him across the mountain.

"What got you to start your company?" she asked, as the trail leveled out and they could stroll side by side. The light was indeed fading and he worried they were going to be hiking home in the dark.

"My aunt. And yours?"

"The elders."

"Elders?"

"I have some Chippewa blood—not much, though. But the elders weren't Chipewyan—they weren't *my* elders..." She shook her head as though clearing her thoughts, forcing them to fall back in their square-pegged holes. "I'm getting lost in semantics, because they're everyone's elders. But it was the Ute people who taught me how to make the creams and soaps. They taught me which plants can provide the medicinal effects I want."

"Why?"

"Because I helped them pick flowers one day," she replied simply, almost as though it had been a silly question.

"Tell me more," he requested gently. She got a faraway look in her eyes and he slipped his gloved hand in hers, hoping she'd share whatever memory was rolling out like a movie in her mind.

She smiled weakly, her gaze drifting to their interlinked hands. "I was up here hiking."

"Alone?"

She nodded, taking her hand back so she could scramble over an exposed boulder in the middle of the snowy path. She moved like a mountain goat, sure-footed and smooth.

"How old were you?" he asked, once he was over the cold, lichen-covered rock.

"Fourteen." She inhaled, taking in the alpine meadow they'd

strolled into. The setting sun streaming over the evergreens lining the south edge and he guessed that was where Jill planned to tap for sap. "My mom and sister were incredibly tight. They were into girlie stuff."

"And you weren't?"

"There wasn't room to be. They're avid."

"It seems like you and your dad have a bond."

"Yeah." She had a wistful look to her. "I met the elders while he was reinventing himself."

"Reinventing?"

Jill tried to wave away the subject, but Burke came up alongside her, taking her hand again. That seemed to be all she needed to keep talking. "He was a musician. Mom and Dad were a duo. They had their own band, but Dad got an injury that prevented him from playing regularly. He can still only play half a set before it hurts too much. So after the injury he had to find a new way to support our family. He didn't have a backup plan."

Ah. No plan. Was that why Jill was so into them?

"Was it rough?"

"They did a good job of hiding the financial strain, but they fought a lot and then Dad took a ranching job he hated. Then one for the forest fire detection patrol. He was gone a lot."

Leaving her with the princesses.

"Did you have a boyfriend?" he asked, knowing he'd turned to the girls in his class when he'd felt lonely.

"No, that was Jodi's thing."

"I thought that was everyone's thing."

"The guys were more interested in her." Jill was watching her footfalls too closely for the fairly even path they were on. "I played football with them, and she sat in the bleachers and cheered, and hugged them at the end of the game."

Jill took a deep breath. "Anyway, I was up here one day, and I came across some Ute elders singing, laughing and harvesting.

Their voices were so rich...and I just wanted to be nearby and listen."

She glanced at him as though making sure he wasn't judging her.

"I followed them all afternoon," she said, looking embarrassed, "staying hidden in the bushes, eating berries, enjoying being in their presence."

"You stalked them?"

"Well, no." Her nose wrinkled adorably before she admitted reluctantly, "Sort of."

"And then what?"

"Rebecca called me over. I was mortified, but intrigued. They showed me what they were doing and why. I knew that what they were doing was special."

"How do they feel about you selling products made from their formulas?"

"They suggested it."

"Do they get a royalty from each sale?"

"They don't want it." The flesh between her brows tightened and he wondered what that was about.

Burke paused to take in the glowing mountain peaks above them, reflecting orange from the setting sun. In the distance was the town, behind them the rolling meadow, a deer standing at the opposite end, eating the lower branches off a coniferous tree, unconcerned that they were there.

"Nirvana," he announced.

"What?" Jill had stopped at a line of evergreens lit up by the setting sun, taking in the open surroundings behind her as though gazing at it all through fresh eyes.

"This," he said, turning around, his breath coming in clouds, "is my church."

"Hmm."

"What's that look for? I believe in nature. Serendipity. Karma."

He held out his arms, finding the crisp evening air bracing, refreshing. "This is what we should protect."

She was watching him.

"You don't agree?"

"I do," she said quickly, taking the pack from him.

"If only I could get paid for being up here," he said, inhaling deeply.

"Ask Jen Kulak. She runs a guiding business out of the sporting goods store and could use someone in the summers to make sure the hikers don't fall off the trail or get eaten by bears."

"Perfect. I'll send in my résumé."

"After you sell Sustain This, Honey for big bucks, of course."

"I really wish I'd named the company something different."

"Why?"

He shrugged. "Most people don't get the name—and for a good reason. I was feeling cheeky and a bit like in-your-face-world right about then, and so when Gulliver suggested it, I went with it. I had a lot of ideals."

"You said your aunt got you started?"

"She egoed me into it."

"Is that a real word? *Egoed?*"

"She appealed to my ego, pushing me into action. It's a verb. I was pretty pleased with myself. Then I almost lost…"

"What?"

The company. My employees. My chance to make a difference.

All because he'd believed Neila loved him. That he was capable of giving her what she needed—other than his company, which was all she'd seemed to want in the first place.

"Nothing," he said casually. "It's all good."

"No, it's not." Jill stopped unpacking the supplies she needed from the bag—there was more in there than just her previously listed safety gear, he noted. She reached over and squeezed his hand, playing his earlier game where he'd done the same when trying to get her to open up.

He smiled. It wasn't happening. Nope.

She was wordlessly demonstrating what to do to collect the sap. He crouched beside her, helping.

"I feel responsible," he blurted out.

"For the planet?"

"For my staff." He could feel the stress emanating off him, the heat from the setting sun on his back. "They need me, the job, the company. And it isn't easy making money the honest way, the right way."

She placed a hand on his cheek, cupping it. She said nothing as his eyes searched hers.

He dipped his head down, not wanting her to see this part of him, the part that could fail, or break.

CHAPTER 9

Jill kept finding herself staring out the window of her All You office the week after her hike with Burke. He'd been so real and almost vulnerable. She'd wanted to pull him into her arms and tell him it was all going to be okay. Which would have been silly. The man was fine and could own the world. He didn't need her reassurances.

Especially when she was in the process of trying to scale her life for the big time, thanks to his help.

She already had Rebecca producing more product for her, and she'd brought her son, Joseph, on board as well. Jill felt responsible for them, and couldn't imagine the pressure Burke must feel being responsible for so many more. He cared so deeply about each and every one of his employees, as though they were family. The stories he'd told her as they'd hiked down the mountain in the growing dusk had made them feel so real to her it was like she'd already known them for years. From Gulliver and his steadfast loyalty, to Andrea and her dry humor.

Jill had also felt connected to Burke. She'd never told a soul about spying on the Ute elders all those years ago, but she'd told him. She had to admit she was drawn to Burke, and his newly revealed side made her love him. Just a little bit.

Jill sighed and closed her eyes, allowing herself to relive his goodbye kiss. He'd gently placed his hands over her hips, his fingers spanned as the two of them had gazed at each other. Speaking without speaking.

And then he'd thanked her for the afternoon before wetting his lips and—

"Uh-oh."

Jill's eyes flew open as she jolted out of her reverie to find her boss watching her.

"Someone's a smitten kitten." Emma smiled and set a slice of chocolate pie in front of her. "Shh. Don't tell anyone. It's Leif's chocolate maven pie."

"What? How did you get a piece? He stopped making this when Benny's Big Burger burned down." Jill lifted the fork and dived into the dessert. She closed her eyes as the rich chocolaty flavors rolled over her tongue like a fond memory. Leif's pie used to be the top of her best-thing-ever list, but after Burke's goodbye kiss, it was just a mere second place.

"Leif promised me free pie for life if I convinced Lily to rebuild the restaurant after the fire." Emma smiled and perched on the edge of Jill's desk, obviously satisfied with herself.

"Well done. The women of Blueberry Springs thank you. However, our waistlines do not."

"Are you kidding me? You have some serious va-va-voom now that you've got a little bit of junk in your trunk. No wonder Burke can't keep his eyes off of you."

"Don't lie," Jill said, feeling pleased.

And yet she couldn't help but feel a burst of apprehension. She was daydreaming about a man who didn't want marriage. It was like high school, when she'd been set up by Mandy, who had convinced her that Scott Malone was interested and was waiting for her to ask him out. He hadn't been. He'd been interested in Jodi.

Jill still got hot with embarrassment thinking about how she'd asked him out when his gaze kept trailing over her shoulder toward Jodi. He'd looked at her when she was finished and said, "You're Jill, right?"

She'd nodded.

"Sorry, I'm interested in someone else."

He had dated Jodi for three months before Jill's twin tired of him and moved on.

"What's up with you two, anyway?" Emma asked, ruffling her pixie cut. "You guys got married in secret but are living apart?"

"That's about it."

"I don't understand."

"Speaking of getting married in secret, is Lily okay?" The woman had eloped with Ethan as part of a business deal regarding her new restaurant—which he had owned at the time. The marriage hadn't been meant as anything more than an exchange of assets. It had turned into true love, as if Cupid was hiding somewhere around Blueberry Springs, striking unsuspecting pretend lovers with his arrows.

Jill froze. *She* had a pretend lover...

No. Cupid was not interested in her and Burke.

"Why wouldn't she be okay?" Emma asked. "Is she pregnant?"

"What? Is she?"

"I don't know."

"Blueberry Springs is getting to you."

Emma had grown up in a city in the South, but was fitting right in to small town life, as if it was her birthright.

"I was just thinking that after being trapped in the burning building like that..." Jill shivered. "I can't imagine rebuilding on the same site. It has to bring back some haunting memories."

"Someone said she's talking to the counselor at the hospital."

"That's good."

Emma swiped a finger through Jill's pie, dipping the chocolate-covered digit into her mouth with a sly smile. "Love this stuff."

Jill pulled the slice farther away from Emma's probing fingers.

"So for real—what's up with your marriage?" Emma asked. Her voice lowered. "Is it a business arrangement?"

"Kind of," Jill admitted, scrunching her nose, fearing judgment even though she knew Emma had originally married Luke for business reasons.

"Well, be careful." Her boss stood.

Jill's stomach dropped. "Why?"

She laughed, lightheartedly. "You're *married*. That tends to divert even the best-laid plans."

"We signed a business agreement."

"So did Luke and I." She wiggled her ring finger with a smile. "We married for business and fell in love. You two have a *business agreement*." Her eyes twinkled as she sang, "I know what's going to happen next."

Jill struggled not to roll her eyes. "You're starting to sound like Ginger." She turned away, waking up her computer so she could get some work done before she started fantasizing about what life would be like married to Burke—truly married.

"Two people don't just get married in secret, then partner their businesses when there's nothing there. Even if it's just hiding under the surface," Emma whispered over her shoulder, her words sinking through the walls Jill was struggling to erect between reality and fear. Or was it hope?

Emma took Jill's empty plate with her, leaving her alone to think about Burke. Their marriage. Their businesses. But most of all, the heat that seemed to build between them whenever they were together.

Despite the situation, she already felt closer to him than she had to any of the other men she'd been with. How could that be? Was it just an illusion? Part of the act?

She slid her bracelet up her arm, taking in her half of their heart tattoo.

Or was it something else?

Burke couldn't concentrate on his work. He wanted to be out hiking with Jill again. She'd been a patient teacher and he'd enjoyed using his hands to extract the right ingredients, then, back at her little apartment, prepare a few creams. It was calming, meditative.

But even more, he'd enjoyed watching how intent she became, how focused on putting her heart and soul into her products. The ingredients and results mattered to her. Authentic. Artisan. No minimum wage workers slaving in a factory or over a machine, bruising and crushing the leaves to make everything more uniform, faster and cheaper—a race to the bottom.

She was preserving uniqueness, a reminder of why he'd taken the path he had, clinging to it through adversity. She embodied everything he valued in his own company, and the moments he'd shared with her were ones he wanted to capture, preserve, savor.

That, right there in her tiny guest room, was the meaning he'd been trying to find.

But instead of immersing himself in that world, he was in his office, in the city, trying to summon enough focus to pore over his proposal for Tiffer.

He needed to get this done now so he could let it rest for a few weeks, then reattack it, its flaws standing out after he'd let it sit.

He leaned forward and took a sip of his organic, rain-forest-friendly coffee. He was going to get the deal this time.

Things were lining up, and serendipity was delivering the win he'd needed, just in the knick of time.

Someone moved in his doorway and Burke looked up.

"Andrea!" He stood, greeting the new mom. She had a tiny infant nestled in a sling. "What are you doing here?"

"It's called visiting," Andrea said.

"Snooping?"

"Gulliver said you were singing this morning."

"I was?"

"Glen Miller."

Burke had indeed caught himself humming one of the big band's tunes under his breath.

"So? Who did you make a deal with?" Andrea gingerly rested a hip against his desk, careful not to wake her newborn, Avani, whose name meant earth. The name was as perfect as the girl's delicate features.

"No deal. How's motherhood?"

"Fine. Sleep is for wimps. So why the singing?" She was watching him from the corner of her eyes as though expecting him to reveal something.

"The beta tests for Jill's Botanicals have continued to be very promising."

Andrea was nodding intently. She looked wired, but exhausted. He had a feeling the high of having a newborn had yet to wane and allow reality to come crashing in. "Yeah? How good?"

"Surprisingly so."

"I'm glad to hear that."

She stifled a yawn, her perkiness suddenly slipping. The baby began to stir and Andrea stood, her hands moving quickly, her expression one of panic.

"You know it's okay if they cry," he said gently.

She bit her bottom lip, her eyes welling.

"Here." He reached for Avani once she was free of the fabric. "Let me walk her."

"What if she's hungry?"

"Then she'll cry." He cradled the baby against his chest and told Andrea to sit. "Close your eyes for a moment."

"What do you know about babies?"

"Lots, actually."

He'd had a girlfriend named River in high school who'd had a baby—not his—and she'd moved out of her parents' home, trying to go it alone rather than face their disapproval for keeping Mika. He'd spent hours babysitting so River could study. Funny how he hadn't thought about the two of them in a long time, or even how River had left him as soon as she'd completed her diploma, even though he'd mourned their loss for a long time.

"We'll cry if we need you," he said to Andrea.

"You sure?" She sank into the couch, looking tense.

"Chill. I've got this." He stepped out of his office, inhaling the gentle scent of the baby. Her crown was covered in the most delicate hair, her skin precious and soft.

"Are you smelling the baby?" Gulliver asked as he passed his desk.

"Want a sniff? She smells incredible."

Gulliver leaned back as though he'd been offered something offensive.

Burke chuckled and walked the perimeter of the office. It was quiet today, with half the crew out at a workshop. He talked to the baby as he moved, telling her about his day, his dreams for his deal with Tiffer. How Jill was helping him and how expanding globally would improve their bottom line and help out Avani's family. That maybe her mom would be able to work from home more, and they could hire an assistant to help with her workload.

"Family is important, Avani, remember that. It's not something you can take for granted."

The baby made a satisfied sucking sound and Burke choked up.

What was with him? Not only was he feeling sentimental, but he'd shown Jill a more intimate side on their hike. The business was what mattered, not whatever it was they were doing together on a more personal level. Focus on the business. Nothing else.

Light and loose.

He cruised by his office and found Andrea asleep, her head propped in her hand.

Burke decided to keep walking.

"Jill's on line one," Gulliver called as he passed.

Burke placed a finger over his lips and stepped to Gulliver's desk, taking the call. He cradled the baby's head as he shifted to sit on the desktop. The man sighed heavily at the inconvenience of having his boss take over his workspace, and Burke smiled.

"I'm going on break," Gulliver said, abandoning his post.

Burke nodded and said to Jill, "Make sure the people you hire understand the artisan aspect of your products, and take pride in creating the best they can each time."

"Why are you talking so softly?"

"Avani fell asleep on my chest."

There was silence on the other end of the line.

"Jill? You still there?"

"Yes, of course." Her tone was curt.

"It's Andrea's baby. My financial officer. She came in today even though she's on maternity leave." He was bemused by the thought that Jill might be jealous, and disappointed that she'd assumed the worst—that Avani might be a woman he'd just slept with.

"Oh."

"Were you jealous?"

"You have a bit of reputation for being indiscreet." There was something in her tone.

"What's wrong?"

"Did you read the papers?" That tone—it was unhappy.

"Which papers?"

Gulliver was standing a few feet away in the break room doorway, nursing a cup of hot cocoa. Burke raised his brows at him and in a flash his assistant was seated in front of his computer, typing furiously into a search engine as Burke mouthed to enter his name.

They both inhaled sharply as the first headline hit them.

"Oh," Burke said.

Well, actually, it wasn't too bad. Pretty much the truth, too.

He was married.

Had been dating Autumn.

But the article made him out as a two-timing schmuck who cared about the planet, but not people.

Ouch. That wasn't good for their brand.

Gulliver clicked to the next article. More of the same.

"It'll blow over," Burke said with an authority he didn't feel.

Jill was quiet. Silent women were often deadly foes and his stress levels rose like the water in a bathtub about to overflow.

He put himself in her shoes. Small town. Mysterious new secret husband—who'd been cheating on her. That wasn't good.

She was strong and capable, but he also knew there was a thread in her life he'd yet to figure out. Something about being unlucky in love. There were men who had let her down, made her look or feel foolish. And now Burke had become another one of them.

He opened his mouth to speak, to apologize, but he didn't know what to say. He glanced at Gulliver for help, but his assistant was gaping at him.

"It's true?" Gulliver mouthed in disbelief, after scanning yet another article. He pointed at Burke, then the phone. He mimicked sliding a ring onto his finger.

Burke waved him away, not wanting to get into it. Not when Jill needed him to say something.

Anything.

No, not *anything*. The right thing.

What was the right thing?

Gulliver hit speaker on his phone. "Jill? It's Gulliver. Are you okay, honey?"

That was, indeed, a good place to start.

She let out a shaky sigh that could be heard over the line.

"Oh, sweetie." Gulliver turned to Burke, scowling at him. "Burke, get lost. Jill and I need to talk."

"She's *my* wife."

"Thanks for telling us, by the way. I suspected, but I thought that was something you would have disclosed to your most-trusted assistant." He turned up his nose and shifted so his back was to Burke. He'd taken the receiver and was talking in quick, hushed tones.

Burke shifted, feeling like a third wheel, until Avani began fussing, at which point he went to his office and woke Andrea.

She yawned, then, seeing her child, stretched out her arms for her. Spotting Gulliver hunched over his phone through the open doorway, she asked, "What's got Gulliver in a tizzy?"

"He found out I'm married."

Andrea nearly dropped her baby. "The newspaper articles were right?"

"It's a long story." One he probably should have shared with his staff, come to think of it. He'd just kind of figured it wouldn't impact a thing.

Andrea had settled on his couch, Avani tucked under her shirt to feed. Burke looked away.

"I thought it was just someone trying to bring your stock down a little further. You know, the competition. Enemy. Unhappy coworker." She angled her head toward Gulliver, eyebrows raised in silent question.

"No," Burke said. "He's upset and worried, but he would never betray me."

But it had him wondering if someone else would.

And if that person was the one he knew Jill already suspected —Autumn Martinez.

Jill wanted to avoid downtown Blueberry Springs. Desperately.

However, Emma had requested she pick her up a cappuccino on her way by Mandy's—which was always busy this time of the morning—when she went to collect the day's mail at the post office.

And on a mild spring day, there were more people out, which meant any time spent on the sidewalks was equivalent to a few miles of running the gauntlet. But instead of soldiers attacking her, it was the gossips who appeared out of nowhere, like ravenous termites catching wind of tasty, dry wood.

Her phone rang and she picked it up, grateful to have an excuse to ignore absolutely everyone she saw.

She just had to get through today and then it would be the weekend and she could hide out for a blissful forty-eight hours.

"Hello?" She ducked her head, pretending not to see Fran waving to her from the doorway of her boutique.

"Jill Armstrong? It's Zebadiah from WWYL."

"Hey, Zeb. Sorry. I've been meaning to—"

"I have a new one. Before you say anything at all, you want to check out this one."

"Does he live with his mom and play video games in his free time?"

There was a telling pause.

"Zeb…" They'd been through this before. And now that she was out about her marriage, she needed to let her subscription lapse.

"You live with your sister."

"No, I *rent* from my sister. There's a difference. And anyway, right now I—"

"Jill, honey. Yoo-hoo!" It was Mary Alice and her sister, Liz.

"I have to go." Jill was going to need more than a phone

conversation to dissuade the sisters from hounding her. She hung up as the ladies called, "We heard the news about Burke."

Jill closed her eyes and turned on her heel, shoving open the hardware store's glass door, acting as though she hadn't heard the women. Inside, she ducked down the paint aisle, knowing there was a very good chance they'd follow.

Yes, she and her cheating husband had made the news.

She'd already suffered through her mother cornering her to talk about Burke, going on and on about all the things Jill needed to change about herself in order to catch someone good—like Jodi's husband, Gareth.

Wade Sinclair from high school still had a crush on her. Why not take him up on one of his dating offers?

Why hadn't she?

Because she'd accidentally married a man who cranked her engine a lot harder than Wade ever could or would.

"I saw her," Jill heard Mary Alice say with determined authority. "She's in here somewhere. Jill? Jill, hon!"

Jill timed her movements around the store like she was playing paintball, slipping past a shelf of paintbrushes before hustling across the end of the aisle into the electrical section, then across to the restroom. She quietly closed the door, locking it.

Jill counted to a hundred, then back down to one. She cracked the door, listening. Then she walked the perimeter of the store before returning to the front. She rounded the end of an aisle, nearly knocking into a man who was tall and smelled heavenly, his strong hands catching her easily to keep them from colliding.

"Jill."

"Burke? What are you doing here?" All he seemed to do lately was burn up the highway between the city and Blueberry Springs. If she didn't know better, she'd think he liked her.

Or that he needed to fix the way he kept messing up her life.

"I'm sorry for how things went down with the press. Gulliver said people are talking here and I..." His expression went blank, as though he was suddenly uncertain why he had indeed burned up the highway in the middle of a workday.

Was this a pity trip? One to placate the wife, to ensure she didn't mess up his business deal, because he'd made her look foolish to everyone she knew—as well as the general public?

"Well, what do you expect?" She let out a huff of self-depreciating laughter. "My husband's been doing the governor's daughter for months. I knew she'd talk to the press. Hence actually admitting to my mistake of marrying you."

Why had that seemed like a good idea, again?

She let out a long sigh, wishing he was still holding her.

"I didn't sleep with her."

"Burke, it's not important." It felt important, though.

"Or anyone else. Not since you."

She wanted to push past him, but she was frozen in place, her heart beating loud in her ears at the prospect of this sexy playboy not being with a soul since marrying her months ago.

She wanted to jump up, wrap her arms around him and kiss him.

"I find that hard to believe," she said.

"So do I," he replied, peeking at her. "But it's true."

"You can't tell me Autumn's just been—"

"I haven't slept with her," he repeated quickly, almost as though he was embarrassed. "She thinks I'm being old-fashioned and respectful, and changing my playboy bachelor ways because I love her."

Jill began walking away. She didn't need to hear this right now.

"But I don't." His voice was clear, strong. She stopped in her tracks and turned to face him. "And I'm not a cheater."

"So you haven't been..." She caught herself. It didn't matter. It wasn't her business.

And that feeling of joy and relief should take a hint, as well as serve as a warning sign that she was in way too deep.

"Have you?" he asked.

She felt herself blush, embarrassed by her true lack of a love life. She glanced left. Mary Alice and Liz were eavesdropping at the end of the seasonal aisle, which was optimistically offering garden hoses instead of snow shovels despite the fact that the mountains no doubt still had another dump or two of the fluffy white stuff in store before spring officially sprang on the small town.

"She hasn't." Mary Alice piped up as she stepped out of her hiding spot. "She hasn't had a date with that kind of action since Devon, back in…" She turned to her sister. "How long has it been? Three years?"

"Five?" offered Liz. "Well, let's see. It was before Amber and Scott got married and just after the Johnsons' barn fell in after all that snow. Remember that Christmas? Katie got snowed in at the hospital with Nash."

"I rescued them. Got her home in time for Christmas dinner."

"That was how many years ago now?"

"Oh, quite a few. I'd think it's safe to call Jill a virgin once again. What's the term? A reborn virgin?"

"I don't think that's it." Liz giggled. "But I like it."

"Okay, thank you, ladies," Jill said, grabbing Burke by the arm.

"And before Devon," said Mary Alice, "she was with that no-good piece of work—"

Jill had Burke outside before he could hear about her failed marriage and how she'd been blindsided.

"The press can say whatever they want," Burke stated. "We know the truth. We just keep our heads high and our backs to each other."

"I don't know, Burke. Maybe it's time to give up the gig." She drove her hands deep into the pockets of her light jacket. "You know Tiffer's going to have his underwear in a knot over this."

Burke's brow furrowed and his gaze lifted to the mountains surrounding them, as though expecting the answer to be carved into their rocky sides. "He sent me an email."

"What did it say?"

"He says he's worried that the instability of our relationship will impact my ability to keep my eye on business."

"Did he retract his offer to meet with you at the Metro Conference?"

"No, but it was definitely a warning."

They walked in silence for a block, Jill keeping her gaze averted any time they passed any townsfolk, so they wouldn't try to talk to her. It mostly worked. That and Burke interrupting them to kindly say, "Not now, thanks."

Jill stopped outside the post office as a thought struck her. "Did you drive two hours to see if I'm okay?"

"Does that win me points if I did?"

"Are you trying to be romantic?"

"Huh?"

She laughed at his expression.

"You deserve better than this," he said.

Her cheeks heated at the sincerity of his comment, and she stepped into the post office, unlocking the box Emma had rented for All You.

"I knew what I was getting myself into."

"I like the photo they chose for the article," Burke said, taking the mail from her as she emptied the box, wrapping it in one of the magazines and tucking it under his arm.

Jill groaned. "Don't be cute."

The city's newspaper had used a photo taken at MacKenzie's, where she was in Burke's lap looking like she wanted to devour him. Of course they hadn't chosen the one they'd posed for a few days ago for Burke's site, where they were shaking hands.

"I think we should frame it." Burke gave her a sly grin that made her insides turn to goo. "Call it our wedding photo."

"You're ridiculous." Despite everything, Jill couldn't help but smile.

"Well?" boomed a male voice. Jill turned. It was her father, standing in the doorway to the room with the mailboxes, arms crossed.

"Hey, Daddy." Jill shifted uncomfortably.

"What's this I hear about Burke having a lady friend on the side?"

"We were separated then."

Jill blurted that out at the same time Burke said, "I didn't sleep with Autumn."

"You two need marriage counseling."

"They need to take their marriage seriously, that's what they need to do," added her mother, coming in behind her husband.

"Oh, we're not—" Jill began, before being interrupted by her mom.

"You haven't even had a party and you've kept him all but hidden. Of course he stepped out on you. He thinks you don't care."

"He hasn't stepped out."

"This is just like with your first husband. You didn't show him enough care at home and so he left."

"He left because he was a thief, Mom. It was part of his scheme."

"He was a con artist," Argo said to his wife. "There was nothing Jill could have done to have changed that fact."

"I didn't mean it like that," Jenilee said defensively. "All I'm saying is that love can change a person and maybe if she'd just—"

"Mom, no."

Her mother had caught Burke's expression of surprise and darted a glance at Jill before saying quietly, "She didn't tell you she's been married before?" She frowned at Jill with what only could be described as disappointment. "Honey, you can't keep holding men at bay. You think you can't find love, but you don't even try when you have it right there in your hands." She fluffed Jill's hair with a frown.

"Mom, stop." Jill inhaled slowly. "Our marriage is fake. It was an accident."

BURKE BARELY HAD time to react to Jill's little bomb about their marriage—and her mother's one about Jill being previously married—before Argo was ushering him out the doors of the post office, calling over his shoulder, "We're going to have a little guy time out at the lake. If you need us, too bad."

Burke wasn't sure what to say, so he didn't say anything. He simply climbed into Argo's truck and rode out to the lake, where his father-in-law pulled fishing rods and an auger from the truck's box. He handed one rod to Burke, and they made their way down to the frozen lake in silence. The snow on its surface had melted with the warm weather, then refrozen, making it gleam in the late-March sun.

Jill had been married. Why did that feel so significant?

Because it made her more like him?

Because it made her flawed and all the more endearing and vulnerable?

The last thing Jill needed was this whole Autumn thing making her look like she couldn't keep a man.

They set up their rods after Argo cut two holes in the ice, going back to the truck for folding chairs. They fished for about five minutes before Jill's father broke the silence.

"What do you have to say for yourself, son?"

Being called son took the air from his lungs. The question was so open-ended Burke merely shook his head, at a loss.

"Well?"

Finally, he said, "Our marriage was accidental. Neither of us recall the ceremony and I'm not proud of that. Part of me worries

I somehow lured Jill into doing something that's caused her a lot of personal repercussions."

He let out a sigh, having unburdened himself.

"It takes two to tango. Two to waltz. You get the picture." Argo shifted to face him. "I do find it odd that my Jill did something like this on a whim." He angled back to the lake. "Then again, I've seen you two around town here and there, and I think I understand."

"What's that?"

"She likes you," he said simply, as if that was all there was to it.

"Autumn and I don't have an intimate relationship and never have. I didn't cheat on Jill."

Argo pulled back on his rod, reeling in his line before letting it out again. "I appreciate you telling me that even though it isn't my business."

"Yes, it is." Burke met his eye, holding his ground. "Jill deserves more than I've given her. I'm trying to reach for a business deal that could change the future of my company, and that of all my employees who've stuck with me since the beginning. The first years were tough, and they took lower than average salaries, deferred bonuses, and made personal sacrifices because they believed in me and the company and what we're trying to do. I was hoping this business deal would allow me to honor those sacrifices at long last."

Burke shook his head, feeling disappointed in himself for making the conversation about money.

"You don't intend to stay married?"

"No. But I hope we'll stay friends." He hung his head, focusing on the line disappearing into the icy water, feeling inexplicably sad about their future parting. "I've told Jill stuff I haven't told anyone, and sometimes I feel like she's done the same with me."

He was going to miss her.

Jill's father smiled, his eyes tracking a bird soaring high above the lake.

They were silent for a while, Jill's father's rod dipping as a fish nibbled, but didn't bite.

"How long will you stay married?"

"A few more months. Jill's agreed to stay until I can pitch to this guy—he believes I'm more stable if I'm married. But this mess might change things."

Argo chuckled. "More stable if you're married? I wasn't. Not until I couldn't play in the band any longer. Used to live on whims and the wind. Those were the days." He pursed his lips as he shook his head, as though further considering the memories and finding them tarnished.

"But I'll stay as long as Jill wants me to. I've upended her life."

"What can we do to help?"

Burke looked up in surprise.

"You're family. Jill chose you and that means something. You two have plans and she saw something in you worth pursuing."

Burke had to focus on the water to hide the emotion that suddenly overwhelmed him. "Thanks. I appreciate the offer."

"So? What can we do?"

Burke gazed out into the distance, where a truck was driving out to an ice fishing hut.

"I'm not sure." He had to convince Tiffer he was stable. He had to protect his reputation, which was taking a beating. But most of all, he needed to protect Jill. "What do you think Jill needs?"

Argo clapped a hand on Burke's shoulder as he stood. "I knew I liked you, son."

"Mom, I can't believe you told Burke I've been married before." Jill was still standing in the post office, arguing with her mother, trying to ignore the way residents were taking their time gathering their mail, watching her out of the corner of their eye and more often than not missing their mailbox's keyhole by a good several inches.

"Oh, for crying out loud, Gloria, just shove the key in the lock already," Jill snapped.

The middle-aged waitress jolted, turning back to the metal box, jamming the key home and retrieving her mail in record time before scuttling from the room with a whispered "Good luck" to Jill's mother.

"I can't believe you didn't tell him," Jenilee said once Gloria was gone. "Jodi and Gareth don't keep secrets from each other. It's not healthy."

Jill pressed her fingertips to her temples, struggling to keep a grip on her patience. She inhaled, the unique scent of tons of mail filling her nostrils.

She hoped Burke was having a better time with her father than she was with her mother.

"It's not a real marriage," Jill explained yet again.

"People do not get married by accident," her mother continued, "so don't you dare try that line with me. You're the most well planned person I know. Why were you trying to hide this marriage from us? Are you ashamed?" Jenilee's eyes filled with tears.

"What?" How had her mother made this all about her?

"You're too ashamed to have us at your own wedding? You had to run off and get married in secret?"

"Mom, Burke and I got drunk at a conference and we woke up married. Except neither of us remembered, and I accidentally borrowed against his credit, which he'd planned to use for his business." Her mother gave her a look of disbelief. "Wini saw I was married and she thought she was doing us a favor, but instead created a giant mess. I was trying to help Burke by going public about our marriage even though we're getting a quiet divorce. As lame as it sounds, it looks better if he's married and stable for a business deal he's working on. This deal is really important to him." She thought of all his employees, the ones that sounded like family to him. "And so it's important to me, too."

"But...this was all a mistake?" Her mother looked confused. "He stood up for you like he was a real husband."

"He's a good friend."

"That woman...the governor's daughter?"

"He wasn't intimate with Autumn, and she's stirring things up in the press because—I don't know—she likes attention and she's used to getting what she wants. But it could ruin everything."

"What are you going to do?" Jenilee asked.

Jill was having trouble concentrating, what with Fran gesturing wildly to her mother from outside the large window behind them, mouthing something Jill couldn't make out.

They both turned their backs to the window, shutting her out.

Jenilee's cell phone rang and Jill half expected her mother to find nobody on the other end of the line; so far Logan hadn't been able to trace the calls for her. Yes, she'd asked.

Her mother talked in crisp tones, mostly disagreeing, before heaving a terribly long sigh and saying "fine," and then clicking off.

She turned to Jill with a purpose that made her cringe.

"Who was that?" Jill asked.

"Your father. We both agree that it doesn't matter if your marriage was a mistake and that it wasn't intended. We need to show this Autumn Martinez that she cannot mess with you and she cannot mess with your husband. If you married this man, that means something."

"It doesn't mean a thing."

Her mother inhaled deeply. "I love your father very much and I trust his judgment. And so we are going to show this Autumn Martinez, and I don't care if her father is the king of Spain." Jenilee made a grand gesture with her arms, sending her gold earrings swinging. "We are going to prove to the world that you and Burke are as tight as thieves."

"Thick as thieves?"

"Are you correcting me, young lady?"

"Yes."

Her mother's eyes roamed over her, quick and assessing as she adjusted the bangles on her wrists. "The first thing we need to do is your hair."

"We are not doing my hair."

"After that we are going to throw a party."

CHAPTER 10

Apparently the answer to their marital problems, according to Blueberry Springs, was to throw a party. A rather large, impromptu one that kept Burke from heading home to make sure his kitten hadn't destroyed his place. A quick call to his neighbor's son assured him that the cat had, indeed, shredded his front mat in protest of his absence.

Considering he'd thought Jill's dad might cut a hole in the lake's ice big enough to stuff him through it and drown him during 'guy time,' Burke still called a ruined front mat a win.

He looked around the small Blueberry Springs café—Mandy's.

"Remember," Jenilee murmured, as she hurried by, "look like you two are solid and united."

"Mom, I told you this is just going to complicate things," Jill said, trailing after her mother, who had a roll of tape, no doubt for the decorations going up around the small restaurant. "We're not staying together forever," she added in a harsh whisper.

"One thing at a time," her mother said, before disappearing into a cluster of women bustling about in the back corner. "Just show that Autumn lady and the world that you two love each other."

"Mom..."

"Your father's usually right about these things, so just play along. Pretend, and that woman will fade like a piece of black construction paper left out in the summer sun."

"What's with the wedding bell streamer things?" Burke asked, clearing his throat as he pointed at the decorations being strung up around the narrow restaurant. There was even a banner congratulating them.

"This is out of hand," Jill said. She looked stressed.

"If I didn't know any better, I'd think this was an anniversary party." Even though the two of them had been married for less than a year.

Jill was studying the room as though looking for the keystone —the one she could pull to suck this whole new marital mess back into the proverbial box. "The only way either of us could make it to a one-year wedding anniversary would be if we didn't know we were married," she muttered.

Burke chuckled. "Your love life has been that bad?" He held out his arms as if to showcase himself, then the decorations.

She began laughing, which caused him to join in. She clutched him for support and he held her tight.

"Nobody's going to believe us for a second," she said, still out of breath from laughing.

"That we're married?"

"Surprise! We are!"

They began laughing again, swiping at the tears rolling down their cheeks.

"How did we end up here?" she asked.

He stopped laughing, worried she might be cracking up. She'd told him that in small towns marriage was one of the biggest moments in a couples' life. While the two of them weren't lying about their status, they were definitely misleading everyone about everything else. Worse still, Jill had been married before, meaning he was taking her down a familiar and painful road where the signposts were judgment and advice. Crossroads filled with awkward moments where you had to explain again and again why you were no longer with your one true love. That feeling of being untethered and slightly lost.

"I'm sorry," he said, his arms still wrapped loosely around her.

"Why?" She looked up, putting them just about nose to nose.

He gave a slight shoulder hitch. She wasn't scuttling off, wasn't anything but present, gazing at him, still glowing from her earlier laughter. For a moment he thought she might kiss him.

"Happy anniversary," a woman said, rattling a gift bag beside them.

"It's not our anniversary," Burke said, not looking away from Jill. He had a feeling that when he did, this moment would be gone, and he wanted to stay in it for as long as possible.

Mary Alice pushed the bag into the crook of Jill's elbow. Jill's hands slid down Burke's arms as she broke contact, trying to save the wrapped item from hitting the floor.

"Forgive the gift. I thought you two would be breaking up after hearing about that floozy."

"She's no floozy," Liz declared, coming alongside her sister. "She's the governor's girl."

Jill stepped in. "It's just a misunderstanding—"

"That's what all con men say," Liz snapped.

Mary Alice and Liz turned as one to glare at Burke.

"Jill," Liz said, "blink twice if you need our help with this one."

Jill didn't blink. "It's fine. Thank you for your concern."

"I always had a feeling about Hayes, and I have a feeling about this one, too." Mary Alice jabbed a finger in Burke's direction.

"You also tried to run our kind doctor Nash Leham out of town, once upon a time," Jill reminded her gently. The man had been on the wrong side of a romance with Beth Wilkinson—now Reiter—according to the women.

"Nice to see you both again," Burke said, hoping to get the festivities back on track.

Mary Alice angled away, saying, "We're keeping an eye on you. One wrong move and we'll run *you* out of town, you hear?"

"Loud and clear, ladies."

"I'm sorry," Jill said under her breath as the gossips moved along. She set the gift on a table, peeking at the bag's contents. A guidebook to divorce, by the looks of it.

"Nice women," Burke said mildly.

Jill chuckled. "A bit protective, but well-meaning even if they do tend to remind people of their past mistakes as frequently as possible."

The small restaurant had filled with people, and the noise was nearly deafening. He quickly scanned the crowd. He'd temporarily satisfied the two gossips, but he could still see chatter rippling through the room, people turning to give them slightly skeptical looks when they thought it would go unnoticed.

He straightened his spine. Sure, their divorce papers might be ready to be signed, but in the meantime he and Jill were partners.

He grabbed a chair and stood on it so he was a head above everyone who'd gathered. Then, thinking twice, he climbed down, slid over another chair and pulled Jill onto it so they were both raised.

"Excuse me!" he called. The room started to hush. "Thank you for coming today. If we haven't met yet, I'm Burke Carver. You all know my lovely wife, Jill Armstrong, who I managed to woo a few months ago." He turned to give her a smile. She looked like she wanted to hide from the world.

Burke lifted Jill's hand, pushing back the sleeve so he could raise her flesh to his lips, giving it a kiss. "Take off your bracelet," he whispered.

She tensed, clutching her fingers around the leather.

"Trust me," he murmured.

She had her eyes locked on his, and after a beat, she hesitantly unsnapped the bracelet. He pushed up his sweater sleeve, then took her left hand in his right. He lifted their joined hands, revealing the way their commas formed a heart when they were together.

The room filled with the sound of tenderly spoken "aww's." Just as he'd thought, the tattoos felt like a serious indicator of their devotion to each other.

Jill inhaled deeply, then said, "I know Burke and I don't have a traditional marriage, and our work keeps us apart. I also know there are a lot of rumors going around, but I want you to know I trust him. He's family."

Burke had to swallow over a lump in his throat. He caught Jill in his arms and kissed her, so deeply that nobody would ever have any doubts about him and his wife.

JILL COULDN'T STOP KISSING Burke. She knew they were putting on a spectacle. Knew she should stop. But the cheering from her friends and family was as heady as the feeling she got tucked in Burke's arms. And the way he'd stood up for her once again made her heart feel so warm and full she was afraid it was going to burst.

"What are you after, Burke Carver?" she whispered breathlessly when they broke apart.

"Just you."

He kissed her again.

"Okay, quit rubbing it in," Amy said. "Come on down. We have gifts for you."

"We don't need gifts," Jill said, stepping off the chair. Gifts were a whole different problem.

Amy lowered her voice so only she could hear, but Burke leaned in, too. "With Liz and Mary Alice talking about Burke playing the field, we thought maybe we'd messed up with gifts, but after that kiss...?" She shook her hand as if she'd touched something hot. "Wowie-zowie. Those two old biddies are off their rockers."

Burke laughed and Jill placed a hand gently on his cheek, rubbing a spot on his chin with her thumb. "He is easy on the eyes."

"Is that all I am? A good kisser and eye candy?"

She winked and followed Amy to the pile of gifts before she got to thinking about how she should be at home filling orders.

And sorting out that horrible one-star review she'd received on Burke's site. She knew negative feedback was inevitable, but that one had felt personal and as though it was an attack from Autumn. Jill shook off the thought. That would be a pretty low and vindictive thing to do, and her mind was probably just going nuts because it was her first bad review.

She pulled her mind from her thoughts to find Liz and Mary Alice, heads bent together, whispering and watching her and Burke.

Jill turned her back, only to find Burke right there, sliding an arm around her shoulders.

"Don't," she whispered, carefully sidestepping him. He wasn't looking for the same thing she was. This wasn't reality to him, it was a game. A PR move.

And that was okay, but she needed a bit more space to help her remember that. It wouldn't be long before she'd be telling the town she'd ended things between them.

He pulled his arm back. "I thought—"

"This isn't real and in a few short months I'll be leaving you..." She couldn't finish her sentence, imaging the way everyone in town would pussyfoot around her, all the while crowing about how they'd *known* all along that it wouldn't last.

Because it never did.

But this time, she'd thought she was going in with eyes wide open. Their marriage was intended to fail, but it was starting to feel like something she wanted to preserve.

And that was an even bigger conundrum than the pile of gifts before her.

Burke went through the motions of cutting the cake with Jill, desperately trying not to inhale the strawberry scent of her shampoo. But as soon as he stopped doing that, he noticed the way her curves felt pressed against his body as they worked together.

It was too easy to believe it was real.

Too easy to hear Jill's words sliding over him like knives.

This isn't real and in a few short months I'll be leaving you.

Their marriage wasn't supposed to be like this. He was doing it again. Making things feel real where they weren't.

But she felt different than anyone else he'd ever been with. She made him relax, smile, and he never wanted to let her go. He needed to find a way to settle his head back on his shoulders and get over himself.

This was all just business, and a way for her to save face.

Jill had a piece of plated cake in hand. She was watching him. And he wasn't sure if her look was playful or vengeful.

"Jill," he warned, as she lifted the piece in her fingers.

"What?" she asked innocently.

"Don't you dare smash that in my face."

"It's tradition to make a mess while sharing the first slice of cake. Don't be a party pooper."

"This isn't a wedding." His chest felt tight, but he wasn't sure why. "And the tradition is to feed each other *nicely*."

"Make a mess!" Amy called.

"Do it, do it!" Amy and Moe chanted, slapping the top of their table in time with their chants. The entire room joined in.

Jill giggled, angling closer, her earlier tension forgotten.

"You wouldn't," Burke said. "This is my favorite sweater."

"I know a good cleaner." She was inches away.

Burke ducked right, but Jill was there with him, the cake's icing brushing his lips.

"Open up, baby!" she cooed.

He straightened, thinking he could move beyond her reach. He couldn't.

He was fairly confident there was now icing up his nose. With one quick step he was at the cake table, grabbing a slice, then pursuing his bride who'd broken loose.

She was laughing, trying to skirt his moves, sliding in the cake she'd dropped on the floor. But there were too many people and chairs in her way, and he quickly caught her with one arm around her waist. She was cringing, laughing, barely looking at him as she awaited the messy disaster.

When he didn't do anything, she opened one eye, watching him. He gently offered her the piece. "Bite?"

"You're going to smush it in my face." She had both hands wrapped around his wrist, trying to prevent the cake from moving closer to her.

"I won't. I promise."

Around them people were watching, waiting. It was quiet, the stereo between songs.

"You said you trusted me," he said.

"Maybe I lied," she replied mildly.

He held his slice between them like an offering. "Bite at the same time?" he asked.

Her eyes softened, as did her body. She leaned her head in at the same moment he did, and together they shared a bite from opposing ends, as though in a scene from *Lady and the Tramp*.

A chorus of sighs filled the room.

"Nobody else," he whispered.

She didn't reply, simply lowered her gaze before bringing it back up to meet his again.

"Nobody," he repeated. "And you have icing on your nose." He reached out with the hand still holding the cake. "Let me just get that for you."

She squealed and ducked, but she was too late.

"You look good in blue icing." He hugged her tight as she laughed, planting a kiss on her cake-free cheek.

"You two are wonderful," Amy said with a sigh. "Open bar! Who's thirsty?"

"Shh! I don't have a liquor permit," Mandy said loudly.

"It's okay, Scott's not here," someone called. It sounded an awful lot like Officer Scott Malone. In fact, it was, and in full uniform no less. But he was grinning, and the crowd moved toward the sound of popping corks.

As Burke handed Jill a napkin so she could wipe her fingers and face, his cell rang. It was his aunt Maggie.

"Sorry," he said to Jill, excusing himself. "Aunt Maggie," he said as he picked up, pushing his way outdoors.

"I saw on social media that you're having an anniversary party with your lovely wife and didn't invite me."

There was a group of smokers laughing and puffing away just outside the doors, and Burke moved farther down the street to gain more privacy.

"It was to show solidarity." He winced. That was almost a lie. "It became something more."

Kind of like that warm feeling inside him whenever he was with Jill. He loved playing with her, and he wanted to find another excuse to kiss her again.

"It was a surprise party. Totally impromptu." He lowered his voice. "You know Jill and I aren't spouses in that way."

"Did you file for divorce?" His aunt was using that stern tone she'd used when filtering through his selective offering of information as a teen in hopes of avoiding trouble.

Burke faced a store window and rubbed his chest, a flash of dull pain reminding him that he still had a bruise from when Alvin's truck had hit his car almost three weeks ago. His chest was going to hurt in a whole new way when they broke up, a little voice inside his head told him.

He shifted, facing the street as though that would block it out.

"Burke? Have you?"

"Not yet."

"Why's that?"

"For business reasons."

"Business?"

He heard the doubt in her tone and added, "Nothing more."

"Are you sure?"

He once had been certain, but he wasn't any longer. He liked being a part of Jill's life, having her at his side to laugh and hang out with, and he liked being a part of her family, too. Part of her world. He wanted to be wherever she was, doing whatever she was doing.

Maybe it was just a feeling of obligation after upturning her life, a need to protect her. But whatever it stemmed from, all he knew was that he wanted to be back in that party, receiving everyone's congratulations and feeling that hope. He wanted that easy feeling of belonging and acceptance he had with Jill.

"We aren't playing house, having babies and living happily ever after," he said gruffly.

"Oh, Burke."

"It's not like that. I'm not doing it again. I'm not putting too much into something that's..."

This isn't real and in a few short months I'll be leaving you.

He was doing it again.

But when he'd spoken the words from his heart, when he'd told her *"Nobody else..."*

And the way she'd looked at him...

She wanted this, too. He'd felt it.

"Does she love you?" Maggie asked.

Will she leave you?

Burke sighed. It was inevitable that she would. It was part of the agreement, as much as them staying together until after the meeting with Tiffer next month.

"Do *you* love *her*?" his aunt pressed.

"What if none of that matters?"

Maggie said nothing for a long moment. Then she said, "What if it does?"

CHAPTER 11

Jill let Burke into her home after the party. The lights were on at her sister's, but she hadn't come to the event, as her girls had been busy at gymnastics. Jill had half expected Jodi to drop by to see about this "cheater" she'd married.

Although they seemed to have quelled the idea of Burke having his eye on someone else, given the way he'd kissed her.

"That was actually quite a bit of fun," he said. "Blueberry Springs knows how to put on a party."

"You should see the surprise birthday parties we put on. We can usually convince Scott to play along and get the birthday person all worried they're in trouble, before popping the surprise on them."

"That sounds...fun."

"It is, actually." She smiled and turned to him in the small entry, kicking off her shoes. Her dog stood like a panting sentinel, watching them with his big eyes before heading off into the house to have a nap.

"Do you think the party will help?" Burke seemed worried, the lines around his mouth deepening.

"Oh, sure. Everyone thinks we're *deeply* in love now."

He cracked a half smile and brushed her cheek, sending shivers through her. "Icing."

"Thanks." She cleared her throat and took a half step back. She knew their game was only going to lead to trouble, but she'd enjoyed pretending it was a little bit real tonight. Kissing. Sharing cake. Being silly. But most of all, having a man willing to enjoy it all with her with a twinkle in his eyes—a twinkle for her.

It was an act, of course. A show.

"You said your aunt heard about it from the city?" Jill asked.

"Because she stalks me."

"Liz grudgingly offered to send photos to the papers in the city, as well."

"Isn't she the mean one?"

"That's Mary Alice. Liz works for the local paper."

"Fitting."

"What else can we do to help your image?" Jill picked at a torn fingernail.

"I think your parents were right about us acting as a united front." He'd crossed his arms across his broad chest, his shirt bunching at the shoulders. "Let's wait and see if it helps everything die down."

The doorbell rang and Jill went to answer it. There was a deliveryman on the step, half hidden by a giant bouquet of flowers. He was someone she didn't recognize.

"What's this?" She turned, glancing at Burke for a clue. He raised his hands in question.

"Sign here," said the man.

Jill signed. "Are you new in town? I didn't realize Blueberry Springs Floral delivered this late at night."

"I deliver from Dakota. Twenty-four/seven."

"Wow." Jill took the bouquet, studying it. Lilies, hydrangea and roses, with an adorable, beady-eyed teddy bear settled among them. She searched for a card. The deliveryman was already retreating down the walk toward his car, which was idling on the street in front of Jodi's house. "There's no card. Who's it from?"

"Enjoy the flowers," he called.

Jill frowned and brought the bouquet inside, setting it on the kitchen table. "Who am I supposed to thank?"

Burke search through the blooms for a card, coming up empty-handed. "Maybe they're from Mary Alice."

They laughed.

"They're probably from someone who came to the party, but didn't have time to get a gift."

Jill went to the freezer to pull out a tub of frozen cookies. Jen Kulak, the local nature guide, had made them for a fundraiser a few weeks ago and they were so delicious Jill had frozen them so she didn't eat them all at once. So far she'd just about broken all her teeth by noshing on frozen cookies.

"Want one?"

"Sure." Burke sat at the kitchen table with her.

"I'm going to miss hanging out with you when you move on," she said to Burke.

"Maybe you'll move on first."

"It never happens that way."

"You've never left anyone?"

"Not even when my ninth grade boyfriend said he got my sister and I mixed up and kissed her 'by mistake.'"

Burke winced. "Ouch."

"Yeah. Good times."

"Have you ever been in love?"

She didn't know whether to look at him or not, wasn't sure what he was getting at. He knew she'd been married before, which made it a stupid question. One meant to get her to talk about what, exactly? Her feelings for him?

"Have you?" he insisted.

"Of course. Haven't you?"

He toyed with the frozen chocolate chip cookie. "I thought I was once or twice. But Maggie thinks maybe I was just in love with the idea of it all." He bit into the cookie and made a face. "These are really hard."

"They did just come out of sub temperatures," she pointed out.

"How do you know if love is real?" His question wasn't tentative, but the look in his eyes was.

She shrugged, then froze, cookie halfway to her mouth. "Wait. Are you falling in love with me?" She was toying with him and he knew it, but he remained serious.

"I got caught up in tonight. It was fun. It's easy to pretend I'm in love with you."

Pretend. Right. That was an important word.

"In case you're wondering, I'm not in love, either," Jill said. "Tonight was fun. But we're just friends."

Friends who kissed like they could set a house on fire with the heat they created.

Burke gripped her hands, holding them tight. "I like that we can talk about anything. I like where we are and I just wanted to make sure you're okay. That all of this is okay."

Jill softened. "You're too perfect, you know that?"

"You know that I'm not."

"And yet I still find you difficult to resist. And that makes you perfect to me."

Burke smiled, the ever-present tension he'd carried as though it was a part of him, suddenly gone.

BURKE HAD SPENT the night in Jill's guest room. They'd stayed up late watching movies and working on filling jars with freshly made botanicals. Once done, they'd sat at the kitchen table eating by-then-thawed cookies and discussing her products. He'd convinced her to pare down her list to the more popular ones, as well as try boosting her prices. More profit, more focus. Streamlined. He'd also convinced her to offer bulk order deals even though she hadn't been so certain about that.

"What are you up to today?" he asked, popping bread into her toaster. He should return home, take care of things. Make sure his neighbor, who was cat sitting, wasn't fed up with Fluke's destructive ways yet.

But a big part of Burke wanted to stay right where he was. Not because he was putting too much into it, as Maggie might try to claim, but to try and figure out why things felt different with Jill. Why he was enjoying being with her so much.

"Are you sticking around?" Jill seemed surprised, but she didn't look away from the egg she was flipping, her focus narrowed onto it.

"Thought I might, if that works for you."

"Well, I have this partnership with this guy…" Her gaze cut to the side.

"And…?" He hated the way jealousy was rearing up inside him, the way he was waiting for her to say more.

"He's totally blown my business wide-open." She smiled. "So I'm working today."

"Oh." He was embarrassed by the relief he felt. She'd been talking about him, not some other guy.

She buttered the toast when it popped, then placed the toast and eggs at the table. Without thinking, he leaned over and kissed her as she moved past him to her side of the table.

"What was that?" she asked, eyebrows raised.

"A kiss." An impulsive one.

"Why?"

"Domestic moment. Sorry."

Jill gave him an amused smirk, but said nothing as she sat with her breakfast. "Fake domestic bliss. My favorite."

It might be just for show, but it felt pretty good.

"It's also my mom's birthday and I still need to get her a gift," she said, taking a bite of her toast.

"Hmm." He reached across the table and hooked his pinkie through hers. She watched him through her lashes.

Unable to resist, he stretched across the table to place a long, wet kiss on her mouth. She responded and before long they were pushing their plates out of the way so she could climb onto the table and crawl toward him.

He kissed his way across her cheek, where she had a smear of homemade marmalade. It was tart and sweet at the same time. "You taste delicious."

"It's the marmalade." She was breathless and he wondered what she was thinking, dreaming of.

"No, it's you."

"You might have to double-check your facts." Her lips were on his, then moving down his neck. Hungry. Impatient.

"I like a woman who cares so much about ensuring a fair assessment."

"Multiple tests."

Taylor barked once, loudly, making them jump. Seconds later, someone knocked at the door.

Jill, who had her hands cupping Burke's face, paused. "I should get that."

"Or not." He kissed her lightly.

The person knocked again, then called, "Jill Armstrong?"

"I guess maybe you should get that." Burke helped her out of his lap.

She padded to the door in her bunny slippers with the big sharp teeth and rabid-looking eyes.

"What's this?" she asked as she opened the door.

She was handed an envelope. It was a different deliveryman than yesterday, Burke noted.

"Have a good day," the man said with a bow before returning to his idling car.

"Idling is hard on the environment," Burke called over Jill's shoulder. He closed the door as she opened the envelope and read what looked to be a congratulatory wedding card.

"'You ruined your first marriage, but I'll ruin this one. He was mine first.'" Jill looked up at Burke, the flush draining from her cheeks.

It seemed as though Autumn Martinez was going to be a bigger issue than he'd realized. And to protect Jill it meant he was going to have to step back instead of what he wanted to do, which was to step closer.

"Burke, I'm not sure us staying married is helping things." Jill paced her kitchen.

"Take a breath," he said.

"I *am* taking a breath! There's no way this isn't going to blow up. There's no way Tiffer is going to see you as a stable man worthy of partnering with. I don't even care what my family or the gossips in town think about me falling into another marriage where…" She waved a hand through the air, unable to come up with the correct words to sum it all up. "I worry everyone is going to think we used them. That our marriage, instead of just being a whoopsie, is going to seem like a big scam."

The large bouquet from the well-wisher caught her gaze. People were happy for them. Offering gifts and congratulations. That was even worse than them thinking she simply kept choosing the wrong kind of men. It was going to be difficult to face everyone once their marriage was over, but not for the reasons she'd originally anticipated. She didn't care anymore if the gossips thought she was incapable of finding love.

Burke pulled her into the comfort of his arms and her feelings of losing control ebbed.

"What are we going to do?" she asked.

"Let me see what I can do. I might be able to settle this down."

"Autumn?"

His hands slid her back as he released her. "Yeah."

"She doesn't want to let you go."

"I heard a rumor that her dad's kicking her out of the mansion, that he's tired of her entitlement and games. I think she's panicking and clinging to me in hopes of me replacing her dad's stability and wealth, if that makes sense. So she sees you as a threat to her own personal security."

"What did you say to her to make her think you want to be that man?"

"I wish I knew. But I'll figure out how to fix this."

Jill leaned in, thinking he was going to kiss her forehead, but instead he stepped away, saying, "But in the meantime, we have work to do today."

For the next few hours they worked diligently, getting ahead of the curve for the upcoming week.

Around four in the afternoon Jill pushed back from her spot at the table. "I'm beat."

Burke checked his watch. He'd been quiet all afternoon, sporting a pensive expression.

"You okay?" she asked lightly.

The expression broke. "Yeah. Hey, didn't you say you have to get your mom a birthday present?"

Jill jumped up. "Oh my gosh. I completely forgot!"

"I'll help."

Within minutes they were walking down a quiet residential street toward the shops, patches of still-brown grass exposed where the snow was melting.

By five Jill had collected a scarf from Fran's boutique, brownies from Mandy's and a voucher for a paddle boarding lesson from Jen at Wally's Sporting Goods. As well, the new librarian had released her latest romance novel the day prior, so she snatched up a signed copy of that, too.

"What else do you need?" Burke asked. He'd been carrying her bags, being a good husband. It made her wish she had more errands to run.

Jill checked off her mental shopping list. "All done."

They headed back the way they'd come, and as they passed the jewelry store, Jill tried to act natural and not allow her gaze to slide toward the window display. Where she instantly noticed a beautiful, discontinued sapphire ring she'd been pining for. It was well beyond her current budget, and she'd placed it on hold almost a year ago, going in every few months to make a small payment whenever they threatened to refund her.

One of these days she would have to let it go and take the refund. Especially since it had made it back into the main display and was no longer tucked away for her.

She shook herself out of her trance, realizing she'd stopped walking to stare at the thin band of diamonds and sapphires. She went to keep moving, but discovered Burke had stopped, as well.

"What are you looking at?" she asked. He was standing in front of the store's glass door.

"I don't think that man is wearing any pants," he said.

Jill looked through the glass. "Oh, no." She pulled out her cell phone and quickly dialing Ethan Mattson. As she waited for him to pick up, she glanced down the street, noticing the helium-filled balloons waving in the breeze outside Lily's newly rebuilt restaurant. It still sported the name of the previous owner, Benny, as in Benny's Big Burger. Only Lily had dropped Big Burger from the name—something that had never fit with the little restaurant that was anything and everything except fast food.

Jill shut off her phone and turned to Burke. "Can you go get Ethan? I think he's probably at the grand opening for his wife's restaurant down there." She pointed toward Benny's.

"And tell him what?" Burke was already walking down the street, looking over his shoulder, waiting for her answer.

"Tell him Gramps is on the loose."

Jill entered the store, not sure how she could help. Gramps didn't get ornery or aggressive, he just sometimes felt the need to not wear pants over his boxer shorts. He was living in the nursing home now, but every once in a while he slipped past the reception desk, keeping the town on their toes.

The clerk behind the counter saw Jill and asked, "Here to try on the ring?"

"No, not today, thanks."

"Make a payment or accept a full refund?" he asked hopefully.

She shook her head. "But soon, okay?" She turned toward Ethan's grandfather. "Hey, Gramps. How are you?"

"None of the Mattsons are answering their phones," the clerk whispered, referring to Gramps's family. He gave the man's lower half a pointed look and Jill nodded.

"Pretty good," Gramps said over the clerk's whispers. "Was feeling a bit warm earlier. I had some of Lily's wonderful mashed potatoes, but they were a bit hot. Got me sweating."

"The weather is unseasonably warm again today," she said supportively. "How's Lily's grand opening?"

"Good, but she's been having nightmares. Hopefully, they'll pass now. It was my need for mashed potatoes that had Ethan saving her from that fire in her restaurant, you know."

"Really?"

"I don't quite remember, but that feels about right. How is that new husband of yours? I heard he's some big deal."

"I think he is."

"Don't leave him."

"Sorry?"

"Us men don't deal well with that."

Well, they seemed to do well enough with leaving her.

"My wife left me almost fifteen years ago and I'm still trying to get over it."

"Oh, I'm sorry. I thought she'd passed on."

"Same thing. Left me here all alone."

Feeling a rush of emotion, Jill gave him a tight hug.

"Oh, no. Don't go all leaky eyes on me. I'm a tough one." He hugged her back just as tightly.

"Love sucks."

He chuckled, his voice deep and raspy as he answered, "Well said, my dear Jill."

The door to the street opened, and Ethan came rushing in. "For the last time, Gramps, those are not shorts."

"They have shorts in the name, buster. *Boxer* shorts."

Ethan went to his grandfather's side. "Where did you leave your pants?"

"In the restaurant. Lily's mashed potatoes made me hot."

"Thank you," Ethan said to Jill, as he guided his grandfather from the store. "Let's get you back into them."

"I'd rather have a nap. I have the best naps after a dish of potatoes."

Jill headed toward the door, where Burke was waiting for her.

"Sure you don't want to try on the ring?" the clerk called.

She gave a small shake of her head, hoping Burke hadn't overheard.

"Ring?" he asked, once they were on the street.

"Just a gift to myself."

"Oh."

"I haven't bought it yet. I've been admiring it for some time, but so far can't afford it." Now it sounded like she expected him to buy it.

"It's nice to treat yourself. Especially if it's something you really like."

"Thanks."

He smiled and Jill felt relief that he didn't seem to be freaking out over the fact that his wife-who-wasn't-his-wife was drooling over rings.

She smiled back. He really was the best fake husband there ever was.

As they reached the flower shop, Burke tugged her inside.

"What are you doing?" she asked.

"I want to get something for your mom."

"I thought you were heading back to the city?" She hadn't presumed he'd be joining the Armstrong clan tonight.

"I thought we were doing this marriage thing?" he asked.

"Well, if we are, then these presents should be from both of us, don't you think?" She gestured to the bag he was still carrying.

"Let's add flowers to the mix. As a hostess gift if nothing else."

"All right." She went to the cooler to select a prearranged bouquet, touched by how thoughtful Burke was. Even though it would make it harder to explain when they broke up.

She sighed, staring at the flowers.

"Let's arrange our own," Burke suggested, coming up beside her.

"Let's not."

"It would be special. Can we or are you closing soon?" he asked Sasha, the woman behind the counter. She'd recently completed her online course in floral arrangements and had shifted from waitress to florist.

Burke rewarded Sasha with a charming smile and within seconds she was showing them how to create a bouquet despite Jill's protests.

Burke flirted and goofed around, his hands deft as he built the perfect arrangement. He took a sprig of baby's breath and tucked it behind Jill's ear.

"Beautiful," he announced.

"The bouquet is definitely passable," she said.

"I was talking about you."

The florist sighed softly. "You two give me hope that if I wait long enough the right man will come along."

"Oh. Um, good," Jill said awkwardly.

ACCIDENTALLY MARRIED

Burke chuckled and kissed her on the forehead. "The best comes to those who wait."

"Ginger has a sale on dresses in her bridal shop," Sasha said, as Burke paid for the bouquet. "You should buy one."

"We're already married," Jill said, backing toward the door.

"No, no. You have to do the whole wedding thing for the town. Everyone is so excited that you finally found someone. I mean, Mary Alice isn't convinced it's real, but it's easy to see why you two came together." Sasha beamed at Burke. "You're both so in love."

"Right. Very in love. Thanks." Jill hit the street, Burke following behind.

"You all right?" he asked.

"Everyone in town is going to be so confused when we break up."

He sobered, giving her a look that seemed to mask something deeper. "I think we all are."

BURKE DIDN'T KNOW what to think. Was he getting in too deep? Or was this meant to be? Maybe the two of them were just fabulous actors who had fooled the town...

Or maybe there was something hiding in their relationship, just waiting for him to notice it.

Instead of heading home like he should have in order to talk to Autumn and deal with his kitten, as well as work, he'd invited himself along to the Armstrong family dinner.

He followed Jill inside her parents' home, the scent of roast beef overpowering the bouquet he was carrying.

"It smells wonderful," he said, as the birthday woman peeked around the corner from what must be the kitchen. Her hands were deep inside large oven mitts and her hair was done up like she was going to a gala.

"Come in, come in. I'm just pulling the roast out of the oven. I'll say hi in a minute."

Burke steadied Jill as she removed her boots, the gift basket wobbling in her arms. He glanced up when someone said, "You must be Burke."

The woman coming down the hall looked so much like the Jill he'd married almost a year ago that he found himself taking a step back. She was gorgeous like Jill. Combine that with Jill's spark and it was a double whammy that made it obvious to him why they'd gotten together in the first place.

Only this woman was somehow flatter, lacking the spark and appeal that drew him to Jill. And not just because she didn't have the curves Burke had come to love.

"You must be Jill's sister, Jodi," he said.

"So pleased to meet her new man at long last," she said, placing a hand on her slim hip and twisting slightly as though showcasing herself. "I can't believe Jill's been keeping you hidden away like she thinks I'm going to steal you." She laughed, hand against her cleavage. "I'm *married*. Have been for years." She wiggled a finger laden by a rock that must have sent her husband back a decade or two in his retirement fund contributions.

"I'm married, too," he found himself saying. "Have been for months."

He heard Jill let out a snort of amusement.

"Is there anything I can do to help?" Burke asked as they entered the kitchen.

"Oh, I do like you," Jenilee said with a smile. She placed a hand on his cheek. "Thank you, but we're ready to eat." She flashed a glance at Jill, who set her gift basket on the table. "I really wish you could find a way to keep this one."

"What does that mean?" asked Jodi. Jill's eyes darted to her mother and Burke thrust the bouquet in between the women, figuring they hadn't let Jodi in on the secret.

"For the birthday gal."

Mrs. Armstrong's expressions softened and she gave him doe eyes. "Oh, Burke, honey. You're such a keeper." She sent Jill a pleading look.

"I try, Mrs. Armstrong."

"Call me Jenilee."

In the dining room Mr. Armstrong was already at the head of the table, a man Burke assumed to be Jodi's husband to his left. Two small girls ran to the other side of the table, falling into seats, leaving an empty spot between them.

Burke made a point of shaking Argo's hand. He went to do the same with Jodi's husband, but the man was watching something on his phone.

"Hi," he said in a tone the man couldn't ignore. "I'm Burke Carver." *Your brother-in-law, for the sake of all appearances and technicalities.*

He looked up. "Oh, hey. Gareth." He offered a loose handshake and went back to his phone.

What a dud. This was the superstar husband everyone was going on about? It made Burke want to try harder just to show him up. A lot.

"Auntie Jill, sit here," one of the girls said, patting the vacant seat.

"Yeah, sit between us," chimed her sister.

Jill shooed them into new seats so she could sit beside Burke. "This is Priscilla and Penelope," she said, making the introductions. "I call them the princess and the pea."

"I'm the pea because I bug Prissy lots," the youngest said with a giggle, getting a dark look from her sister.

Before long they were all settled at the table, Burke across from Gareth, Jill to Burke's right.

"So the two of you used to work together?" Burke asked Jodi in a lull in the conversation. She'd been fairly quiet, sizing up Jill and him through most of the meal.

"She told you about that?" Jodi asked, giving her sister a curious look.

An awkward silence fell over the table.

"They used to run a café together," Gareth said at long last. "Jill brought in her husband to help manage the finances. He neglected to pay the bills, then stole months' worth of income from the owners. Then he left." He gave a slight shrug and went back to shoveling food into his mouth.

Wow.

Jill was staring at her plate, strangely still.

The table was too quiet and Burke felt for her.

"Did you know I was married once, too?" he asked. "My ex took everything. I just about lost my business. It's a good thing she didn't or I never would have met Jill." He squeezed her hand and she glanced at him in surprise. "Maybe that's why we've connected the way we have." Her chin lifted and her eyes warmed with gratitude. "I've learned that sometimes failure takes us where we were truly meant to go and shows us what really matters." He leaned toward his wife, giving her a gentle kiss.

"Ew, kissing," Pea said, sliding lower in her seat until she was on the floor. "So gross."

Burke chuckled and released Jill, only to find that Priscilla had carrot sticks shoved up her nose. He let out a burst of surprised laughter.

Pea crawled out from under the table to see what was going on.

"It's a rare, horn-nosed flubber buster," he said.

"No, it's me!" Prissy pulled the carrots from her nose. "See?"

"Huh. You looked just like one." Burke took two of his own carrot sticks and shoved them under his upper lip so they hung down like fangs. "Guess what I am."

The girl scrunched up her face, thinking.

"Sabre-toothed booger nugget, obviously," Jill said, leaning closer to him.

Pea laughed, as did Burke, losing his carrot sticks. He glanced at Jill. She was smiling despite the rest of the table being completely serious.

Jodi sighed. "That's enough," she said to the girls. She turned to her sister. "Jill, you still owe me for the chocolates."

"Right." She stood. "I'll get that now before I forget. How did the fundraiser go?"

"The ballerinas were so precious at the trade show. Did you see them?"

Jill was fishing around inside her purse and frowning. "I must have left my wallet somewhere today. I'll pay you later."

Burke fished into his wallet. "I've got it."

"No, it's okay." Jill caught Jodi's curious glance and quickly changed her mind, adding, "Thanks."

"So? I hear you two got tattoos?" Jodi asked. "I thought you'd get the ring you have on layaway?"

"That's something Jill will treat herself with soon enough," Burke said. "We went with unconventional for our unconventional marriage."

Jill, to his surprise, wasn't wearing her leather bracelet, and had turned her wrist to display her half of the heart. It was a move that opened a spring of tenderness inside him, and without thinking, he leaned in, tangling his hands in Jill's long locks as he lowered his lips to hers and put on a show for all to see.

JILL TURNED to Burke under the porch light outside her apartment. She felt breathless and inexplicably happy. She wanted to throw her arms around him and laugh.

He'd been so wonderful it made her want to kiss him.

Again and again.

"Thank you for being Mr. Perfect."

"Perfect? Not complicated?"

"Oh, everything to do with you is complicated, and I'm sure my sister will get the whole story of our marriage soon enough. But it was fun pretending I had what she does. I fear that makes me a petty person."

"Sibling rivalry at its finest."

"Ever since the café, things have been a bit tense. I think she blames me for losing her job and I don't blame her one bit. I had blinders on."

"Don't be so hard on yourself. It sounds like the guy was a piece of work. And as for your sister, I think she's jealous."

"Of me?" Jill nearly laughed. That would be the day. Her twin had the perfect life and family. She got to stay home with the girls, make pretty scrapbooks of their lives, help out at school, and had a husband who hadn't stolen from the town she loved before leaving her high and dry. That looked pretty perfect to Jill.

"Yeah." Burke put his hands around her waist, holding her close.

"Yeah? Why?"

"You've got me, for one."

Jill laughed.

A window opened in the main house and Jodi hollered, "Quiet! I'm putting the girls to bed!"

Burke smiled. "See? Jealous that you're out here laughing like a newlywed, while she's inside with Mr. I Don't Care."

Jill quirked her head, then gazed over at the big house with the perfect garden, the shiny minivan in the driveway.

"Think about it," he said. "Jodi is stuck at home with the kids and a dud for a husband, and you're out living life. Career, handsome husband…"

"Who happens to have an oversized ego."

"Naturally, but I carry it well. Your dad looks out for you. Everyone loves you. You're the dauntless one out there, accomplishing things. Making a difference, working hard and risking change." He'd tugged her closer and she snuggled in, ready for another of those wonderful kisses. She'd been a bit embarrassed kissing him in front of her family, but at the same time had been thrilled, caught up in the moment and filled with such gratitude and love it had been difficult to care.

"You were married before?" she asked, her mind flitting back to that surprising news.

"Years ago. It's difficult, isn't it?"

She nodded.

"So this guy who stole from you? Do you want to talk about it?" he asked.

"Do *you*?" She looked up at him in surprise.

He shrugged and reached over to let them into the house. "You go first. Abbreviated version."

"Okay. I fell in love with what seemed like a great guy. He swept me off my feet. Wasn't part of the plan," she added wryly, knowing it would make Burke smile. He didn't disappoint her, the skin around his expressive eyes crinkling. "My sister and I were running and managing a local coffee place called The Café, and he offered to help. He seemed like a godsend." She paused, letting the old, familiar pain and humiliation slide over her. "Then things started to go south. He'd miss a vendor's payment. Someone's paycheck would bounce. But the place seemed to be doing okay. His excuses all seemed reasonable and he'd fix things right away. I didn't realize he was stealing until after he'd run off."

She collected herself before continuing, "He left me, left town. Jodi and I both lost our jobs, and it looked really bad that I'd not only married him, but let him have control over what I should have been managing on my own. The Johnsons—the owners—had said it was fine when they heard his credentials, but I was the one who'd vouched for him." She crossed her arms.

"My turn?" Burke asked.

Jill let out a soothing breath and nodded, glad for the lack of judgment and follow-up questions about how she'd overlooked every one of the warning signs.

"I, too, had thought I'd found someone trustworthy. I was ready to settle down and have a family. We were in love. We didn't fight. She left me a Dear John six months into our marriage. I didn't see it coming. She took everything that wasn't nailed to the ground, whether or not it was legally mine, and fought tooth and nail for everything else."

"My story's better."

Burke moved to Jill's side, taking her in a loose embrace once again. "And how's ours going to end?"

"Hopefully, a lot better than either of those. Then again, neither of us expects some glamorous happily ever after like you see in fairy tales."

Burke watched her for a moment. "That's true," he said at last, making her wonder what he'd been thinking, contemplating.

"I understand your desire to play it light and loose." She kissed him. It was a long and lingering kiss full of meaning. When she gently broke free, she said, "Sometimes it's safer to be alone."

CHAPTER 12

"Safer to be alone *together*." That's what Burke had said to Jill last night. Right before he'd taken her to bed, instead of heading home like he should have.

His night with Jill had been unlike anything he'd ever experienced. They'd been slow and patient, showing each other the things they remembered from their wedding night, reminding each other of what had brought them together in the first place.

He'd woken in the predawn light full of hope. Instead of slipping out to drive back to the city, he'd rolled over, pulling Jill close and falling back asleep.

Why not?

Nobody was going to break anyone's heart here. They knew what they'd signed on for, right?

But now, hours later and in the solitude of his car, driving away from Blueberry Springs, with nothing but the hum of tires on pavement for company, he felt as though he was on the verge of panic. Every blissful second of being with Jill last night was flooding through his mind. The feeling of being connected. The give and take of a true partnership. The trust.

With each new snippet of memory from the night before, one from his wedding night came up, swamping him and his ability to shove it all aside, and tell himself that none of it mattered. It felt as though his chest was going to crack open, and he had trouble catching his breath.

This was supposed to be light and loose.

She was going to leave him.

Leave him.

He'd put too much into it.

Burke pulled over suddenly, sending gravel flying as he slammed on the brakes, yanking on the wheel to park across the roadside turnout for the Blackberry River Trail.

He struggled to hold it together, but fear was hitting him like that pickup had his car: full force. Unrelenting. Leaving him helpless as it plowed into him, knocking him sideways.

He pulled at the neck of his sweater and stretched back in his seat so his lungs had more room to expand. He was having a heart attack. He needed oxygen. He needed 9-1-1.

He opened his car door, sucking in great gulps of the crisp mountain air. He stumbled, landing on his hands and knees on the gravel. The pain of his tearing flesh covering the heels of his hands grounded him. The pain was real. This was real.

He was still himself. He still had a home to go to. Still had a business she couldn't steal, due to their contract.

It was going to be okay.

He was still Burke Carver.

Slowly, his breathing began to regulate. Now all he needed to do was pull himself together.

An SUV drew up beside him and the driver got out, his movements stiff, giving Burke time to get to his feet, his knees screaming in pain.

"You okay? Oh, hey, Burke. Where are you off to?"

Of course it was someone he knew: Ethan Mattson, his techie.

Burke brushed the dirt from his pants and tried to act like everything was cool.

"You lose something?" Ethan was watching him, looking concerned. He'd definitely caught Burke sprawled on the ground like a baby.

"Yeah, probably just my mind. How's your morning so far?"

"I'm heading a few towns over to pick up some hothouse cucumbers for Lily. Her grand opening for the restaurant cleaned her out yesterday. She's freaking out, so I'm pretty much game to drive anywhere on the planet just to avoid the craziness." He chuckled, crossing his arms. "So you and Jill figuring out this long-distance marriage?"

That tightness in Burke's chest was back. "Trying to," he wheezed.

"She's a catch, and strong enough to keep your you-know-what in line." Ethan climbed into his vehicle with a grin. He put down his window. "By the way, I'm going to open up her test for the full site online tomorrow. Are you ready to hit the roof?"

"Surprise me."

"I won't have to." He sent Burke a grin full of meaning. "Jill will."

Ethan drove off, and Burke said to the whiskey jack perched in the evergreen towering above him, "I'd say she already has."

The question was what was he going to do about it?

JILL SNIFFED the bouquet of flowers that arrived at her All You office first thing Monday morning. Burke was seriously the best accidental husband ever. Her ex had never sent her flowers, nor had Devon. Meanwhile Burke, the husband who wasn't supposed to be, even recalled that she loved calla lilies.

Although what was it with yet another bouquet with beady-eyed teddy bears? Cute but strange. Though she definitely wasn't complaining.

And what was with having flowers sent all the way from the city? The deliveryman had said they were from Mr. Carver, as the card was unsigned. But didn't Burke shop local? Maybe it was because the local florist didn't deliver until after noon. Then again, she was certain they'd make an exception for Burke, as he'd been such a charmer on the weekend. He'd gone home yesterday and she'd missed him, wanting to call and see how his Sunday afternoon was going. But she hadn't. She'd shown maturity and restraint.

The weekend had been all about shoring up a facade, and yet it had felt so real. She wanted every day to be like that. They'd worked together, played together and more.

She sighed dreamily at the memory of Saturday night. Every moment had seemed full of meaning.

Jill adjusted the flowers on her desk, caught in a world of what-ifs, all of them circling around the possibility that their accidental marriage was actually meant to be.

It would be easy to brush it off as Burke simply playing a role. He was protective of his employees, and of her in turn, because he was protecting his assets, his business, his reputation. Not her personally.

She pulled labels off a sheet fresh from the printer, sticking them to her fingers as she got ready to place them on the orders for bulk cosmetics. She knew it wasn't him simply playing a role. Somewhere along the line things had shifted.

Her cell phone rang and her caller ID showed Zebadiah from We Win Your Love.

She tapped the green button, then the icon to put him on speaker so she could continue her task. "Hey, Zeb," she said, knowing the sound wouldn't carry beyond her office. "I was hoping you'd call." It was time to cancel her account once and for all.

"You didn't tell me you're married," Zeb said, a sharp edge to his tone.

Jill stopped placing stickers on order sheets.

"Oh. Right. That." She hadn't even thought of how it might look with her still having a WWYL account.

"Yeah, *that*. I didn't realize you liked cheater-cheater-pumpkin-eaters. You misrepresented yourself."

"It's not..." She caught herself before saying it wasn't real. To the outside world, it was. At least real enough.

Jill put a hand to her forehead, leaving the last sticker from her fingers behind. "I'm sorry, Zeb. Things got away from me." She peeled off the label, placing it on the order sheet in front of her. Wrong order. She set the papers aside, concentrating on the call.

"Your husband cheats, and you're on a dating site looking for someone on the side."

"It's not like that." Her voice was tight, surely making her sound like a liar.

"Being married goes against our terms of service. We've charged your credit card your nonrefundable annual subscription, and banned you from our site, as well as terminated your We Win Your Love contract. You should be ashamed of yourself."

He hung up and, trembling, Jill put her phone in her desk drawer, hoping that having it out of sight meant out of mind in regards to how she'd just been chewed out for her dishonesty.

She hoped Burke was doing better in the city and had managed to find a way to calm Autumn. Jill could understand how the governor's daughter might be reaching out to Burke if things were going south in her own life. He was the kind of man who made you feel as though everything would be okay even if logic told you otherwise. He just had that...certain something about him.

The card that had come with the flowers said one word. *Thanks.*

Jill smiled. The weekend had meant as much to Burke as it had to her?

Aw.

That made everything seem better.

Emma entered the office, bringing with her the scent of spring. It was late March and the earth, like Jill's heart, was full of hope, everything coming to life once again after a long period of dormancy.

Emma stopped when she saw the flowers. "Those yours?"

"They're from Burke."

"Things are going well?"

Jill nodded.

"So secretive."

"There's not much to say. We're an old married couple." She grinned like a fool.

"Sure. Nothing to say." Emma smiled, but let her off the hook by changing the subject. "How are your orders?"

"A bit slow over the weekend." Jill handed Emma a printout of the All You orders that had come in. Typically, it was slow over the weekend, as most businesses did their ordering midweek.

"I meant yours."

Jill felt the familiar jab of worry at the thought of filling the orders that were streaming in. There had been a few hiccups. Today was the first day her products were being offered to the entire site and also the first day she'd ever had a return—a large one at that. It had been a bulk order that had to be tossed out, as she couldn't risk resending the product since she didn't have anti-tampering packaging in place. That had hurt. All that wasted product.

There had also been a few new negative reviews. Originally she'd wanted to blame Autumn, as she felt like an easy target, but to have this number of bad reviews had to be due to more than some woman with a vendetta. Poor reviews were a part of business though, right? Emma got a few, as did Burke. And having no poor reviews might even look suspect, as no individual shopper loved everything.

But the one about the rash? She'd seen that post last night, and hadn't dared bring it up with Burke yet. The reviewer had even shared a photo, which looked ugly and scary. It could be an allergy, perhaps. That could happen, and Jill couldn't blame herself.

Anyway, she had to focus on the customers who loved her stuff and were leaving raving reviews and placing orders for their friends. Lots of friends. Ethan's system had sent her pages of orders that morning. And there would be more again tomorrow. And the day after that, keeping Rebecca and Joseph busy for even more hours than she'd initially promised them.

"What's wrong?" Emma asked.

"There are so many orders. It's great. I love it, but it's overwhelming."

Emma nodded in sympathy.

"How did you deal with everything when All You suddenly took off?"

Last spring Emma had released some honest, soul-baring videos on her beauty blog that had reached viewers around the world, causing a flood of orders for her all-natural cosmetics. Practically everyone in Blueberry Springs had stepped in to help, Jill even leaving her job at the town office to help Emma full-time. It had been exhilarating, but at the end of the day Jill had been able to leave her desk and put it out of mind until the next morning.

"On a personal level or a business level?" Emma asked.

"Personal level."

"Luke was my support system, handling many of the details to make sure everything at work went smoothly. With him taking care of business it meant that things in my personal life drifted back into place."

Jill nodded and twisted the end of her ponytail around her

fingers. She could see that she and Burke were going to have to realign her system once again, possibly taking out the bulk order option he'd been insistent upon, making her feel like a failure, as she couldn't seem to get it perfect. Things just kept interfering, messing with it all.

"Have you spoken to Burke about how you're feeling?" Emma asked gently. "Because if the business side is taken care of, the personal side will resolve itself, too. And vice versa. Just know that you're going to be very busy as your business grows. Be patient with him and your relationship. Everything will change from day to day."

They sat in silence for a moment, then Emma leaned forward. "So? Will there be a real wedding in the future, like Luke and I had in South Carolina at Christmas? Ginger has this most adorable dress that would look so cute on you. It's the one in her window." She caught Jill's expression. "If you don't like the long sleeves, Olivia could shorten them."

"We're already married." Jill began shifting papers on her desk, desperate to change the subject, her mind circling around their unsigned divorce papers. Papers she was no longer itching to sign.

"It's okay if you don't have a big wedding. I'm just happy how he's made you smile more."

The two women settled in to work, organizing a marketing campaign until noon.

"I'm heading down to Lily's restaurant for lunch. Did you want to join me?" Emma finally asked.

"I lost my wallet on the weekend and it hasn't shown up yet." Jill waved her brown paper bag lunch. "I'll eat here. I have some catching up to do, anyway."

"My treat."

She contemplated the peanut butter and jam sandwich she'd made for herself versus some of Lily's good cooking. "Okay, you've twisted my arm. Just give me a moment to finish sending these emails."

"Meet you there?" Emma said. "I have to make a stop along the way."

Jill finished her emails, and was reaching for her coat when her cell began ringing in the drawer.

It was Burke. Smiling, she answered.

"Jill?" Burke's tone pulled the smile off her face. "We need to talk."

"You've stopped singing Glenn Miller," Gulliver said, standing in the doorway to Burke's office. He came the rest of the way inside and closed the door. "Do you need me to send flowers?"

Burke shook his head. When he spent time with Jill in Blueberry Springs it became easy to become distracted and forget about the real world. But now, back in the city, with a little distance between them, he'd come to realize that not only was he losing his grip on his business and reputation, but he'd also taken his fake wife to bed and it had meant something. Maybe it was the way she approached him with hope lighting her eyes. The way he lost track of time when he was with her.

Jill couldn't leave him.

They were a team. A very good team. Except...now he had to tell her some bad news, and their mixing of business and pleasure might make a mess he wasn't ready to deal with.

"Maybe jewelry?" Gulliver asked.

"No, no gifts. But I need you to call Autumn. Tell her we need to discuss some things."

Gulliver sat down on the couch. "Think she'll take your calls after the press marked her as the wounded and betrayed?"

"I think she may have been behind it, actually."

"Really?" Gulliver was all ears.

"Yeah, and her meddling is the last thing I need."

"Especially with the pitch to Tiffer coming up."

Burke nodded. He was getting a stress headache just thinking about it.

"What are you going to do as counter-publicity?" Gully glanced down as though expecting his notebook and pen to be waiting on the couch cushion beside him. "Hang on. Your little weekend party that made the news...?"

Burke nodded.

"Smart. By the way, love the matching tattoos." He winked.

"Well, hopefully it's enough." Burke handed over a document sent from Ethan twenty minutes ago. "Because look at this."

"What are these?" Gulliver scanned the ratings and reviews from the website on Jill's products. A third of the ones that had come in over the weekend weren't what he would consider good. Plus the return rate had skyrocketed, thanks to a bulk order that had come back immediately—simply stating they'd ordered the wrong products—and putting a ding in their profits.

"Are they all this horrible?" Gulliver began flipping through the stapled sheets, reading the headlines.

"No, but a good chunk of them are. And Ethan just opened up the site so everyone gets the pop-up for her products today."

"Well, Monday mornings are usually slow at least," Gulliver said. He kept flipping, skimming. He winced when he came across one with a photo, claiming that the rash was caused by her products. "This isn't good."

"I know," Burke barked. He strived to push down the panic that kept threatening to rise up.

One star—would have given it zero if that was an option.

Worst money spent this year.

I can't believe Sustain This, Honey allowed this crap on their site. I used to think this was a good store and a company who cared about their customers.

"There are some good ones, though," Gulliver said supportively.

The good still outweighed the bad, but for how long?

"Call Ethan, tell him to pull back on going wide and to temporarily shut off the review feature. And curb the bulk orders, too. Jill can't afford returns." Burke pinched the bridge of his nose. "Never mind. I'll call."

He cursed and dialed Ethan, giving him the commands. "You know what? No. Just pull all of Jill's products until further notice."

"What?" Gulliver was gaping at him, and the techie's own verbal surprise echoed over the line.

"Don't hit yourself in the chin, jerking your knee in reaction to this," Ethan said. "It's probably a troll."

"How could it be a troll? This is way too pervasive." Hadn't Jill tested her products? Why hadn't he demanded more from her before subjecting his own brand and reputation to this onslaught? He knew better than this.

He'd already learned this lesson before. Never partner with a woman who has less to lose than you do.

"I'll suppress reviews for now," Ethan said, "and I'll put a size limit on the site so people can't order bulk."

Burke could hear the reassuring sound of fingers clacking over a keyboard through the phone's speaker. Ethan was already on it.

Burke owed him a bonus. A bonus he hoped to pay all his employees if he could just survive the next six months.

"I'll also go back to the test version, where only a fraction of site visitors see her stuff at checkout."

"Thanks." Burke tapped a pen on his desk. This was going to put them behind their projections, but they might still be able to raise enough capital to get where he needed to be in time for next month's pitch to Get There Media. Assuming Tiffer was still taking his calls at that point.

"Did you notice the increase in cart abandonment for those who didn't get Jill's pop-up at check out over the weekend?" Ethan asked. He sounded half-distracted, his typing still echoing through the phone.

"What? No." Burke hadn't gotten that far into the reports.

"Yeah, totally up. It's like customers were trying to get the pop-up with Jill's products when they were checking out, and if they didn't, they abandoned their cart and started over."

"Really?"

"Yeah, maybe. Keep watching the numbers. Don't throw the baby out with the... Hey, I gotta go. Zach is calling."

"Who's Zach?"

"Forrester. He does digital investigations for Logan Stone's personal security business here in town. If there's a troll, he'll find it. I'll add his services to your bill."

Burke hung up, more confused than ever.

He imagined his employees on the other side of the wall. Their lives. The way they depended on this job, on him. Just like his aunt had when he'd been nineteen and scared of failing her. Scared she wouldn't get better, that he'd lose their home by not figuring things out in time.

But he always figured things out in time. He was Burke Carver.

JILL HAD ENDED up canceling lunch with Emma, as well as taking the afternoon off so she could meet with Burke in the city. He hadn't disclosed why he needed to talk to her, but his tone of voice told her everything she needed to know—it was bad.

By the time she reached his office's building she was a bundle of nerves.

Tiffer had to have told him no deal, and so Burke was going to cut her loose. The fear and hurt she felt at the idea told her everything she needed to know. She'd fallen for Burke.

As she opened the doors to the building, she whispered to herself, "Breathe, Jill. Don't assume the worst. Just keep breathing."

She walked past the reception desk toward the elevators.

"Ma'am? You need a visitor pass for security and identification purposes," the guard called.

"I haven't needed one yet," Jill grumbled to herself. It was the same scrawny guy who had given her a difficult time outside the workout room last month. That already felt like years ago. "I'm here to see Burke Carver."

"Is he expecting you?"

Her nerves getting the best of her, Jill marched over, placing both palms flat on the counter separating her from the security agent.

"Yes," she said clearly, "my husband is expecting me." She turned on her heel and marched to the elevators, grateful when one opened as soon as she pushed the up button.

Gulliver wasn't at his desk and she opened the door to Burke's office, letting herself in. "Your building's security is over-the-top."

"They warned me you'd breached the gate and were storming the castle."

She sat in the chair across from him. "What's so important I had to come immediately?"

At one point during the drive she'd let herself fantasize that the desperate, firm edge to his voice over the phone had been borne from his need to kiss her. One glance at his expression killed that fantasy faster than a bird hitting a window.

He pushed a pile of papers across the desk.

She hesitated, then accepted the stack and began to read.

They were reviews for her products and every single one was horror inducing. They were like the one about the rash…only lots more of them. She'd never heard anyone say anything so horrible and she found it difficult to inhale past the pain.

"These are all from your site this weekend?" she managed to croak.

She'd done as Luke Cohen, the former CEO of his family's major corporation, told her. She'd stretched, reached and challenged herself. She'd relinquished some control and left room for the unexpected.

This wasn't the "unexpected" she'd been seeking.

"I had Ethan suppress the review feature. These came in over the past thirty-six hours or so."

Jill lifted a hand to her mouth. Noticing it was trembling, she lowered it again.

"I am so sorry," she said quietly.

"Did you test your products?"

"In a laboratory?"

"At all?"

"They're centuries-old. Nobody's ever complained."

Jill looked at the papers trembling in her left hand. How had she allowed this to happen? What if someone got hurt? She could be sued.

This was horrible for Burke's reputation. Everything she did now seemed to affect him and his reputation. And yes, she knew the possibility of Autumn being the one to drag his name through the mud wasn't her fault, but it felt like it was. Just a little bit.

She looked at the reviews again. *This* was definitely her fault. This wasn't one person having a hissy fit and trying to pull her down.

But why now? She'd been making these products for years without any customer complaint. But she hadn't been selling them in these quantities. Had dissatisfaction been happening, just on a smaller scale, and because she'd been selling mostly to family and friends they hadn't told her?

How could she shield Rebecca and her fellow Ute from the

bad publicity that was surely coming down the line? And what would happen to Burke and his company?

Jill swallowed hard. This was where she lost everything. Not just for herself, but for those she cared about. She could feel the chill seeping into her bones.

There was only one thing she could do.

BURKE SAT at his desk in silence for a good fifteen minutes after Jill had gone home, his mind refusing to engage. She'd vowed to come up with a plan.

Another plan.

He was so sick of plans. Sick of them not working out. Sick of her feeling like she had to have everything perfect. Life wasn't perfect. Business wasn't perfect. Hadn't she learned that yet? The biggest mistakes were often ones he'd never regret because they'd taught him what had gotten him to where he was now.

The way Jill had refused to meet his eye after reading the reviews left him with a sense of unease like he'd never felt before.

Something wasn't right. And not just the email that popped up on his monitor, shaking him from his trance. It was from Tiffer, with the subject line: *U 2 R perfect 4 ea other.*

The short preview of the text inside said, "Unfortunately, this isn't providing the image..."

Burke almost deleted the email before catching himself. He'd read it.

Later.

He pressed the button that connected him to Gulliver. "I need the idea files."

Moments later his assistant appeared with a stack of dog-eared blue file folders, worn with use. This pile of picked over ideas might be all he had left.

"We need just one thing," Burke said, as he spread papers across his desk. "Just one thing."

One thing to make his business boom, and keep his mind off the woman and plethora of problems that had appeared after a weekend of bliss. Because if he'd learned anything during his years of dating, it was that if it started to look good, it meant it was about to fall apart.

CHAPTER 13

At nine o'clock that night, Jill worked on shoveling ice cream from the carton straight into her mouth, then moaned and clutched her head when brain freeze set in. So much for the whipped cream, syrup, cookie dough chunks and sprinkles saving her.

Emotionally, everything felt numb. She wanted to cry, but the tears wouldn't fall. How had she failed Burke so spectacularly? How had the ancient formulas gone so wrong and for so many? She couldn't blame Burke or Rebecca or Joseph for that. It had been her. All her on those batches. She couldn't even blame a distraught Autumn.

What was she going to tell the elders? They'd been excited to hear she was reaching a new audience and through a company that respected Mother Earth. They'd trusted her. And she'd failed. Failed them all. Everyone.

Not only that, but Zeb had told someone that she'd been using his dating service while married. The story was all over social media despite him being bound by a privacy agreement, and without a doubt Tiffer Garbanzo had heard about it and was ready to cut Burke loose.

She was losing everything. She ought to sue Zeb. And yet she knew that wasn't the answer to her problems. Not by a long shot.

Her phone rang and she idly flipped it over to check the screen. Caller ID said it was Gulliver.

"Gulliver?" she asked, half worried, half intrigued. He'd never called her before.

"Jill? I only have a minute before Burke comes back for more brainstorming."

"Did he see the thing about the dating service? I wasn't...cheating."

Why was she defending herself? She should be defending her products.

"According to Andrea's replacement there's been something strange with Burke's credit. She said that you borrowed additional funds."

"I didn't. I only took that first amount." Jill felt cold. Colder than the ice cream working its way through her digestive system.

"Well, somehow every last dime of his available credit has been claimed—by you."

"But..."

"It happened this morning."

"But I—I didn't do it. I'll talk to Wini at my bank. It has to be a mistake."

"I'm going to have to tell Burke about this in the morning. You have until then to sort things out."

"Thanks, Gulliver. I really appreciate the heads-up."

"I know."

"Why are you doing this?"

"You're good for him." He lowered his voice, his words quick. "I really hope my gut is right about you and that you'll protect him like I trust you will."

She nodded, even though he couldn't see her and had already ended the call.

She hadn't had a chance to protect her sister from the

firestorm of gossip after Hayes had left her and ruined the café. But Jill had a do-over this time. A shot across the bow. If she was going down, she wasn't going to take the person she loved along for the ride.

Burke used to like mornings. He used to find them full of optimism and hope. Things to get done, goals to reach. But today he didn't feel any of that.

It was all straight uphill. All crap, and fires to put out.

Jill had borrowed even more against his available credit. There hadn't been that much left—not even enough for a nice new car—but she'd taken it.

He hadn't expected that.

He'd thought this time was different, but he'd been blinded once again by the way she made him feel. Just like his ex-wife had.

Burke rubbed his eyes. How many times did he have to play the fool before he'd learn?

"Burke, Jill is on line one." It was Gulliver, through his intercom's speaker.

Of course she was.

Burke picked up the phone, hitting the blinking light to patch him through. "Gulliver, hang up." He waited for the click before continuing.

But it was Jill who spoke first, her tone sure and determined. "Wini says she didn't request more credit against you. She said the loan came from a branch in the city. Logan Stone said he's requested footage from their cameras to see who came in for the meeting."

"Wini? The Blueberry Springs bank manager?"

"Yes."

"And Logan?"

"He works security with Zach Forrester—the man Ethan has looking into the possibility of a troll. But Burke...?"

"Yes."

"I think with everything that's gone on it would be best if we pulled our deal." She continued on before he could react, like if she stopped talking she might forget what she was going to say. "Because what if it isn't a troll? What if my products do cause rashes? I'm not helping you or STH, and every day that I stay with you and your business is another day I make things worse. Zeb told the world I was using his dating site while married. I didn't date anyone, but my resulting reputation isn't one Tiffer Garbanzo wants you to have."

He was losing her. She was leaving him. She'd taken what she could and now that their very short honeymoon was over...

When would he ever learn?

"The world thinks I was cheating on you with Autumn," he said quietly. "Yet Tiffer emailed and said you and I are perfect for each other. We're still in this together."

"Did you see today's news?"

He turned to his computer, dreading what he might find. After the dating site thing he'd told Gulliver not to bother forwarding the daily sweep of social media buzz around him and the company. Or at least not to tell him about it unless it was absolutely vital. Maybe that had been a bad idea.

"Everyone knows about our fake marriage."

"Are you kidding me? How?"

"I don't know."

What was next? The shoes he'd stolen in high school? Who had he ticked off?

Other than Autumn.

Because this felt big. This felt personal.

Jill's voice had gone quiet, flat. "There's also buzz about my products not meeting federal guidelines, even though they're exempt. You don't need that kind of media focus on you right now as you try to expand. If you have a chance it's without me. Pull my products from your site." There was a pause before she added, "I've signed the divorce papers and I've had them couriered to the city. They should be there by noon."

No tears. No emotion. Nothing. She hadn't even tried to find a way to resolve things.

Get out while the getting was good.

His chest hurt where the air bag had thumped him. He rubbed the spot, knowing it wasn't the already healed bruise that was causing the pain.

It was Jill.

JILL CALLED IN SICK.

Emma asked if she was okay and she squeaked out a yes before ending the call and sobbing into the fur of her worried pooch.

Hours later, after her dad came by to walk Taylor as usual—Jill stayed hidden in the bathroom so her puffy eyes wouldn't give her away—there was a knock at her door. She half hoped it was Burke here to beg her to stay. That's how pathetically she'd fallen for him. The man who'd said nothing when she'd told him she was couriering the signed divorce papers.

The knock came again.

"Jill, I know you're home," Jodi called. "Dad told me."

Jill unlatched the door for her sister, knowing Jodi wouldn't leave otherwise. While her dad would use his key and march in, Jodi would just knock. And knock. And knock. Jill figured she might as well let her gloating sister in, and get the humiliation over with.

Jodi took one look at her and said, "I'll be right back."

Jill shrugged and kicked the door closed with her foot, heading back to bed.

A few minutes later her sister let herself back in. She had a full chocolate maven pie from Benny's.

"How did you get that? Leif said he'll only sell it by the slice."

Her sister shrugged and smiled, not saying a word as she turned to head to the kitchen. Despite the warm, secure comfort of her bed, Jill got up and followed her.

Jodi had gone to the cupboard and was getting down plates, dishing them each a generous slice. She sat at the kitchen table across from Jill.

"Are you okay?" Her sister was uneasy, but the genuine kindness and concern set Jill off and she began to sob. She didn't know whether to wipe her eyes or her nose first. Her sister was beside her in a flash with tissues, rubbing small circles on her back and making soothing noises.

"I'm getting a divorce—" Jill hiccuped "—*again*. Our marriage was fake. An accident, but I thought—"

"That wasn't fake."

"It was. It felt real, but it wasn't. We got drunk, got married, then pretended it was real so he could get a business deal to better his company, but I messed it up."

Jodi rubbed a circle, her palm warm and comforting. Jill could hear the confusion in her tone as she said, "But it looked real. More real than what I have."

She looked up in surprise. Jodi gave her a sheepish half smile. "As much as I talk up Gareth...I feel like I'm the one always putting in the effort." She sighed, sat down again and shoveled a chunk of pie into her mouth, her eyes so sad. "But what can I say?" Jodi added lightly, "I've always been unlucky in love."

"You? You've always had a boyfriend. And you're about to celebrate your tenth wedding anniversary."

"I always had a boyfriend because someone was always leaving me, making room for someone new."

"Oh."

"You connect with men. I could never figure out how."

"Because I'm one of the guys," Jill said bitterly. "Burke didn't even fight for me."

Jodi toyed with her spoon. "I was really jealous of you two, you know. The way he looked at you." She shook her head. "I can't believe..."

"Yeah." Jill kept her eyes averted. She'd seen that look, too. Believed it enough to allow herself to fall.

Jodi's palms smacked the top of the table. She looked ready to jump up and take on the world in Jill's defense. That was the sister she missed. The sister she'd had before she'd lost the café.

"I'm sorry," Jill said, feeling herself tense. They'd never really talked about the whole café thing, or what Hayes had done to them and their reputations. She'd been too afraid to, and whenever she'd broach the subject her sister would usually get kind of weird and change the topic.

"For what?"

"For the café. I'm sorry I lost you your job."

Jodi watched her for a long moment. "You know I don't blame you."

"How could you not?"

"I didn't see what he was doing, either. I don't know. It's in our past."

"But I know that my mistakes must have affected your image around town," Jill insisted.

"So do all the good things you do. The good with the bad, right? Sure, I was mad at you for trusting him. But I was also mad at myself." Jodi wouldn't look up and for a moment Jill forgot her own problems, reaching across to take her sister's hand.

"Why?" she probed gently.

"Because I felt like I'd let you down. You were always looking out for me, telling me what the guys were saying, letting me know before someone dumped me so I'd be prepared. But I felt like I'd let you down by not being able to do the financials for the restaurant. You had to ask for his help. If I'd been better at math then maybe it wouldn't have happened. Maybe you'd still be married."

"He was a con artist, Jodi."

"I know…" She rolled her spoon between her fingers and shrugged. "But maybe he wasn't before he met us. I don't know." She looked embarrassed at her confession.

"You can't blame yourself for what he did."

"I know. But it's hard."

"True." Jill let out a tremendous sigh.

"But good can come from bad. Because I had nothing else to do after losing that job, I had two wonderful girls." Her expression softened, revealing genuine love and gratitude. "So don't ever feel bad. Everything happens for a reason, and it doesn't matter how much we plan, the things that were meant to be happen. And always will."

"Way to make a gal feel powerless." Jill stood to take their empty plates to the sink.

"So what happened with you and Burke?" Jodi asked. "Is it just that social media stuff?"

Jill came back to the table and lowered her head to its surface and groaned. "And my products suck."

"What do you mean?"

She quickly filled her in on their marriage deal and all the ways since then that she'd torpedoed Burke's business life, from borrowing credit to the latest credit mystery to the bad press to the bad reviews and bad products and her inability to make everything magically perfect.

"So you filed for divorce?" Jodi asked, looking surprised.

"I'm trying to prevent things from becoming worse than they already are."

"I admire that you're trying to protect him, but did you try asking him what he wants?"

"He wants that deal. It's important, and everything to do with me takes him one step further from reaching it."

"So you're divorcing him?"

"Yes."

"Even though you love him?"

"Yes." Jill's eyes filled with tears. Oh, why did she have to love him? That complicated everything.

"So you're overanalyzing and overcompensating by creating a million plans to ensure life doesn't happen."

"No."

"Life *happens*. Every misstep you've ever made brought you to where you are now. Not just your plans, but the mistakes, too. They brought you to Burke."

"That's a romantic thought, but you know why I stopped going to riflery meets? Because I showed up that one time thinking I was good enough, that I didn't need a backup plan, and I embarrassed myself when things went wrong. I know when I'm in over my head and when it's time to back out."

"You're afraid to fail."

"No, I'm just preventing it."

"You thought he was going to leave you, so you left him first."

"We're not talking about my marriage. We're talking about business."

"You were free with Burke. You never were with Hayes or Devon. You let yourself go and be who you truly are with him, and it was like watching you grow and shine."

Jodi reached across the table, tapped the leather bracelet Jill had slapped over her tattoo. "He's the right man. What if you're wrong about this?"

Jill wanted to be wrong. With all her heart.

She just couldn't see Burke's world being better for having her in it.

"So what am I supposed to do?" she asked Jodi.

"Stop caring about what everyone else thinks for once. Seriously, Jill. And go win him back, of course. Don't you ever watch movies?"

"Just *Die Hard*. And the plan is to get my life back, not mess up his even more."

"No wonder Dad likes you best. *Die Hard?* Really?" She was teasing, none of that resentment that used to be there showing itself.

"And you're suggesting romantic movies as a way to solve my life's problems. No wonder Mother loves you best."

Jodi laughed and Jill felt the world fall back into place.

"I missed you. Missed this."

"Me, too."

They sat quietly for a while, until Jill, feeling the need to pull her life back together, began tidying the kitchen. The first bouquet she'd received was fading, a sad reminder of how things had changed since their party at Mandy's. She pulled the bear from the dying arrangement and put him on the table while tossing out the flowers.

Jodi was staring at the bear when she turned around. "Why do you have a nanny cam?"

THE DOOR to Burke's office opened and Gulliver marched in.

"Gulliver, not now." He shut down his laptop and checked the time. He had a flight in less than two hours and he'd planned to hand-deliver a proposal to a local marketing company on his way to the airport. It was small potatoes, but if they could somehow create a cult brand around his products it would be a step in the right direction.

The last few days had sucked. A lot.

He was divorced. Again.

He'd hated every second of it.

Gulliver tossed a sheet of paper onto Burke's desk.

"I said *not now*."

"Profits are down because you cut Jill's Botanicals loose."

"Are you trying to make me angry? Because it's working. We don't talk about Jill in the office."

"The office is the only place I ever see you," Gulliver said. "Because you never leave."

"And for the record, she cut herself loose."

"Well, in case you are curious, it was a troll."

"I don't have time for fairy tales. I'm trying to save this place," Burke grumbled, hating the way he'd perked up over the idea that a troll had caused havoc on the way Jill's products had been slammed.

He stood, shoving things into his briefcase.

"Ethan's guy, Zach, ran a program—Ethan's really cute, by the way. Totally gruff and wounded, but he has this sweet center—"

"He's married and straight," Burke stated, struggling against the thread of hope that had lit up inside him. What if Jill truly was innocent? Was there a way he could convince her to come back?

He might as well take his hopeful heart and smash it now.

"I merely complimented Ethan, I didn't suggest I was going to do something about it," Gulliver scolded. "And anyway, I'm officially engaged. Emilio said yes."

Burke reached the door to his office before realizing he'd forgotten the marketing proposal on his desk. He snagged it and exited his office, Gulliver at his side.

"Oh, don't be a poopy pants, Burke. Be happy for me," Gulliver said with a pout.

"I'm happy for you," he replied grudgingly.

Gulliver handed him pink papers. "Don't forget your boarding pass."

"I have it on my phone already."

"I don't trust technology." He pressed the colorful papers into Burke's hand.

No, he didn't trust *Burke*. Gully had found Burke's lost phone twice in the past week and was likely afraid his boss would end up at the gate without a pass.

"Put it in your briefcase now so you don't lose it."

Burke did as he was told. "Seriously though? Pink?"

"Sorry, I had it in the printer from the breast cancer awareness campaign brochure mockup and I didn't want to waste more paper than I already was." Gulliver continued with his original conversation thread as though he hadn't missed a beat. "Anyway, Ethan's brilliant man figured out the troll thing. I told you not to assume the worst in Jill."

"I didn't."

"The troll was hired by someone here in town."

"How do you know?"

Gulliver bowed in a graceful flourish as Burke headed for the elevator. "I know everything." He handed over a folder Burke hadn't noticed he'd been carrying. "It's also in the report from Ethan and Zach. I took the liberty of forwarding a copy to Jill."

Burke got into the elevator and pushed the down button, thinking. He didn't like this. He also didn't appreciate the implications. He'd been too quick to distrust Jill and she'd been too quick to cut herself loose.

Neither of them had fought for what they had.

The fact was, she hadn't tested her products, and he hadn't performed due diligence before subjecting his brand's trust and image to the partnership.

No. Wait. That was all the troll's doing, wasn't it? The products were in fact good. He flipped open the report, kicking his foot out to prevent the elevator door from closing.

"Everything I need is in here?"

"Everything."

He gave a sharp nod. "Thank you, Gulliver."

"Should I call Ethan and give him the go-ahead to reinstate her products and the reviews feature?"

"No."

"No?"

He let the elevator door close this time.

When he reached the lobby he was met by an out-of-breath Gulliver.

"How did you get—"

"Ethan says we could sue whoever it is for loss of sales and defamation. They're messing with your business, Burke." He added quietly, "Your marriage, too."

"It wasn't like that."

"You liked her."

Burke felt the weight of sorrow and loss settle over him again. He missed her. Missed believing it was real and that she'd been genuine.

But he'd also learned a hard lesson. It was never genuine even when it felt like it was.

"The fact is, Gulliver, she stole from me by using my credit. Twice." He held up his hand, knowing Gulliver would argue that she hadn't meant to dive into his financial credit and use it for herself. But Burke wasn't born yesterday. He knew accidents didn't happen twice. "I'm not going to welcome someone back into my life if I can't trust them."

CHAPTER 14

"I don't know," Jill said to her sister. Jodi was standing at Jill's closet, trying to choose an outfit for her to wear to the Metro Conference. "I don't know if I can put myself out there. Burke was happy for me to leave. Maybe this is a bad idea."

Her sister paused thoughtfully, a hanger dangling off her finger. "Didn't you say that his company is like family to him? Maybe it's not about you. Maybe it's about him feeling as though everything he holds dear was being threatened, and so it was easier to let you go than to fight for you."

"Yeah, but still. I was his *wife*."

"Wife before life?" Her sister laughed at the joke. "Oh, I like that. Let's make that a saying. It's better than 'happy wife, happy life.'" She resumed flipping through Jill's wardrobe. She held out a dress, her eyebrows raised.

Jill shook her head, then let out a shuddery sigh. "I think nice pants and this peasant thingy is good enough."

Jodi pursed her lips, holding a different blouse in front of Jill. "You definitely need to go to him," she said. "This is an amazing second chance. One year later. Same conference and everything."

She tilted her head to the side, analyzing Jill's appearance. "What about some mascara?"

"Burke liked the real me." The one she didn't have to try to be. It was wonderful. "And I'm trying to win him the contract, Jodi. Not win a pageant."

"I don't see why those have to be mutually exclusive."

Jill ignored the comment. "He got the report about the troll and didn't invite me back into his life, or offer to renew our business partnership even though it was profitable. Maybe he doesn't even want the Tiffer pitch now. Maybe he found something better."

"Yeah, yeah. Business is boring. Go win him back like they do in the movies." Her sister began putting the rejected outfits back into Jill's closet, giving up on trying to dress up her twin. "What are you going to say when you see him?"

"I'm going to show up at his meeting with Tiffer and pretend I'm his wife so he gets the deal."

Without thought she caught herself peering around the small space, on the lookout for something that might be spying on her. Like the nanny cam her sister had found. The beady-eyed bear in her office had been spying on her the whole time, as well, just like the one at home. She felt violated knowing that the bear had been reporting back to someone...somewhere. The sense of invasion of privacy had left her chilled. And paranoid.

"And then what are you going to do or say? To Burke? To win him back?" Jodi prompted. She was really hoping for a happily ever after. So was Jill, even though she knew that was a very long shot.

Would she have the courage to put her heart out there? She'd been missing Burke something terrible and she loved him.

"What will you tell him?" Jodi prodded, coming at her with a pair of shoes—flats, thankfully.

Jill hated feeling so hopeful, of having people on her side, knowing her plan could fail and she'd disappoint not only herself, but everyone else, too.

"She's going to tell Burke the truth," said a deep Australian voice. A man darkened the bedroom doorway with his bulk. It was Logan Stone, with Taylor beside him, panting happily, pink tongue lolling out. The investigator handed her a dossier. "This is everything Zach and I found. And might I suggest you find yourself a real guard dog?"

"He specializes in planting land mines out in the yard. I'm impressed you got past them." The dossier felt heavy in Jill's hands and she sat on the edge of the bed, contemplating the document's girth. "So what is the truth?"

"Tell him about the identity theft as an icebreaker."

"I already did."

It had been that call that had given her hope, then dashed it like a sudden storm throwing a schooner helplessly against the rocks. She'd needed all her resolve to reach for her phone, and had been relieved when Gulliver patched her through immediately.

Burke had promptly picked up, cool and professional.

"Burke, it's Jill. I'm sorry for any grief the credit situation caused."

He'd grunted in reply.

"It turns out my missing wallet ended up in the hands of an identity thief. I've filed a report with the police, filed an identity theft report, and let my bank know."

"So will the bank relinquish the available credit to me?" She'd heard the hope, the softening in his voice.

"It takes time. Months maybe. I want to—"

"Thanks for your call." And he'd hung up. That had been the rocks her proverbial schooner had been helplessly tossed against.

It had been a week since then and she'd been silly to think he'd treat her otherwise. She'd ruined his life, destroyed his chances of success, then divorced him to boot.

She was silly to think going to the conference would change any of that. That she'd be wanted there. Needed.

She clutched the stack of papers from Logan. But maybe with this dossier she could find the truth, sort through it all and show Burke that beneath the mess there was something still between them that was worth exploring and saving. Something unrelated to business. Something that felt a lot like love.

"There's one person behind everything," Logan stated. "Everything from the calls with nobody on the other end of the line, the leaked personal information, to the stolen identity, bad reviews and bulk product returns. You made yourself a sizable enemy who hired some professionals. This person is going to have a lot of protection. The good news is that you have Zach on your side and he did everything on the up-and-up. We'll catch them. Make them pay."

Jill flipped open the dossier and saw the name she'd feared seeing. The culprit.

She closed it again and stood. "I need to talk to Burke."

BURKE STRAIGHTENED his tie and smoothed his shirt. He'd spent Easter alone with his aunt, feeling lonely and as though he was barely going to make it through. It had been three weeks since his divorce and he felt off his game.

Not a great way to feel when about to go into the biggest pitch of his year.

"Here goes nothing," he muttered to himself as he let himself into the suite Tiffer had booked for his Metro Conference meetings.

"Tiffer!" he called boisterously as soon as he entered, spotting the man sunk deep into the cushions of a sofa parked near the floor-to-ceiling window overlooking the city below. "How are you doing? Good trip over?"

"Look what the cat dragged in." Tiffer stood, buttoning his suit jacket. "No wife?"

Was this where he got kicked out? The expression on the businessman's face proved he hadn't expected him to come, even though he'd technically never canceled. The email he'd sent ages ago had been sour. Saying Burke and Jill deserved each other because they had no clue how to behave like two stable business partners.

Which was probably true.

"Jill can't make it." Burke offered him an awkward handshake. Tiffer barely completed it, his lack of interest apparent.

"Because she divorced you?" he asked.

"Mutual parting. Never mix business and pleasure," Burke said mildly.

"Funny you say she can't make it, because I saw her in the lobby earlier. We had a good chat."

Jill? She was here? Why? And why had she chatted with Tiffer?

Burke avoided eye contact as he sorted through the implications of Jill being here. He gestured to a cart with what looked like fresh brewed coffee. "May I?"

"Help yourself." Tiffer gestured to his team, who were crowded around a laptop in the dining nook off to the right. "Boys?" He tipped his head toward the sitting area.

The group settled in and Burke tried to keep smiling, act as though this was the deal he'd always wanted. That everything was fine and that he had the money should Tiffer say yes.

"So what do you think you have that we can't live without?" the man asked. He pushed back in the cushions, uncrossed his arms to check his smart watch, then crossed them again.

"As you know, Sustain This, Honey is a—"

"You need to change your name. Rebrand."

Burke bit his tongue. "My assistant and team—"

"Sith Lord."

ACCIDENTALLY MARRIED

"Pardon me?" Burke was struggling to keep up with Tiffer, to not react to the disdain that was thick in the room.

"STH. Sustain This, Honey. All you're missing is an *i* and you're the lord of Sith. A Sith Lord. Linked to the dark side like you're a part of *Star Wars*. Not the look you're going for, I'm sure." He smiled tightly. "And your sassy rebranding idea has potential, but it narrows your niche."

"Actually, we've been working on that and the feedback from our community has been quite positive. We've also lined up some local marketing contracts and the outlook for growth has been very positive." Just not quite as positive as it had been when he and Jill had been partners.

"So far nothing has been amazing about your trajectory. Jill's Botanicals were doing well and yet you pulled them. Why?"

Burke inhaled slowly and focused on the question, knowing Tiffer was really asking about his ability to handle risk. "We had a troll. An attack."

"One? Isolated, I hear?"

Tiffer checked his watch again, exposing a wrist tattoo that made Burke think of his own, of Jill's. He still hadn't had it removed, but he'd finally gotten as far as making the appointment.

Burke cleared his throat. "Yes, just one attack as we promptly shut things down. Jill thought it would be better for STH if she no longer partnered with us."

"Didn't you have a contract?"

"We did. I let her out of it."

"One attack and you rolled over and gave up?"

"It was complicated."

Tiffer smirked at his word choice.

"I think our track record and growth show we're a viable company, ready for global expansion." Burke passed sales data and projections to the man beside him. "Since talking to you last we've partnered with a few local businesses, and our new marketing contract is working on reaching a few select niches that you'll see on page five."

Tiffer didn't look at the packet before he said, "You aren't profit oriented."

"I have people who depend upon me. I churn a profit."

"So do I." Tiffer leaned across the small table that separated them. "You need to stop thinking about everyone else and start thinking about lining your pockets. About the real world and what you can take from it."

"I run an ethical company and I believe in treating my employees the way they should treat our customers. Like family."

"I hear you have credit issues."

"My wife's identity was stolen."

"I thought you were divorced."

"We are."

"So you give up when things get tough?"

"No."

"But you did."

"No, she did."

"Why?"

"To…" Burke closed his eyes, opened them again, knowing that what he was about to say was the truth. Truth that wasn't about him and his past or even his fears. It was about Jill trying to do the right thing for him.

Because she loved him.

Truly loved him.

"She wanted to protect me as well as the company."

He felt ashamed of himself, the truth was so blatant. A truth he didn't want to see. Instead of battening the hatches to weather the storm together, they'd taken separate lifeboats and cut the lines that had tethered them, made them stronger and more stable.

"Have you seen this?" Tiffer held up what looked like some sort of file with Autumn Martinez's name on it.

"What's that?"

"Your troll. The thing your wife was protecting you against." Tiffer paused to let it sink in.

Autumn had been behind all this? That hardly seemed possible. When Burke had finally managed to meet with her, she'd been pale, distant. Not clingy or needy. He'd been relieved and hadn't questioned it, but now he did.

Had she known the gig was up?

"I told you playing around was going to get you in trouble," Tiffer said. "But I like your determination, Burke. Not a lot of men would have the balls to come in here today. That shows me something. That and the loyalty you build in those around you. Well, not in Autumn's case." He gave a wry smirk. "But in the case of your ex-wife. She went to bat for you today, to convince me that you and your company were what I'm seeking."

Burke wasn't surprised that Jill had done that for him, but it added to his own sense of failure for assuming the worst in her and letting that taint everything he saw—or thought he saw.

"However," continued Tiffer, "your reputation is in the toilet with this governor's daughter business. If we're going to work together you'll have to go through a severe overhaul. Join a church. Do something big to show you've changed your ways."

While Tiffer talked, Burke flipped through the file on Autumn. She was in some serious trouble. Identity theft, public mischief, harassment, invasion of privacy. She'd been spying on Jill with cameras and it all felt a bit overwhelming. What had Jill ever done to deserve all that he'd heaped upon her?

The woman he loved?

He wanted to run to her, wrap her in his arms and ensure she was safe.

He stood, carefully placing the file on the table. "Did you say Jill's here?"

"Are we not ironing out what you need to do to grow your company? To protect your employees?"

"You think you can do all that?"

"Yes."

"Really? With me?"

"Well, not as you are..."

"Because Jill can. And she was." He cursed under his breath. And he'd blown it. But maybe there was still time to make it right again.

"She was using you to propel herself," Tiffer said simply.

"Did she say that?" Burke challenged.

"She didn't have to."

"You don't know her. And you don't know me, either. Your values are all messed up."

The man got to his feet. "I believe in marriage and devotion to those we love."

"So do I. I just suck at showing it sometimes."

JILL SAT in the hotel bar, where a mariachi band was pumping out cheerful music that normally would have her up and dancing—and had a year ago when she'd been here with Burke. She'd reacted on instinct when she'd spotted Tiffer in the lobby hours before Burke's meeting. She'd walked up to him, pressing the dossier into his hands despite it being confidential, and vouching for Burke. She'd been desperate for the businessman to know the truth about Burke and to see beyond the poor reputation he was no doubt judging him for.

She'd wanted to go home after that, and had skipped out on crashing the meeting between the two men. But she hadn't been able to convince herself to leave, and had instead wandered the booths set up by conference vendors, half hoping and half afraid to bump into Burke. When everyone packed up for the day, she still hadn't been able to leave the hotel, knowing she had to speak to Burke about Autumn before she headed back to Blueberry Springs.

"This is yours, I believe," Tiffer said, placing the dossier on the bar beside her. She'd been here for forty-five minutes and still hadn't ordered anything despite frequent enquires from the bartender. He kept his hand over it, watching her. "You all right?"

"Yes, thanks."

"You sure?"

There was a genuine kindness in his expression and she felt choked up at his unexpected concern.

"How did the meeting go?" she asked.

"He walked out."

"*What?*" Burke had walked out of the meeting? She wasn't sure how she felt about that. Angry? Proud? Worried?

"You haven't seen him?" Tiffer seemed surprised when she shook her head. He placed a fifty-dollar bill in a shoe that was going around the room as part of a wedding celebration. The wedding party was why Jill had come into this bar tonight, and had last year, too. It was loud, full of life, and had very few people from the conference in it.

It was also the hotel bar that Burke was the most likely to choose of the three on the large property. The idea of him showing up sent butterflies romping through her stomach.

"Well," Tiffer said, "Burke walking out is likely for the best. We wouldn't have lasted long before one of us told the other to take a long hike off a short pier."

She nodded in agreement, unsure what to say.

Tiffer tapped the dossier. "He's lucky to have you." He squeezed her shoulder as he stepped away. "Good luck to you both."

"Thanks."

There was no "both," though. That was the problem. She tucked the file in her shoulder bag, knowing she and Burke would have to talk about Autumn at some point and decide whether they were going to press charges, and if so, which ones.

But what was really puzzling was why Burke had rejected Tiffer. On one level it didn't surprise her. They weren't a good fit. But on the other hand, there'd been so many sacrifices and he'd just thrown it all away.

She should get back in her car and head home, regroup, pull her life back together. If she left now she could be in Blueberry Springs in time to curl up in her pj's and watch a movie with her dog.

She lowered her left hand to the bar, wishing she'd brought her leather bracelet. She'd left it at home, baring her wrist as a symbol to Burke. Stupid hope.

She was going to have to tell everyone she'd divorced him. Currently, only her family knew. But soon word would begin to travel, as it always did.

The bartender came by and Jill finally flagged him down for a drink and a burger which she knew wouldn't be as juicy and all-around amazing like the one Amy and Moe made back in Blueberry Springs.

"Tequila's on the house as part of the wedding celebration," the bartender said, after he put in her food order. He gestured to the party going on behind her as he set her up with the shot, lemon wedge and salt. He was peering at her like he should know her. "You were here last year, weren't you?"

"I was."

"You got engaged."

"I suppose I did."

"Just over there." He smiled as though enjoying the memory. "Did you get married?"

"That night."

"Wow." He chuckled. "And?"

"Divorced."

He winced, and the sympathy in his eyes made her heart ache.

Jill licked the back of her hand, then sprinkled it with salt. Morosely, she ran her tongue over the grains before knocking back the tequila and sucking on the lemon wedge. The last time she'd had a shot of tequila was at this bar with Burke.

It looked like her drive home was going to be delayed.

That had been a stupid move.

Spontaneity still wasn't her friend, was it?

Her sister's words roamed through her head, about how our mistakes bring us to the place we're supposed to be. She had gone full circle, hadn't she? Same bar, one year later. But this time there was no Burke beside her as the wedding celebration went on behind her.

"Take it easy tonight, okay?" the bartender said as he took away her empty shot glass.

"Always."

He raised his eyebrows.

"Okay, so last year I went home married."

"So did I," said a deep voice from behind her. A masculine hand pointed to her wrist as shivers rippled up her spine. "Nice tattoo. I have one just like it."

Jill breathed Burke's name, her heartbeat stuttering.

"Jill."

The bartender gave her a secret smile, and passed a few more shots their way.

Jill sent him a questioning look and he simply shrugged, as if to say *"Hey, it worked last year."*

"On the house," Jill whispered, as Burke turned to her. He didn't touch his shot. She didn't touch hers, either. This year she wasn't going home married.

"I heard you refused Tiffer's offer?"

Burke knocked his shot back without touching the salt or lemon. If she recalled correctly, he'd done the same last year, too. "He's not the kind of man I want to work with," he stated.

"I thought he was your company's big hope?"

"He wouldn't treat my employees right. And he made me realize a lot of things. As did that file you left with him."

Jill hadn't really expected Tiffer to share it with Burke, and she wasn't sure what to say. In her peripheral vision she saw Burke turn on his stool so he was facing her.

"I want to work with someone who cares about me, my business, my employees. So much so that they'd shoot their own foot off before mine."

"Wow," she said. That sure wasn't Tiffer.

"Our business partnership was good," Burke said, and she knew he was referring to his and hers. "That mess with the reviews and press scared me. It became a catalyst and gave me a reason to pull away and give in to my fears. Because I care for you, and that made me vulnerable. I don't like being vulnerable."

Jill held her breath for a second, his words giving her hope. "What are you saying?"

"Would you consider partnering your botanicals with my business again?"

She shook her head, knowing that wasn't what she wanted, wasn't where she was now heading.

"I'm sorry I blew it then," he said, his eyes filled with a sadness she wanted to erase.

"You didn't."

"I didn't trust you."

"No, I didn't trust myself. Or you, either."

Burke's tone became professional. "What can I offer to convince you to bring your products back to STH? We won't be working with Tiffer, but we've recently signed new partnership contracts with local businesses that has gotten the team excited. I think some of our marketing efforts could really help your botanicals as well."

"It's not that," Jill said, shaking her head. "I recently realized something important about myself. My passion is in organizing. It bugs me when things are out of place—remind me to tell you

ACCIDENTALLY MARRIED

about Don and his reindeer cup back when I worked at the town office." She shook her head, regaining her focus. "What I discovered was that I'm good at putting systems into place. But I don't enjoy the pressure of making them work."

"I don't follow."

"I'd rather put a system in place to keep someone's closet organized than be there all the time making sure they used it. I like the idea of having a business and expanding it, and being this amazing businessperson. But it stresses me out trying to make it happen."

Burke was watching her. "Sell me your company."

"What?"

"I'll take over, but you'll still receive a healthy chunk of the royalties."

She shook her head. "I've partnered with Rebecca's son, Joseph. He's doing all the stuff that stresses me out, and I do all the stuff I love. He's a full partner, so I'll have to talk to him."

Burke's jaw had gone tight.

The mariachi band was been moving around the bar, serenading couples, and they paused by Jill and Burke. A fatherly looking fellow with a giant smile stopped, took one look at them and said, "You two are lovers?"

"Uh..." Jill glanced at Burke. "We were."

"You still care for each other, yes?"

She felt a small smile escape.

"Ah, yes. You two are meant to be." As the band played a melodic love song, the man wrapped a cord loosely around Burke and Jill, forming a figure eight. It was a lasso. "Now your futures are intertwined," he told them simply. Eyes twinkling, he dropped one end of the cord, freeing them, before moving on.

"Somehow I always thought Cupid would be taller," Burke murmured, causing Jill to giggle.

Burke had shifted in his seat to face her better. "Jill?"

She hesitated, then turned, the space between them disappearing as he slid forward and wrapped his arms around her. Nervous energy built inside her as she waited for him to speak.

"I missed you," he said. "And I'm sorry."

She placed her hands on either side of his face, breathing him in, her forehead pressed against his. This was the first step. The one to their happily ever after.

They had work to do as a couple, but she didn't doubt that they could accomplish it if they stuck together.

"I missed you, too."

He kissed her, slowly and sweetly. He tasted like tequila and memories of happiness. She wanted that again. The spontaneity of not knowing what the next day was going to bring for them. She'd trusted in that part of her that wanted to have it all, that felt strong enough to break away from who she'd always thought she was. The part that believed she could reach for happier times.

"Can I take a risk?" he asked.

"I think you just did, by kissing your ex-wife."

"Can I ask you out on a date?"

Her heart sang. "Yes."

"Will you go to supper with me?"

"As long as it's not at MacKenzie's. Not after what happened last time."

"But MacKenzie's was fun."

"Fun?" Mortifying was more like it. She'd lost such control in that heady kiss.

"I've never been kissed like that before."

"Really?" She liked the idea of him charting new territory with her, and of being able to knock him off his feet.

"Have you?" he asked.

"Only by you."

He gave a satisfied sound of approval.

The burger she'd ordered earlier arrived and Burke glanced at it. "I was thinking we could go out to eat tonight, but it looks like I'm too late."

"We can share."

He kissed her again, and she didn't in the least bit mind that her burger was getting cold.

When they broke apart, she whispered, "Kissing isn't going to fix everything, or sweep our problems away, you know."

"I tend to approach things wrong from start to finish."

"I know. You didn't even buy me a ring."

He chuckled. "I love you, you know that?"

She pulled back to look at him. The way he'd said it, it was like a passing comment and not what it should be: a life-changing proclamation.

"I really do," he said soberly. "And that scares me beyond belief. I'm really hoping that tonight we can talk. Figure out how to figure out what's real and what's—"

"We'll do all of that. And as for what's real..." She kissed him with longing. "This is real. And it always will be."

This was a new beginning, and it would be even better than the last one. They just had to trust and let go. Something she knew they could do. Together.

WITH A GROAN, Burke reached out to silence his buzzing phone.

"Burke?" He felt someone stir in the bed behind him, and glanced back to find Jill smiling at him. He rolled over and kissed her, taking his time and enjoying every moment.

"So we remarried?" he asked in a husky voice. Last night was a blur. Dancing. Laughing. Kissing. Lots of kissing.

Jill pointed over his shoulder. There was a top hat sitting on the bureau on the other side of the room, as well as a bridal veil. "I think that's a good sign we did."

"Tequila, Mexican weddings and us." He frowned. "Why does my hip hurt?" Burke twisted to take a peek. The skin there was red, and tattooed with a blue puzzle piece.

Jill laughed.

He craned his neck. "I remember everything this time. Even this puzzle piece." If he recalled correctly, it fitted perfectly with the tattoo on Jill's hip. She rolled over, exposing her own new artwork, just under where the waistband of her panties would come if she was wearing any. Her puzzle piece did indeed interlock with his.

"Nice. That's actually rather naughty."

"Is not!"

"But the truth is, they fit together. Like us."

"Burke!" She was blushing.

"That must be why we had them tattooed out of sight this time." He waggled his eyebrows, making her cover her face. So he rolled her over, peppering her with quick kisses until she was laughing, the best sound in the whole entire world.

EPILOGUE

*J*ill swished the skirt of the dress she'd bought out of the window display at Ginger's bridal shop. Her friends had been right; it *did* look amazing on her. A bit much for her twin's tenth wedding anniversary party, but seeing as the event combined their dual celebrations, it was perfect.

"Third time's a charm!" she sang to Burke as she turned from the mirror in the Blueberry Springs community center's back room.

"Who would have thought either of us would get married three times?"

"My last two husbands are my favorite."

"That's because they're both me," Burke replied smoothly, landing a quick kiss on her lips.

Jill smiled and hooked her arm through his as they marched out to the party being held in their honor.

Burke had agreed to press charges against Autumn, who'd been arrested for driving under the influence only a few days after the news of their remarriage hit the papers. It was also public knowledge that her father had turfed her out of the house and she'd been charged for stalking two different men—other than Burke.

The woman had big problems on top of taking an image of a rash off the internet and posting it as a valid review for one of Jill's products, hiring someone to steal her identity—including her signature via signing for the flowers—then taking out money against Burke's credit. That was on top of stalking and spying on Jill with the nanny cameras. All the info about We Win Your Love, their fake marriage—all the leaks had been from Autumn and Jill had provided it all through the cameras.

Everything had come out in a teary confession to Logan and Zach, who had confronted her at a black tie affair where an undercover agent had been recording her via a corsage given to her by Zach who'd posed as her date.

Jill was still happily working at Emma's, and she and Joseph were in the final stages of negotiating a deal with Burke. She wasn't sure who was the harder bargainer—Joseph or Burke. Jill loved it.

As well, a new friendship center had been designed by a local architect. Things were moving at long last, even though Jill wasn't footing the bill. In fact, a government grant she'd applied for after returning from the Metro Conference had come through.

"Oh, I forgot something," Burke said suddenly, halting in the doorway to the large hall, where their guests were turning to watch them enter.

"Burke!" Jill whispered, afraid he was about to head back to the staging room.

"I forgot something important," he said to the room at large. He got down on one knee. "I forgot to propose."

"We're married," Jill said, giggling.

"Jill Armstrong, will you marry me?" He was holding a thin, white-gold band that supported the most gorgeous and familiar looking line of small sapphires and diamonds.

ACCIDENTALLY MARRIED

"I already did. Twice," she said, clearly so all could hear. Everyone in the room laughed. "But yes, I will marry you."

He slid the jeweled ring on her finger and straightened. It looked even more fabulous as a gift from the man she loved.

"I figured you were never going to treat yourself, so I thought maybe you wouldn't mind if I did."

Off to her right, Jodi and Amy were standing with Burke's aunt Maggie, and Jill heard all three of them heave a collective sigh.

"They're so right for each other," said Maggie.

"He just keeps on sweeping her away," Amy said dreamily.

"You're next," Jodi said in a hushed voice.

"Moe? I don't think so. I'm going to have to do something drastic and hire Ginger to find a match for me."

"Shh!" Jodi said, "I don't want to miss this. It's like the end of the movie where everyone gets what they want."

"Except for me," Amy said.

Jill pulled her attention back to Burke. "But this isn't a wedding band."

She was only teasing, but he replied, "Since when do we ever do anything by the rules?"

She moved to head on into the room, but he stopped her. "I also forgot something else."

Jill patiently tipped her head.

"A real wedding band," he said, not revealing one.

"I thought we were being *cheeky* and only doing tattoos?" She displayed the one on her wrist, and Burke twisted his lips in a secret smile, knowing she was referring to their newer body art.

"We did. Twice. But..." He pulled his hand from his pocket, turning serious. "I want us each to have something more traditional, too."

He revealed a fatter white-gold band. Two of them. Each with an arch of alternating diamonds and blue sapphires that, when resting beside each other, formed a heart. He separated the bands. One half of a heart for her, one for him.

Just like their tattoos.

"Oh, Burke. These are perfect."

He slid the ring onto her left hand, nestling it beside her dream ring. They were perfect together.

Just like she and Burke.

Jill took his wedding band and placed it on his finger, where it fit exactly. The ring shone on his strong hand, claiming him for all the world to see.

Claiming him as hers and hers alone.

Her other half.

"Never stop being you," she whispered, kissing him tenderly.

"I won't, as long as you don't, either."

"Well, I was thinking I'd plan things out a tad less. Leave a little room for opportunity to nudge in her nosy little head from time to time."

"Really?"

"Yes, really."

"Because I heard you already have the dishes and curtains chosen for our new little place here in town."

She gave a good-natured harrumph, knowing he had her on that one. "But what I realized is that all those mistakes I was agonizing over in my past taught me some very important lessons. Like showing up to win a riflery competition and take home a scholarship without a backup rifle…not smart. Planning is good, but within reason—and so you know, I got a great deal on those curtains. And yes, I could have chosen better men sometimes, but they taught me what I needed." She met Burke's soulful gaze. "They all led me to you and made me who I am today—the woman *you* chose."

"Twice. And I'll keep on choosing you day after day." He pulled her into a long, slow kiss that drew cheers from the crowd of family and friends surrounding them.

"This might be the biggest day of my life," she whispered.

"I told you I was a part of it."

Jill smiled. "I hope you always will be."

"Told you they wouldn't stay apart long," Mary Alice said to her sister from the sidelines.

"Oh, shush. You're so full of it, and you're ruining the moment," Liz retorted, dabbing at her eyes.

"We got you something," Mary Alice exclaimed, waving a bag at Jill and Burke as they headed into the room at long last, to take their spot at the head table alongside Jodi and Gareth.

Jill accepted the bag, while her husband placed a warm hand on her lower back, then gave her a quick, chaste kiss on her temple.

Jill pushed aside the tissue paper and pulled out a picture frame. It held the photo from MacKenzie's with them madly kissing, the one that had hit the papers.

"It's a good picture," Mary Alice said defensively, when the two remained silent.

"It is," Burke aunt's agreed, coming over to join them.

Burke turned it to face Mary Alice. "Did you know we'd been joking about framing this photo?"

The woman simply gave him a knowing smile. "You're welcome."

"I married her twice, you know. That's more than I've married any other woman," he called as she walked away.

"I'm keeping my eye on you," Mary Alice said, glancing back as she went. But Jill saw her teasing wink, telling them both that she now considered Burke to be one of her own, one of the town's.

"Then keep an eye on this," Burke called, bending Jill backward in a dramatic kiss that blew her mind and told her everything she needed to know about her own happily ever after. That it was going to last forever.

GET MORE BLUEBERRY SPRINGS!

Keep reading Veils and Vows with the next book in the series: *The Marriage Pledge*—Amy and Moe's story. Dive in today and continue the adventure and find love in the most unexpected places!

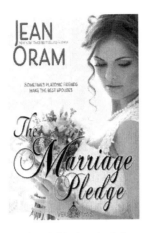

Sometimes platonic friends make the best spouses.

MORE BY JEAN ORAM

IRRESISTIBLE & ADDICTIVE
THE LATEST FROM BLUEBERRY SPRINGS...

Veils and Vows

The Promise (Book 0: Devon & Olivia)
The Surprise Wedding (Book 1: Devon & Olivia)
A Pinch of Commitment (Book 2: Ethan & Lily)
The Wedding Plan (Book 3: Luke & Emma)
Accidentally Married (Book 4: Burke & Jill)
The Marriage Pledge (Book 5: Moe & Amy)
Mail Order Soulmate (Book 6: Zach & Catherine)

Companion stories set in the Indigo Bay series:
Sweet Matchmaker (Ginger and Logan)
Sweet Holiday Surprise (Alexa and Cash)
Sweet Forgiveness (Zoe and Ashton)

BLUEBERRY SPRINGS

Have you fallen in love with Blueberry Springs? Catch up with your friends and their adventures...

Blueberry Springs

Book 1: Whiskey and Gumdrops (Mandy & Frankie)

Book 2: Rum and Raindrops (Jen & Rob)

Book 3: Eggnog and Candy Canes (Katie & Nash)

Book 4: Sweet Treats (3 short stories—Mandy, Amber, & Nicola)

Book 5: Vodka and Chocolate Drops (Amber & Scott)

Book 6: Tequila and Candy Drops (Nicola & Todd)

Companion Novel: Champagne and Lemon Drops (Beth & Oz)

THE SUMMER SISTERS

Taming billionaires has never been so **sweet.**

The Summer Sisters Tame the Billionaires

Love and Rumors

Love and Dreams

Love and Trust

Love and Danger

Love and Mistletoe

ABOUT THE AUTHOR

Jean Oram is a *New York Times* and *USA Today* bestselling romance author. Inspiration for her small town series came from her own upbringing on the Canadian prairies. Although, so far, none of her characters have grown up in an old schoolhouse or worked on a bee farm. Jean still lives on the prairie with her husband, two kids, big shaggy dog and fluffy cat. She can often be found outside playing in the snow or hiking.

Connect with Jean:

Newsletter: www.jeanoram.com/FREEBOOK
Goodreads: www.goodreads.com/jeanoram
YouTube: www.youtube.com/AuthorJeanOram
Twitter: www.twitter.com/jeanoram
Facebook: www.facebook.com/JeanOramAuthor
Become an Official Fan:
www.facebook.com/groups/jeanoramfans

Website & blog: www.jeanoram.com

Made in the USA
Lexington, KY
23 March 2018